RED AS A ROSE

Hilary Wilde

Chivers
Bath, England

•

Thorndike Press
Waterville, Maine USA

This Large Print edition is published by BBC Audiobooks Ltd, England, and by Thorndike Press, USA.

Published in 2003 in the U.K. by arrangement with the author.

Published in 2003 in the U.S. by arrangement with Juliet Burton Literary Agency.

U.K. Hardcover ISBN 0–7540–7255–X (Chivers Large Print)
U.K. Softcover ISBN 0–7540–7256–8 (Camden Large Print)
U.S. Softcover ISBN 0–7862–5410–6 (Nightingale Series)

The text of this Large Print edition is unabridged.
Other aspects of the book may vary from the original edition.

Set in 16 pt. New Times Roman.

Printed in Great Britain on acid-free paper.

British Library Cataloguing in Publication Data available

Library of Congress Cataloging-in-Publication Data

Wilde, Hilary.
    Red as a rose / by Hilary Wilde.
        p. cm.
    ISBN 0–7862–5410–6 (lg. print : sc : alk. paper)
    1. Ocean travel—Fiction. 2. Australia—Fiction.
    3. Large type books. I. Title.
    PR6072.E735R44 2003
    823'.914—dc21   2003047377

CHAPTER ONE

As she gazed up at the white liner towering above them, Elinor felt a strange new excitement. It was an adventure, after all. This thing she had dreaded and fought against—this upheaval to a new land. Everything would be all right, she was suddenly sure of it. This strange six-thousand-mile journey to Australia, to live with an aunt she had never seen—this leaving South Africa, the land of her birth, it was all for the best, she was convinced in that moment. It was almost too wonderful to be true—the sort of thing girls dreamed about, things that didn't happen to people like her sister and herself. Elinor turned to look at her sister and saw that Valerie's lovely face was radiant with happiness. From the beginning, this was what Valerie had wanted—and Elinor had fought it, convinced that Valerie was wrong—but now the two sisters, so totally different from one another, were agreeing, as Valerie turned to meet Elinor's gaze and then nodded wisely:

'You're not sorry, Elinor? Tell me you're not sorry,' Valerie said eagerly.

Their hands clung for a moment. 'No, Valerie,' Elinor said, in her soft, hesitant voice. 'I'm glad. Very, very glad.'

They were always being teased because they

1

were so utterly different, and yet they loved one another dearly. Valerie, who was seventeen but looked far more sophisticated than her elder sister, had always found Elinor a tower of strength in times of trouble. Elinor, just twenty, always felt a sense of responsibility for Valerie. Their mother, who had died just two months before, had always said: 'Elinor, you're the quiet reliable type—Valerie is so flighty that she needs you. You'll always look after her, won't you?'

Elinor had promised gladly but the responsibility she consequently felt was often a burden. Valerie was indeed 'flighty'. She did the craziest things; made friends with most weird types of people, was completely unafraid, and was apt to think that at times Elinor was being 'stuffy'.

They also looked so different that few people took them to be sisters. Elinor had an ethereal look. Not beautiful, not even pretty, but she had a gentleness about her mouth that was always conflicting with the firmness of her small chin. Her eyes held a look of compassion; she had dark eyes that seemed to fill her small face. Her dark hair was softly brushed and curled naturally round her head. A gentle person, you might think, but you could be wrong. Elinor had a strong character. She firmly believed in right and wrong, and was not afraid of expressing her displeasure if she thought it necessary.

Now, as she smiled at her sister, she was thinking affectionately how very lovely Valerie was, standing there, her slanting green eyes dancing with excitement, her red-gold hair worn like a challenging banner, brushed up into designed untidiness. For once she was wearing simple clothes and her white blouse and green pleated skirt made her look quite young as also did the tremulous, vulnerable look she gave as she said breathlessly:

'Is this really true, Elinor? Can this really be happening to us?'

Even as Elinor laughed, she knew what Valerie meant. Their life for the last ten years since their father died had been so drab. They had been so short of money, so sad, for their mother was delicate and she never ceased to mourn her husband who had died on a fishing weekend. Their whole life had been revolving round the motif of sad memory; their mother had never let them forget the horror of that day when they first heard the news that he had been drowned.

'Elinor—look . . .' Valerie said breathlessly, her hand closing like a vice round her sister's wrist.

Obediently Elinor looked and it was as if her heart skipped a beat as she saw the man again. It was almost as if he was haunting her—only of course, he wasn't. Now he was striding through the crowd, head and shoulders above everyone else. He was extremely handsome . . . no wonder all the women turned to look at him.

'He's gorgeous, isn't he . . .?' Valerie whispered excitedly, and as Elinor turned to look at her, the older girl forgot her own interest in the man as she began to worry about her sister. Valerie's eyes were always roving, her warm smile embraced everyone within sight. Valerie was both a joy and an anxiety. She was not an easy girl to advise or guide for she resented every comment or suggestion. She was convinced she was old enough to look after herself. Indeed, she had even suggested that she was far better qualified to do so than Elinor!

Valerie had forgotten the handsome man already as she stared up at the ship. 'Do hurry, Elinor—I just can't wait to get on board . . .'

'We've got to see about our luggage and . . .' Elinor began, clutching the big white handbag tightly, for it contained everything they had of value—their passports, tickets, travellers' cheques. Now she looked at the crowds of people milling about in the big Customs shed.

'You cope with that—' Valerie said excitedly. 'I'm going on board—I want to find out where our cabin is . . .'

'Val—wait for me . . .' Elinor said quickly. The crowds were gathering round the gangway—the sun blazed down on a scene of noisy confusion. 'You'll get lost . . .' Elinor cried distractedly as she saw that Valerie was

4

on her way.

Through the crowd she caught a glimpse of Valerie's flushed angry face. 'Oh, for Pete's sake, Elinor, stop fussing. I'm not a child. How can I get lost when I have our cabin number? See you later . . .' With a last toss of her red head, she was off, weaving in and out of the people hurrying, obviously impatient to see the joys that lay ahead of them.

Elinor watched the red head as long as she could see it, as Valerie sped up the gangway, and then it vanished from view.

Turning with a small sigh, for she wished she could do as Valerie did, Elinor turned towards the crowded shed and again she saw the man. He was talking to another man whose back was turned so that Elinor could not see his face. Not that she was interested in him— she had eyes only for the tall, broad-shouldered man in the tropical pale-grey suit as she stared at his face that was a deep sun-tanned brown. How very fair his hair was—as if it had been bleached by the sun, and yet his eyes were dark. What a stubborn sort of chin he had and an arrogant way of holding his head. He had a mouth that could show disapproval very strongly as she well knew. Several times she had annoyed him and yet she still could not see what she could have done to offend him.

Elinor took her place in the queue and waited her turn to be seen by the men in white uniform who were asking questions and examining papers. Finally it was her turn, she had to show travellers' cheques, pay dock charges and watch their luggage seized.

'It will be taken to your cabin,' a harassed official told her, and turned away immediately, leaving Elinor to watch rather worriedly as the suitcases were carted off. After all, everything they possessed in the world was in those cases. It made her realise how very little they possessed.

She still had not recovered from the shock of knowing that they had all been living on such a small income. After the funeral, she had learned that, although they owed nothing, they possessed no money at all. Just her salary as typist in a solicitor's office and Valerie's even smaller salary as a clerk in a bank. The little money her mother had had vanished with her death. Elinor shivered despite the heat, remembering the cold desolate panic that had filled her. How could she earn enough for them to live on? How she would feed Valerie, who was slim as a wand but ate as much as any man, she did not know—nor how she could ever curb Valerie's wild ideas and her reckless friendships. In that moment, Elinor had been really afraid—afraid of the future and of how she could face it.

Slowly now, she climbed the gangway to the ship, trying to forget those frightening days when she had faced the fact that they were alone in the world and practically penniless. It had been Valerie who had reminded them that they were not quite alone. That their father's family in England would help them.

Again Elinor shivered. She had been torn in two—although she had been desperate, yet she had felt it was disloyal to her mother when she wrote that letter to England.

Valerie had said she was mad—that it was disloyal to their father not to write. Elinor had been forced to admit that he would have wanted them to keep in touch with the family, for he had written regularly, sending them photos of the children, telling the girls about his family and his old home, promising to take them 'home' one day. But after his death, their mother, who had always disliked the English relations, had ceased to answer their letters, even returning them, marked 'Gone away, address unknown'. She had seemed to delight in doing it, making no attempt to hide her hatred of them. It had often puzzled Elinor— but Valerie had called it plain stupid and had said their father would have been furious about it. So, in the end, not knowing what else to do, Elinor had written to England and had an immediate reply, saying that her grandmother was dead but that her father's sister would write to her from Australia. Aunt Aggie's letter had soon followed, a warm loving letter saying how thrilled she was to hear from them, but she was longing to see

7

them, and that they simply must go out to live with her. She had included two first class passages for them, and even sent them money for extra expenses and clothes.

'It's like having a fairy godmother,' Valerie had said excitedly.

It was. Elinor could relax, could know their troubles were over. Best of all, that someone wanted them. And yet she still had the chill feeling of disloyalty to her mother. Yet what else could she have done? Maybe it was this mixture of feelings that had made her so fear the journey that lay ahead, so dread the last severance of the ties that bound her to the mother she had loved so deeply.

At last she was on the ship and the mournful thoughts vanished as she hurried out on deck, gazing round her with wide eyes of delight. Somehow, it was all so clean and exciting. She looked up quickly at Table Mountain as the clouds rolled over the top of it and streamed down the sides. The city nestled at the foot of the mountain with the wide coast line stretching away on either side. The blue sea sparkled and danced in the sunshine as everyone leaned over the railing and waved down to the crowds gathering on the quay. Soon the ship would be sailing and they would be starting out on their great adventure . . .

Again her heart seemed to skip a beat. There was that man! Now he was there, not far

8

away, leaning on the rail and talking to a tall lovely girl. He was grave, his face concerned. She was nearly as tall as he, but slender, and elegantly dressed in a blue silk suit with a tall white hat and long kid gloves. It made Elinor feel her simple yellow frock was cheap and shoddy, her little white hat and carefully darned white gloves made her feel self-conscious. The lovely girl seemed to be annoyed for she was tapping her foot on the deck. The hat hid most of the girl's face, but Elinor caught a glimpse of golden hair . . . Was she his wife? Elinor wondered.

Leaning against the rail, gazing blindly at the crowds below, Elinor wished that she need never have seen him . . . It had been queer—almost uncanny. Almost as if he knew she was near, he turned and she saw, in a hasty glance, that he was very angry indeed. He seemed to make a habit of it, she thought miserably, still writhing from the memory of his displeasure. There was a white line round his mouth and although she could not hear what he was saying, he gave an impression of controlled anger.

Elinor moved away swiftly, afraid he might turn and find her staring at him. She did not want to have to meet those strange eyes again, to see that look of distaste, so she went to stand on the other side of the ship, gazing out at the dancing Indian ocean under the pale blue sky while a small white boat bobbed about on the waves like a small cork.

It was strange the way that man seemed to appear in her life like a thread in a pattern. All in the last few days, too. The first time had been at the East African Pavilion in Johannesburg where their friends had given them a farewell party and everyone except Elinor was laughing and talking loudly. She had felt very blue for the next day they were leaving the Johannesburg that had always been her home, and going to a strange land to live with strange people. She had been upset, too, about Max, a very young journalist, head over heels in love with Valerie and quite unable to accept the fact that Valerie did not want to settle down yet and get married. So that was why when Max, his dark handsome face alight with laughter but his eyes heavy with misery, had asked Elinor why she was so quiet, she had made an effort to become very gay, lifting her glass and calling a toast loudly: 'Here's to our unknown future . . .'

It had been a strange thing for her to do, for she was normally quiet and diffident, leaving it to Valerie to be the gay one, but that night she had wanted to cheer poor Max up and, in the very moment she spoke, she had looked across the room and had seen a man staring at her. A tall, impressive-looking man, immaculately dressed in a dark suit, with very fair hair and dark eyes and a strange look in them as he stared at her. And then—his mouth a thin line of distaste, he had turned away and she had felt absurdly hurt and dismayed. Had he thought she was making herself conspicuous?

She had forgotten all about him afterwards. No, that was not quite the truth. That handsome sun-tanned face had stayed provocatively in her memory. She had wondered who he was, where he came from. He had looked so very different from the other men. But she had never expected to see him again.

And then, they had met again on the train— if you could call it a meeting. She and Valerie had been walking down the dining-car as it rocked and jolted and she had been flung against a table and had found herself staring down into his dark eyes. He had lifted his thick fair brows and had not even smiled as she mumbled a hasty apology and almost fled down the dining-car to the safety of their compartment. Had he thought she had fallen against him deliberately? Her cheeks had flamed at the terrible thought. Could he imagine that she had tried to . . .

Even the memory of it was disturbing enough so she began to walk along the deck. Maybe he would have gone by now. In any case, she simply had to make sure that their luggage was safely on board.

Everyone round her was laughing and chatting, standing in little groups, waiting for the last minute call to leave the ship. As she

11

hurried a little, seized by the fearful thought that she did not know what to do if the luggage was not there, she found herself remembering the third time she had met that man. It had been the worst time of all. It had been on the Blue Train, the fabulously luxurious train that ran between Johannesburg and Cape Town, and she and Valerie had loved it all, especially as the countryside got wilder and more beautiful. She had left Valerie painting her nails in their compartment and had gone to stand in the corridor, to gaze at the vast ranges of grey mountains, to look at the twisting curving railway line, seeing the notice that said *Fifteen miles per hour* and realising how very dangerous it must be for the train to crawl like this down the mountain side. Far, far below lay a deep green oasis of trees and green grass on which stood a group of white houses.

For a moment her love for her country filled her and the thought of leaving it, perhaps for ever, dismayed her and when she heard a footstep she said impulsively: 'Oh, Val—isn't it lovely? How can we bear to leave it—the most beautiful country in all the world.'

'What absolute nonsense . . .' the deep drawling voice had said, and gave her the fright of her life. 'Australia is every bit as beautiful.'

She could remember now how chilled she had felt as she swung round, startled, embarrassed to find herself staring at the handsome, arrogant man who was surveying her with amused, cold eyes.

Her cheeks had burned. 'I'm sorry . . . I . . . I thought it was my sister.'

His thick fair brows had lifted again. 'Indeed?' he had drawled. 'It's the first time I've been mistaken for a girl.'

Her face had felt as if it was on fire. 'I didn't see you. I . . . I heard a step and . . .'

'Jumped to conclusions,' he drawled. 'Dangerous thing to do.'

How stern he looked. And yet she had had the uncomfortable feeling as well that he was amused, making fun of her. He looked so strong, so disapproving, so unyielding. Yet he was very handsome. The most striking-looking man she had ever seen. She had struggled for composure, determined not to let him see how confused she felt.

'You must admit it is beautiful . . .' she said, turning to look back through the window, at the lovely countryside, still uncomfortable under his gaze.

'Of course I will admit it,' he said, almost snapping the words. His fingers gripped the rail before them. 'Have you ever been out of this country?' he asked unexpectedly.

Startled, she shook her head, her mouth dry.

He frowned. 'Then what right have you to make such a sweeping statement?' he demanded.

13

Now she was sure he was mocking her. Anger drove out fear so that she could answer him. 'It was not meant as a sweeping statement,' she said in a rather prim, and, she hoped, dignified voice, and then spoilt the whole effect by adding: 'In any case, you've no right to lecture me and . . .'

How young and horribly naïve it sounded, she thought miserably.

One corner of his mouth had seemed to quirk. 'I would like to point out to you that I did not start this conversation . . .' he said coldly. 'You spoke to me first.'

Now as she stood on the deck, looking warily along in case he should still be there, Elinor could remember vividly the anger that had swept through her. She had opened her mouth and firmly closed it again, afraid she might say something childish she would later regret, uncomfortably aware that she was no match for this sophisticated man, and then she had brushed past him, almost running down the corridor, going into their compartment, sliding the door shut. Vividly she could remember Valerie looking out through a cloud of hair—she was passing the time by experimenting with a new hair style—and saying:

'Anything worth looking at?'

And Elinor had replied. 'Nothing at all.' And she had sat down, opening a book, hoping Valerie would not notice her trembling hands

14

or ask her questions. Valerie would never have described that man as not worth looking at. What would Valerie have said? The girl was afraid of no one.

With a sigh of relief—or was there a little disappointment mingled with it? Elinor saw that the man and lovely girl had vanished, so she could walk along freely. She went to the side of the boat and gazed over anxiously. Luggage was coming on board. Was theirs? Everything was noisy—cranes moving, people talking. Maybe the luggage was in the cabin—and where was Valerie? Elinor hurried below, past the purser's office, down the stairs. It was like a rabbit warren of doors with numbers on. At last she found theirs, 361, and opened the door. It was a pleasant cabin—but no luggage. And no Valerie . . .

For a moment, she felt apprehensive. Where was Valerie? Suppose that Valerie had made one of her lightning friendships and wandered ashore, 'and then the ship sailed without her? What would her sister do . . . she had no money . . . she was so young. Elinor's hand pressed against her mouth, and she gazed around her wildly. Their luggage? What could have happened to it? Supposing it was lost—how could they manage without it? Luckily she had their passports and money with her, but . . .

She gave one last quick cursory glance round the cabin, thinking how Valerie would delight in its luxurious fittings, and then she hurried back to the promenade deck, carefully searching for her sister, gazing into the empty drawing-room, the enormous lounge where groups of people were sitting, talking, back to the deck again, just as a deep voice came over the tannoy.

She caught her breath with dismay. Everyone who was not sailing on the ship must go ashore. That meant they were sailing . . . A huge crane was slowly moving to lift away one gangway, and people began to hurry to the other. Near her were a young couple, clinging to one another. By the rail stood an elderly woman frankly weeping as she kissed two small children goodbye.

Desperately Elinor stopped an officer who was passing. 'Our luggage hasn't arrived . . .' she said anxiously, gazing up into a lean brown face and blue eyes which suddenly twinkled.

'Don't worry,' he said gravely. 'It'll be in your cabin. We never lose luggage, only passengers.'

That only made it all much worse. Suppose Valerie . . .

Elinor swung round and found herself gazing up into the face of the man she had hoped never to see again, the man she kept annoying, the man she could not forget.

'Don't panic,' he drawled, staring down at her. 'There's no trouble that can't be put right.'

Again she had the irritating feeling that he was laughing at her. But in her fear for Valerie, she forgot to be nervous. 'My sister . . .' she gasped. 'She came on board before I did but I can't find her . . .'

'Is your sister the girl who was with you on the train?' he asked, drawling his words. 'The pretty one with red hair?' When she nodded, his face seemed to relax and he was nearly smiling. 'She's safe, having a wonderful time. You'll find her in the verandah café . . .' He paused. 'Is that all the trouble?'

Elinor was so relieved about Valerie that for a moment she could not speak, so she shook her head. 'Our . . . our luggage . . .'

He smiled, then. It gave her quite a shock to see that stern unyielding face suddenly lit up by his smile. It made him look years younger.

'Don't fuss. It'll be in your cabin. No need to panic . . .' he said and then lifted his hand as if in farewell and strode away towards the gangway.

Elinor almost fell down the stairs to the cabin, in too great a hurry to wait for the lift. And there was the luggage. Just as he had said!

She looked in the mirror. Her nose was shiny and her hair all blown about. What a sight she looked. What must he have thought of her after the beauty and elegance of the girl he had been talking to? Anyhow he had gone ashore—he had just walked into her life and then walked out again.

As she carefully brushed her hair, washed her face and then powdered her nose and outlined her mouth, she let herself think briefly—and for the last time—of the man. Who was he? What did he do? He spoke in a strange way. He did not seem to be a South African . . . Why worry—she would never see him again.

In the corridor, she studied a plan of the ship and found out where the verandah café was. She stood in the doorway and stared round anxiously but there was no sign of Valerie. Could he have lied to her? Yet why should he? But he had noticed Valerie—had said she was pretty and had red hair . . .

She walked past the tables and stood by the window above the swimming pool and looked down at it and, for a moment, forgot to be worried about Valerie, realising that she had fifteen days of luxury ahead of her. Good food, meeting people, having fun. It was like a dream come true—a dream made possible by Aunt Aggie's generosity. After all, she need not have paid for them to travel first class. Valerie had been excited, suggesting that perhaps Aunt Aggie was a millionairess—she had heard there were many in Australia. There had been a warmth in Aunt Aggie's letter, also a little wistfulness, for she had said she had no children and her husband was an invalid and that she was thrilled by the thought of having two nieces to love and look after. It was

18

wonderful to know that Aunt Aggie wanted them—that she was not doing this out of a sense of duty. That would have been unbearable . . . Even so, Elinor wished she could lose this feeling of disloyalty to her mother—if only she could feel that her mother would approve of what they were doing. Yet what alternative had they?

Elinor wandered along the decks, getting glimpses of cabins through open doors, looking in at the gymnasium, climbing to the boat deck, where already a few people were playing deck quoits. It was all so huge, so white, so exciting. But she simply must find Valerie . . .

Rounding a corner, she walked slap-bang into her sister. Valerie's red hair was all wind-blown and she looked even lovelier than usual with her green eyes shining like stars and her cheeks rosy.

Valerie grabbed Elinor's arm excitedly. 'Darling—where have you been? I've been hunting the whole ship for you—I even began to wonder if you'd lost courage and left me stranded . . .' Her laugh was gay and happy. 'Oh, Elinor, isn't this absolutely too wonderful for words? I just can't believe it's happening to us . . . And what do you think? I've seen the most exciting man in the whole world . . .' Her words tumbled eagerly out of her mouth. 'He's just so wonderful—I could have swooned. No, honestly, darling, he really is the last word.

Just to look at him makes me feel thrilled. Could it be love?'

Elinor had to laugh. 'Oh, Val, what a girl you are. Last week it was Max . . .'

'But this is different . . .' Valerie said excitedly. 'This is a man. Max was so young, much too young. Oh, Elinor, wait until you see him, but remember he's mine . . .'

Elinor chuckled. 'I'll remember . . .' As if it mattered. As if any man would look twice at her when there was someone like Valerie around. Why, look, even that stern, quick-to-anger stranger had noticed that Valerie was pretty and had red hair!

There was a sudden blast from a tug and the two girls ran to the side of the ship to watch the two tugs easing the great ship out from its moorings.

'You can feel it moving . . .' Valerie said excitedly, as the wind tugged and tore at their hair, wrapping their skirts tightly round their legs. They hurried over to the shore side. People were shouting. Coloured streamers were being flung down from the ship's side.

'Look, Val . . .' Elinor said quickly, pointing to two small coloured boys who were fighting on the quay for the pennies the passengers were throwing down to them.

'We're off . . .' Valerie cried, her face radiant. 'Oh, Elinor, isn't it just too wonderful?'

They stood by the rail, watching the coast

slide away, looking up at the great mountain, its flat top hidden now by clouds. Elinor said a silent farewell to many things she loved dearly. She knew Valerie had no regrets at leaving, but then Valerie was very different, Valerie had not this desolate sense of disloyalty to their mother, this fear lest they be doing the wrong thing.

'Elinor . . . let's go down to our cabin. I haven't seen it yet . . .' Valerie said eagerly, How soon Valerie lost interest in anything, Elinor thought. Valerie loved everything new. Would she always be like that when she fell in love? What was this 'handsome, wonderful man' like? Would he prove to be horribly unsuitable?

In their cabin, Valerie swooped on a card, crying in dismay: 'Oh, no, Elinor. We can't. It's out of the question . . .'

Elinor had put one of her suitcases on the bed to start to unpack.

'What's wrong?' she asked cheerfully. Valerie always veered between the ecstatic and the dismayed.

'They've given us first sitting in the dining salon. We can't . . . We simply must have second sitting, Elinor,' Valerie said, her voice shocked.

Elinor sat on the bed and stared at her sister. 'I imagine we have to take what we're given,' she said mildly. 'After all, most people got on the boat in England.'

21

Valerie was standing, stiff as a poker. 'We must change it,' she said firmly.

'Does it matter so much?' Elinor said, surprised.

'Does it matter?' Valerie cried in a shocked voice. She curled up on one of the beds, hugging her knees. 'Of course it matters. You meet all the wrong people at the first sitting. Darling, be an absolute angel and go down to the dining salon and have it changed. The Chief Steward is the man to see . . .'

Elinor stared helplessly at her sister. 'How do you know these things, Val?'

Valerie waved her hand vaguely. 'I've been talking. I've already made some nice friends on board . . .' There was the faintest hint of defiance in her voice and Elinor stifled a sigh. How had they drifted into such a relationship as the one Valerie always implied? Elinor had no desire to be the stern, fun-destroying elder sister, yet sometimes Valerie . . .

'I'll try to change the sitting if you like,' Elinor said now, placatingly, trying to see Valerie's side of it, wanting to please her.

Valerie nearly throttled her with a bear hug and then leapt back onto the bed again. 'Angel girl,' she said happily. 'I knew I could count on you. Just smile sweetly and with that oddly pathetic little face of yours, you'll do the trick,' she added.

Her hand on the door knob, Elinor paused, looking puzzled. 'Now, what exactly do you mean,' she asked, 'by my oddly pathetic little face?'

Valerie was examining her nails carefully. 'Golly, they need doing. What do I mean? Well, look in the glass . . . you'll see.'

Elinor obeyed. She stared at her reflection worriedly. What a horrible expression. She had no desire to look 'pathetic'.

Could there be a more glamour-destroying word? She stared at her huge, rather mournful dark eyes, saw the way her mouth drooped at the corners, looked at her very ordinary hair style and saw how very drab she looked. It was not a happy face . . . certainly not . . . Glancing at Valerie, Elinor heard again that man's voice saying: 'That pretty girl—the girl with red hair.' How would he have described her? Elinor wondered. Surely—oh no, surely not— as 'pathetic'!

She forced herself to smile and saw that the smile had not reached her eyes. Well, she had nothing much to make her smile. Yet Valerie, no matter what happened, managed to be gay and laugh. Was it because they were so different—because Valerie could shrug off the day's troubles and hope for the best—or because Valerie had none of the responsibilities, because she could leave everything to her sister?

Inconsistently irritated by her sister, Elinor suggested that Valerie do some unpacking while she was gone and then hurried away,

23

telling herself she should be ashamed. Valerie was right, she was naturally the optimistic type, and being the younger, was perfectly entitled to leave things to Elinor.

The Head Steward, apparently, was not available, and the Assistant Steward, very young, his cheeks flushed, his voice exasperated, told her patiently that he was sorry but the sittings could not be changed. There were a number of people worrying him to do it and he kept pointing out that most of the passengers had travelled from England and would object most strongly to changing their sitting.

Feeling snubbed, Elinor looked round the large room at the tables that sparkled with glass and silver. After all, what did it matter? They would make friends at no matter what sitting they sat.

Back in her cabin, she saw that Valerie had not started to unpack but was reading a letter. Valerie looked up when she heard her sister and there was an odd look on her face, as if she was not sure whether she should be pleased or sorry at what she was reading. 'Look, Elinor . . .' she said, handing over the letter.

The letter was written on the ship's headed notepaper. The writing was large—big letters sprawled across the page impatiently. The ink was heavy black and the words seemed to stand out.

'Dear Miss Johnson,

I have received a letter from my old friend, Aggie King, and she tells me that you and your sister are her nieces and are going to make her home yours. She asked me to keep an eye on you and see that you enjoy yourselves. As a start, I would be pleased if you would come to my suite at about six o'clock for cocktails so that we may meet.'

It was signed *C. Anderson*.

'But how kind of her . . .' Elinor said, a little startled.

'Her?' Valerie asked. 'I think it's a man.'

Elinor studied the letter again. 'it could be . . . I suppose. I wonder what he is like.'

Valerie curled up on the bed and began to paint the nails of one hand, the tip of her tongue protruding through her lips as she concentrated.

'Probably some elderly retired colonel,' she said casually. 'Or maybe a wealthy sheep-farmer . . .' she added, looking up, her eyes twinkling. 'Bound to be pretty aged as he is a friend of Aunt Aggie's. If he is single, he might make you a good husband, Elinor . . .'

'Thank you very much,' Elinor said a little curtly. 'I can find my own husband, thanks . . .'

'I wonder . . .' Valerie mused. 'You always look so scared when a man speaks to you.'

'I do not . . .' Elinor said indignantly and began to unpack, her hands unsteady. What was the matter with Valerie today? Saying such mean things. Or maybe she was trying to be helpful—trying to tell her sister things she ought to know. *Pathetic look . . . always look scared when a man speaks to you.* Was it true?

Suddenly she thought of something. 'Oh dear . . .' she began as she looked up in dismay. 'We have to go to dinner at six-thirty . . . they refused to change the sitting. Said it was quite impossible.'

Valerie waved her hand about to dry it. 'Maybe we'll get so bored, we'll be glad to have an excuse to get away,' she said cheerfully. 'Pity we can't be changed but thanks for trying, Elinor.'

'That's all right . . .' Elinor mumbled, bending over her unpacking. That was one of the sweet things about Val—she was always so grateful when you did anything to help her.

'What shall we wear . . .?' Valerie said, starting on the other hand, her face absorbed in the task. 'You never dress for dinner on your first night out, but then this is a cocktail party, so we must wear something a bit smart. Bless Aunt Aggie for sending us money for clothes. She must be quite a honey.'

'She seems very generous and kind . . .' Elinor commented, her voice muffled as she hung away the clothes. Even that seemed absurdly disloyal to her mother, who had hated all their father's relations. Why? They had been unkind to her, she had said. Very, very unkind.

'I think I'll wash my hair,' Valerie said suddenly. 'It'll soon dry and it got pretty dirty on the train.'

Elinor hurried to finish the unpacking. She had a sudden longing to be out in the fresh air-to feel that they were finally going somewhere—to see the beautiful expanse of sea. 'I'm going up on deck,' she said.

'Oh no . . .' Valerie cried. 'I thought you'd set my hair for me.'

Elinor had to laugh. 'Oh no, my girl. I've done your unpacking but there are limits.'

'Okay, you win,' Valerie said cheerfully. 'Just watch out on deck. You might run into a wolf.'

For a moment, Elinor did not understand and then she laughed. 'Wolves need a certain amount of encouragement . . .'

Valerie was rummaging in her sponge bag. 'Then you'll be quite safe,' she said. 'That air of dignity of yours will keep them at bay.'

Elinor took the lift up to the promenade deck, chatting with the lift boy who looked about twelve but was actually seventeen. She went to lean against the rail and gaze at the coast line they were following. The blue sea sparkled and danced, the wind whipped at her, tugging her hair into a mad disorder. What

27

was it Val had said? *That air of dignity will keep them at bay.*

Really, Val was being most disturbing that day. Who, at twenty, wanted to be 'pathetic', 'scared' or 'dignified'? That was no way to live. Was it true? Maybe she had been a bit scared of that man—but then, she told herself, he was different. He was an older man, so very impressive, so frightening when his mouth tightened with anger, when his voice became icily cold. Oh, she must forget him . . .

She gripped the rail, letting her body go with the movement of the ship. Was that why she had so few friends and Valerie so many? She had thought it was because she had worked in the same office for five years in Johannesburg and there was no one else there under the age of forty-nine. But then Val had made friends at the bank, she had gone to dancing classes and squash, she had gone skating and swimming. Or was it because Elinor had formed the habit of going straight home to be with her mother—for she had known that, to her mother, the day had stretched endlessly and with a desolate loneliness. Not that it had ever been a bind, for her mother's warm welcome had been reward enough. So she had no regrets—but suddenly she wished she found it easier to make friends . . .

She walked round the deck, feeling lonely. Thinking that Valerie would have smiled at people and immediately got into conversation with them. If only she herself found it as easy . . .

Rounding a corner, she met the wind full on. Instinctively she ducked, pulling her head down, fighting the wind, and bumped into someone, who steadied her for a moment and then quickly pulled her behind a sheltering wall.

She gazed up into the face of the man she could not forget . . .

Gasping, she blurted out the first thing that came into her head.

'I thought you'd gone ashore . . .' she said. 'I didn't know you were sailing on this boat.'

He closed his eyes and sighed. 'Ship,' he said patiently. 'Don't you know better than to call this a boat? It seems your education has been sadly neglected. I am sorry I did not tell you my plans. You did not ask me and I must confess, I did not think you would be interested.' Again there was that odd quirk to the corner of his mouth as if he was trying not to laugh. 'As you once pointed out to me, it is none of your business.'

She stared at him helplessly. Why had they the power to irritate one another so?

Before she could find words, he went on: 'I take it that your luggage arrived all right? And that pretty madcap sister of yours?' he asked, his voice suddenly warm and indulgent. 'She was enjoying herself all right. It seems odd that you should be sisters. You are so completely unlike one another . . .' With that, he lifted his hand in the abrupt manner he had and walked away.

Elinor stared after him, gasping a little. Breathless, with a strange anger, fighting the curious sensation of helplessness she always felt when near him, wondering why his words had sounded like an insult.

She turned and hurried back to the cabin. It would be far better to set Valerie's hair than run the risk of another meeting with that man. How on earth was she going to avoid him on the voyage? She seemed doomed to bump into him and he always gave her the impression that he thought she was doing it on purpose!

Val looked up as the door opened and she laid aside her book.

'I guessed you'd repent,' she said saucily. 'I've got everything ready.'

Elinor began to laugh. 'You're impossible!'

Valerie's voice came muffled through the towel she was draping round her. 'But nice, Elinor? Your impossible but nice sister?'

As Elinor's hands began to rub the shampoo into red hair, she said in a mild voice, 'Quite nice—in small doses.'

'You're a honey,' Valerie said as Elinor's deft fingers twisted the soft red hair and imprisoned it with grips. 'Your trouble is you're too gentle and kind, Elinor. You get imposed on. But all the same, I'm jolly glad you're as you are.'

Later they dressed and the ship was beginning to roll a little so that, even with the best will in the world, they got into one another's way.

'We'll have to arrange a dressing rota,' Val said as she struggled to get into the tight sheath green frock. 'You first, of course, for I loathe getting up early.'

Elinor was brushing her own hair, trying to make the simple style look more sophisticated. She had chosen to wear a tangerine coloured shirt-waister and she added a pearl choker and ear-rings.

The two girls surveyed one another carefully.

'You look lovely,' Elinor said warmly. It was true, too. Valerie, so tall and slim, with the lovely long legs models need, had chosen a dress that clung to her, but not too tightly. She had twisted a string of amber beads round her neck, a matching one round one arm.

'Max—' Valerie said briefly as she touched the beads.

For a moment, Elinor's face clouded. 'Max made me promise on the train—when they all came to see us off—not to let you forget him.'

Valerie found it very amusing. 'He hasn't a hope. He's far too young. Why won't men accept these things?'

'I don't suppose it is easy for anyone to accept them,' Elinor said thoughtfully. 'It must

31

be hardest of all for a man. Do I look all right?' she asked anxiously as she looked in the mirror, half-afraid of what Valerie might say.

Valerie swung round and gave her a brief glance. 'You look sweet,' she said as she opened the door. 'A perfect lady.'

Elinor caught her breath and then controlled her feelings quickly as she followed her sister. Valerie did not mean to be unkind. But who on earth wanted to look like 'a perfect lady'? Was she really so dim, so drab? A lady—'dignified'—afraid of men— 'pathetic'? Was that really the right description for a girl of twenty? There must be something very wrong with her if she really looked like that . . .

They found Suite Three and for some reason Valerie stood a little behind Elinor and left it to her to knock on the door. It opened immediately as if someone had been standing on the other side, waiting for the knock.

Elinor found herself staring up into the strangely dark eyes of a very blond, sun-tanned man. A pair of eyes that looked as surprised as her own must . . .

'Are you Miss Johnson?' he drawled, opening the door wider, and then he looked past her and suddenly he was smiling, his whole face altering, becoming softer, friendlier, even pleased. 'And this is your sister?'

Valerie swept past Elinor who stood

transfixed with horror. 'Are you C. Anderson?' she asked gaily. 'We thought you'd be an elderly sheep farmer or a retired Colonel . . .'

Elinor stood, unnoticed, as the man shook Valerie warmly by the hand. He was even laughing. 'I am a sheep farmer,' he drawled. 'Whether elderly—or not.'

CHAPTER TWO

Afterwards, Elinor knew she must have automatically reacted, but she could never remember how she found her way to the deep comfortable arm-chair, holding a small glass of sherry in her hand, watching Valerie as she sat, curled up on the couch, turning to talk to Mr. Anderson easily as if she had known him all her life. Valerie's eyes shone excitedly, her cheeks were flushed as she leaned forward eagerly.

Elinor, ignored by the others, took time to glance round curiously. As Valerie had said when the invitation arrived, you had to be wealthy to afford a suite. It was most luxuriously furnished with thick golden curtains, deep plum red carpet, huge deep chairs, great vases of flowers. There were many gladioli of different colours. They reminded her of the enormous bunch of pink gladioli Max had given Valerie at the station

33

when he came to see them off on the Blue Train—and she would never forget the hurt look in his eyes as Valerie casually tossed the flowers on the seat, barely thanked him and then darted back on to the platform to chat with her friends. Valerie had soon forgotten him . . . Look at Valerie now, Elinor thought, as she observed her sister's eyes sparkling and her glorious red hair a delightful muddle when she leaned forward to say:

'Christopher Anderson—what a mouthful of a name.' She pulled a wry face that made her look prettier than ever. 'What shall we call you?'

'Mr. Anderson, of course,' Elinor said very quickly.

The big man turned to look at her, his face suddenly grave. 'My friends call me Kit . . .' he drawled. There was a challenge in his dark eyes that she saw but could not understand.

'Kit . . . that's sort of cute . . .' Valerie said, turning on the couch, kicking off her pointed, spindle-heeled shoes and wriggling her toes. 'What we women suffer to be beautiful . . .' she said, and laughed up at the grave man whose face relaxed every time he looked at her.

Then he glanced across at Elinor and there was a question in his eyes. She felt he was waiting for her to speak, expecting something of her. She plunged into the conversation. 'You know our Aunt Aggie?'

'I certainly do . . .' he drawled. 'My word, I'll

34

say I do. She's the nicest woman . . . You've never met her, I take it?'

He came to offer Elinor a cigarette. When she refused, he looked vaguely surprised, and then jokingly scolded Valerie when she accepted one. Silently Elinor watched as he flicked his lighter—watched Val as she leant forward and held his hand steady and glanced up at him from under her long curling lashes. Elinor wondered why the little quirk showed again at the corner of Kit Anderson's mouth, for he spoke gravely as he leaned back in his corner of the couch and stared at her.

'Your Aunt Aggie was my neighbour until three years ago,' he drawled. 'And a nicer neighbour no man could want. When I say neighbour—she was the nearest person, just on ninety miles away.' He smiled as both girls gasped. 'We farm in a big way here, you know. Anyhow, your uncle was taken ill so they sold their farm and now live outside Melbourne.'

'So we won't have to live on a farm . . .' Valerie began eagerly, pausing in her favourite occupation of blowing smoke rings.

Kit smiled at her. 'Don't you want to . . .' he began, but as the door opened, he looked up with a quick frown.

What an air of arrogance he had, Elinor thought, as she watched him. His first reaction on being interrupted was one of annoyance. Was this man so used to people bowing and scraping before him? Had his wealth made

35

him so proud that he thought he was different from other men? Did he expect everyone to hold their breath when he was near?

Now he was standing, towering above the lean man who had entered the room, an amused look in his humorous face. The newcomer was not a handsome man, but very good-looking in a totally different way from Kit's good looks. He had an easy elegance, a quiet strength that was unmistakable. His hair was blond, he had very blue eyes. He was dressed in dark trousers, a white shirt and a scarlet cummerbund, and over his arm was a white jacket.

'This is my cousin, Hugh Morgan . . .' Kit said formally. 'Hugh—these girls are nieces of Aggie . . . She didn't know they existed until the other day.'

'Well, well . . .' Hugh Morgan said lightly. 'To think that dear ugly old Aggie could be related to such beauties . . .' He smiled at Valerie and then turned to Elinor. 'I wonder what you'll think of Australia.'

Before she could speak, Valerie answered. 'I'm sure we shall love it if all Australian men are like you two.'

Elinor caught her breath but the two men merely laughed and even seemed flattered by the remark. It seemed strange to see Kit's disapproving face crease into laughter lines, his dark eyes dance as he looked at Valerie and then turned away to a table where there were bottles and glasses.

Hugh immediately took Kit's place on the couch. 'Although I'm his cousin,' he said in his quiet slow way, 'I don't live like Christopher. I don't like farm life. I'm from Sydney . . . now there is the most beautiful city in the world . . .'

Kit gave him a glass. 'Too packed with people—everyone rushing about madly, trying to make money,' he drawled.

Hugh's lean face was amused. 'Hark at who's talking.' He turned to Valerie, who was leaning forward, a strange look of amazement on her face. 'Kit is what is known as a pastoralist. One of these multi-millionaires who play about with billions of sheep . . .'

Kit was laughing. 'Don't make it sound too easy, Hugh. Sheep mean work.'

'Nice work if you can get it,' Hugh joked. 'So our dear Aggie wrote and told you her nieces would be on the ship, did she?'

Kit had swung a chair round and was straddling it, gazing into his glass. 'I found the letter waiting for me on the ship. Pity I didn't know on the train,' he added and startled Elinor by his direct look. 'Aggie asked me to keep an eye on the girls. It seems it's the first time they have travelled.'

Elinor's cheeks were suddenly hot. 'You mustn't let us be a nuisance,' she began stiffly.

Hugh nearly choked. Very carefully he put his glass on a small table and looked at Valerie and then at Elinor. 'Somehow I don't think Kit would let you be a nuisance . . . but don't worry, as Kit's cousin, I shall deem it my duty to assist him in the arduous task of looking after Aunt Aggie's nieces,' he said very pompously, his eyes twinkling.

'But we don't need looking after,' Elinor said indignantly.

'I do—' Valerie said gaily. 'I need it very badly. Poor Elinor goes nearly mad, looking after me. You see, Mummy asked her to take care of me so Elinor feels it her bounden duty . . .'

Elinor's face felt as if it was on fire. 'Please, Val . . .'

Kit was staring at her. She did not know where to look. And then he suddenly said thoughtfully, 'I think I shall call you Lady Kia . . .'

Hugh burst out laughing but quickly clapped his hand to his mouth when Elinor turned to look at him, her eyes suspicious.

'It's a compliment,' he assured her. But she went on staring at him doubtfully so Kit said:

'Of course it is a compliment.' His voice was curt. 'Lady Kia is a very dear friend of mine. At times I adore her—at other times I could cheerfully wring her neck.'

Valerie's sweet young laugh rang out. 'Is that how Elinor affects you?' she asked, but at that moment, the door opened and they all turned to look at the tall, slim, beautiful girl

Elinor had seen talking on the deck to Kit.

Now the girl stared at them, her eyes puzzled as she glanced at the two girls. She was beautiful—her deep midnight blue frock rustled as she moved; at her neck and wrists sparkled diamonds.

'Kit, you didn't tell me you had invited . . .' she began, her voice cool and haughty.

Kit was by her side, being very polite, introducing her to the two girls. 'This is my cousin, Alison Poole . . .'

The girl frowned. 'I'm not really your cousin, Kit.'

'Near enough as to make no odds,' Hugh said calmly as he rose. 'Alison just happened to be in South Africa at the same time as Kit and I, so we are travelling more or less together . . .'

Elinor saw the way Alison tightened her mouth as she sat down, and Elinor wondered if she had imagined the slight emphasis Hugh had seemed to put on the word *happened*.

They talked idly, Alison showing little interest in the fact that the girls were nieces of Aggie . . . indeed, she made them both feel that they were intruding and that she was surreptitiously watching the clock to see when they would go and leave her in peace and alone with the two men. It was as if the whole atmosphere of the room had changed. Valerie had hastily sat up, sliding her feet into her shoes. Kit had stopped laughing and looked rather sombre—even Hugh was talking in a subdued manner. It was just as one felt on a sunny day when a cloud hid the sun.

Glancing at her wrist watch, Elinor saw a way of escape and jumped to her feet. 'I'm afraid we must go . . . we are at the first sitting . . .'

Even as she spoke, they heard the rhythmical chimes of the gong. Kit's face was bland. 'No—you're at the second sitting. I had it changed. You'll be at my table.'

Elinor stared at him, her cheeks hot again. 'But I asked and . . .'

Valerie laughed a little too shrilly. 'Money can arrange anything.'

It was as if a shadow passed over Kit's face but he still smiled at Valerie. 'It may seem so to you, at your age, but it can't buy everything. Not quite everything. Not happiness.'

'Happiness . . .' Alison Poole said impatiently, her fingers tapping on the arm of her chair, her eyes darting from Valerie's face to Elinor's. 'Why do people make so much fuss about happiness? What is happiness, anyway? How could you define it?' She shot the question at Elinor who had just sunk down into the armchair and whose legs dangled because the chair went too far back. She felt gawky and ill-at-ease, especially as the elegant cool girl looked at her.

'Happiness?' Elinor echoed, trying hard to think of an intelligent answer and only able to think of the truth. 'Surely happiness means being with the person you love.'

Alison's mouth curled a little. 'How very charmingly put . . .' she sneered and turned to Valerie. 'Do you agree with your sister?'

Valerie looked startled. She had been talking to Hugh in a low earnest voice, her eyes fixed on his face. Now she looked at Alison and seemed, for once, to be at a loss for words. 'H—happiness?' she asked. 'I . . . well, I suppose to me being happy means having fun . . .'

'Fun . . .' echoed Alison, her voice scornful.

'Well, Alison . . .' Hugh asked, stepping into the silence and leaning forward to offer Alison a cigarette.

Alison's mouth tightened. 'I have never thought about it. Happiness comes from yourself. I have always been happy . . .'

Kit rose. 'Like another drink, Alison?' he drawled. 'You don't know what you are talking about—' His voice was faintly scornful. 'You are the unhappiest woman I know.'

Alison's face was suddenly very white. Her eyes blazed as she handed him her glass. 'How can you say such a thing, Kit? It's not true . . .'

He stood before her, staring down at her. 'I've known you all my life, Alison,' he said in his slow, amused voice. 'I have never known you really enjoy anything. Not a beautiful sunset—a flower—a good book—a play. Always you find something wrong with it. You

41

spend your entire time belittling things and people and complaining . . .'

If Alison had been white before, now her face was scarlet. 'Kit . . .'

He sat down beside her, smiling a little. 'Just think it over, Alison—' he said. There was a strange gentleness in his voice—it was almost a tenderness, Elinor thought, as she sat back and watched the little scene. Was he in love with Alison? She behaved towards him as if he was her property—in the way she had put her hand on his arm, the tone of her voice. Now she was looking quite upset as she stared at Kit who went on slowly in that fascinating drawl of his: 'Listen to yourself, Alison, and see if you ever praise anything or anyone . . .' And then, quite quietly, he turned to Elinor and began to ask her questions as to why she and her aunt had never known of one another's existence.

Again Valerie answered, not giving Elinor a chance. 'It was our mother's fault . . .' Valerie said, leaning forward, clasping her hands, her red hair falling over one eye. How young Valerie looked, Elinor thought, how very young, especially next to Alison Poole, who was sitting back now, her face stiff with anger, her mouth a thin line. 'You see, Daddy was an Englishman—one of the bad boys of the family,' Valerie added with a gay little laugh. 'He was sent out to South Africa to make good . . . and he married a South African girl. He took her back to England to meet his family and she hated it . . .'

'Hated it?' Alison said very coldly. 'What a queer thing.'

Elinor's cheeks burned. 'It wasn't so queer when you realise that she was only seventeen and had never been away from home before—' she said quickly. 'And they were all horrible to her—' she added, almost fiercely. 'They didn't like her and they made it plain that she was not good enough for their son and . . .'

Valerie chimed in. 'I know Elinor doesn't agree with me but I think it was Mom's own fault. She was most frightfully sensitive and always imagined snubs and slights . . .'

Kit spoke very quietly. 'I can imagaine that any young bride meeting her husband's people for the first time might be sensitive. If the rest of the family are anything like Aggie, I'm not in the least surprised your mother felt strange and unhappy . . .' He looked at Elinor and gave a small smile. It was the first time he had smiled at her. 'Aggie is quite a character,' he went on slowly. 'She has the proverbial heart of gold but she barks and never bites. Even after twenty-five years in Australia she still looks and talks like a typical Englishwoman. She is blunt . . .'

'I think she is extremely rude—' Alison said stiffly.

Hugh chuckled. 'She certainly spares no punches, but all the same, she is a honey and I am sure you girls will love her,' he said reassuringly. 'I think Kit is right and maybe your mother didn't understand the family sense of humour.'

Elinor had clasped her hands unconsciously. 'It could have been that, I suppose. Mother was strange—once she had an idea, it became an obsession, and she was convinced the family hated her and she was too proud to give them a chance to snub her. I was ten years old when Daddy died and I can still remember the look on Mother's face when she wrote on the letters that came from England—*Gone away, address unknown*, and asked me to post them. I remember saying that we hadn't gone away, and she said that, to them, we had.'

'I think it was wrong of her,' Valerie said bluntly, 'and unkind. To them and to us, don't you, Kit? ' She turned to him eagerly and Elinor saw the quick frown that flickered across Alison's face. 'Dad was so proud of his family, Kit,' Valerie went on. 'He was always talking about when he would take us home to see them. Even I can remember that.'

Kit turned to Elinor. 'Is that why you are so unhappy about going to Australia?' he asked gravely. 'Because you feel it is disloyal to your mother?'

Caught on the wrong foot by his unexpected understanding and the sympathy in his voice, Elinor's eyes filled with tears. 'Yes . . .' she murmured, hoping he would not see the tears.

'I think Mom was disloyal to Daddy,'

44

Valerie said quickly. 'Oh—might as well talk to a stone wall—' she said, her voice exasperated. 'Elinor is just like Mom. Once she gets an idea into her head. Look, there we were, Mom had died and we hadn't a penny in the world but what we earned and, dear knows, that was little enough. We didn't know what to do . . . we couldn't pay the rent of the flat—we were desperate. Yet when I said we should write to England for help, Elinor was about as stubborn as a mule,' Valerie said fiercely. 'What else could we do? Daddy would have wanted us to do it, so why . . . Elinor talked a lot of tripe about pride and so on and how Mom would feel, but what I say is, one must eat and surely pride of that sort is very silly . . .'

'You are, quite obviously, a realist,' Hugh said lightly. 'Some more sherry, Elinor? No? Val? Alison will, I know . . .' He took the glass and then began to steer the conversation into lighter channels. Whether he did it by accident or design, Elinor did not know, but she was grateful for the chance it gave her to get herself under control again. Whenever she thought of her mother, she was filled with this feeling of desolation. She and her mother had always been so close. Sometimes it seemed to her that Valerie hardly missed their mother— but then Val had always been a little difficult, restless, defiant. In a way, Elinor sympathised with Valerie, for their mother had been very possessive and also intolerant, quick to dislike

45

their friends, to discourage the girls making any. Elinor had accepted the situation because of her deep pity for her mother, always ailing, always unhappy, but Valerie had a different nature.

The second gong sounded and the two girls went into the luxurious bedroom of the suite to tidy up. Valerie grabbed Elinor's arm.

'Isn't he absolutely super—smooth . . . out of this world?' she whispered excitedly. 'That's the man I was telling you about . . .'

Elinor experienced a familiar feeling of apprehension. Was Valerie falling in love with Kit?

'He knows it . . .' she said rather sourly. 'So arrogant and . . .'

Valerie looked startled. 'I wouldn't call him arrogant . . .' she began, and stopped talking as Alison came to peer into the mirror, to pat her immaculately groomed golden hair, to look with cold indifference at the silent girls before she left them.

There was quite a hum of excitement as they went into the dining salon, Elinor noticed. The stewards appeared from nowhere, fussing round Kit, shaking napkins, handing the beautifully decorated menus, hovering . . . So this was what happened when you were very wealthy, she thought, a little bitterly. Nice work if you can get it . . . Wasn't that what Hugh had said? How very different the two cousins were, she thought, looking at Kit's grim, unapproachable face and then meeting Hugh's friendly twinkling eyes with an answering smile.

The food was delicious and Valerie made no bones about enjoying it.

'Isn't it scrumptious, Elinor?' she would say. Or: 'Oh, boy—can I really have a second helping?'

The cool wine they drunk with the meal was also very pleasant and Elinor found herself enjoying herself very much indeed, especially as she was lucky enough to have Hugh next to her. He was so easy to talk to and he shared himself between the two sisters, keeping them amused, making them feel happy. Kit was silent and Alison had an aloof air as she played with a salad as if food bored her.

After coffee in the lounge, there was dancing. Alison walked, her hand on Kit's sleeve, as she talked to him earnestly, enclosing them in a world of their own, shutting out Hugh and the two girls who followed them. Hugh was teasing them, making them promise to dance at least once with him before he lost them to younger, more handsome men.

'I think you're handsome . . .' Valerie said in her outspoken way, and then she looked startled and almost afraid for a moment as her face coloured vividly.

Hugh chuckled. 'Thank you, Val—for those few kind words. I know I'm no Adonis . . . like

47

my cousin Kit.'

'I think you're better looking than Kit . . .' Valerie said. 'Don't you, Elinor?'

Startled, Elinor stared at them and then at Hugh. In a way, Valerie was right. Kit was handsome in a vibrant, overwhelming way. Hugh had a more gentle face, lean, almost aristocratic. The sort of face she would have imagined that the Scarlet Pimpernel would have had, the hero of her childish readings.

'Yes, I think you are,' Elinor said slowly.

'Well . . . well . . . I am covered with confusion . . .' Hugh joked as he led them to a table on the verandah café, the floor of which had been cleared for dancing.

The small orchestra was tuning up, people were strolling in to find a table to sit at. Through the windows, they could see the ocean as the ship rolled very slightly.

Elinor danced first with Hugh. 'Sorry I'm not a Victor Silvester,' he said cheerfully, 'but I've got a gammy leg. Hurt it on a motor-bike when I was young and foolish.'

'It's hardly noticeable . . .' Elinor said. She had been nervous about dancing, for she had done very little, but Hugh was so easy—easy to talk to, easy to be with. You were not afraid with Hugh, somehow. 'Is Alison Kit's cousin?'

'In a way, but then, in a way, she isn't,' Hugh said as he danced her round the floor. Not many couples were dancing yet. Kit was dancing with Valerie and Alison was talking,

48

her face a white mask of annoyance, with a very good-looking tall officer. 'It's all rather complicated,' Hugh went on. 'Kit's aunt married a man who was later divorced by her and he remarried and they had Alison. Well, when he and his wife were both killed in a car smash, Kit's aunt adopted Alison. I think she has always loved her husband and having Alison was like having a bit of him. Anyhow that was the way it was. So Alison isn't a blood cousin, if you know what I mean, but they've been brought up as cousins.'

'Why did she deny it, then?' Elinor asked curiously.

Hugh chuckled. 'You noticed that? Well, our dear Alison is afraid Kit's mother will trot out the old story about cousins not marrying . . .'

Elinor felt as if her heart had stopped. 'Are they engaged?'

Hugh chuckled. 'Well, they are and they aren't, if you know what I mean. Alison thinks they are but Kit just says nothing at all. If he is going to marry her, he'll do it in his own time and way. He's a dark horse, is Kit. Never can seem to tell what he's thinking about. His mother and Alison don't hit it off, at all. You'll like his mother. She's a dear . . .' his voice softened as he spoke.

The dance was over and he took her back to the table. When Elinor was asked to dance by Kit, she went into his arms with mixed feelings. In spite of herself, she was apprehensive lest

49

she dance badly or trip over his feet and yet she was conscious of a thrill, to feel his arms round her, the touch of his firm hand. She closed her eyes tightly as she danced, telling herself it was nonsense to feel like this about such a man . . . a man who was more or less engaged to be married . . .

Kit danced stiffly but very well. Elinor found herself able to follow him without difficulty. Once he apologised.

'I'm afraid I don't dance very well,' he drawled in that arrogant way she was beginning to expect. 'I don't get much practice, for I never go to dances if I can get out of it.'

She looked up at him. She had to look up a very long way.

'You don't like dancing?' she asked.

'On the farm I'm much too busy,' he said curtly and she felt snubbed. 'Now Hugh, he's different,' he went on. 'Hugh practically lives in night-clubs.' His voice was tolerant, affectionate.

Valerie was swinging by them, laughing gaily, smiling provocatively up into the face of a young ship's officer. For a moment, Elinor frowned worriedly and Kit's arm tightened round her.

'Surely,' he drawled, 'you're not worried about Val?'

Elinor's cheeks were hot for a moment as she looked up at him defensively. 'I am, sometimes. After all, I am responsible for her and she is so young and she does the silliest things without thinking . . .'

He executed a neat turn, deftly avoiding a couple as they danced past. 'So do you . . .' he said.

Elinor was startled. 'I do?'

'Don't you?' he drawled. The music stopped and they were near the door that led to the deck. His hand on her arm, he led her out of the crowded café and to the cool deck. They leant on the rail and watched the shimmering water as it seemed to dance in the moonlight. 'You speak to strange men on the train . . .' he drawled.

Startled by the unexpected attack, she swung round to stare up at him. 'I . . . honestly, I really thought on that train that it was Val . . .'

He went on slowly: 'You practically fall into their arms in dining-cars . . .'

She looked at him sharply, wondering whether he was being funny. Or was he seriously blaming her? It was difficult to know, when a man had that dead-pan sort of face, when even the twinkle in his eyes that might give you a clue could not be seen because he was steadfastly staring at the water.

'That was an accident,' she said.

'I'm not doubting you for a moment,' he drawled in his maddening way. 'But another man might have taken it for an invitation.'

'What nonsense!' she said, trying to sound

51

indignant.

'Seriously,' he went on gravely, 'I think you need protection far more than Valerie does. Her natural gaiety is its own protection and she loves life, is honest and without guile. Also her head is screwed on all right. No, Elinor, I don't think you need worry about your sister. I'm much more concerned about you . . .'

'Me?' she cried. His remark really stung her. 'Please, Mr. Anderson, don't worry about me. I am perfectly capable of looking after myself and I refuse to be a nuisance to you . . .'

'You're wasting your breath arguing with me . . .' he said quietly, his drawl more apparent than ever as he took her arm. 'I intend to keep an eye on you, make no mistake about that!'

CHAPTER THREE

At breakfast next day, Elinor and Hugh were alone at their table. Hugh jumped to his feet when he saw her, his thin face friendly as he greeted her.

'Kit has his breakfast in his cabin,' he said cheerfully. 'That poor mutt has been up writing letters since the crack of dawn. Who'd be a wealthy sheep-farmer!'

Elinor carefully considered the menu and gave her order to the steward.

'Orange juice and . . . and a cereal and then sauté kidneys.'

Hugh chuckled. 'How nice to meet a girl who doesn't diet.'

'I'm lucky,' Elinor told him honestly. 'I don't have to.'

Hugh helped himself to marmalade. 'The fair Alison has only black coffee and half a grapefruit. Is life worth living?'

'I suppose it is,' Elinor said thoughtfully, 'when you are as beautiful as Alison.'

'Do you think Alison beautiful?' Hugh asked. 'I find her much too cold and stiff. She always looks as if she has found a bad smell . . .'

Elinor dissolved into laughter. Somehow Hugh made everything such fun. He went on: 'Now I call your sister beautiful. Maybe not strictly but she has that air of vitality, of loving life . . .'

'Yes, Val is lovely, I think,' Elinor agreed warmly. 'She is a darling.'

Hugh smiled. 'I can see that. She's very young, isn't she?'

'Seventeen . . .' Elinor said. 'I think it's very young . . .' She sipped the coffee slowly. 'Kit doesn't think so . . .' Somehow she always called him *Kit* in her mind but she found it almost impossible to call him that to his face. He had scolded her the night before for being *unfriendly*, had told her she must call him *Kit* or he would be offended.

'Oh, Kit . . .' Hugh shrugged as if Kit's

53

opinion was unimportant. 'I suppose Val is sleeping off last night's gaiety? She had a good time?'

Elinor's eyes shone. 'She enjoyed every moment of it—I had practically to drag her to bed.'

'And you?' Hugh's voice was suddenly grave.

'Well, I did and . . . I didn't . . .' Elinor said slowly, twiddling a fork on the shining white cloth to avoid looking at him. She thought of the evening after Kit had taken her back to the verandah café. Shortly afterwards he had vanished from the scene and although she had plenty of dancing partners she had missed him, and had been very conscious of the fact that Alison, too, had gone. She had thought of them together—of Kit taking Alison in his arms, kissing that beautiful, disdainful face . . . Now she looked up suddenly, meeting Hugh's enquiring look. 'Hugh—why does Kit dislike me so?'

He was very startled. 'Kit—dislike you? What on earth gave you that idea?' he demanded sternly.

Her cheeks were hot. 'Nothing I do is ever right . . .' she said. 'I do try not to annoy him but . . . well, last night, he told me I was very young and silly and that I needed looking after far more than Val . . . I certainly don't . . .' In spite of herself, the words rushed out indignantly as she saw Hugh beginning to smile. 'I'm three years older than Val and I

54

have been working since I was sixteen and . . . well, I can look after myself,' she finished defiantly.

Hugh folded his napkin slowly. 'I think Kit is right. You do need someone to look after you. But in a loving way. You need someone to care what you do . . . to want your happiness.'

'I . . .' It was Elinor's turn to be caught off balance as she stared at him, not knowing quite what to say. 'Oh, Hugh . . .' she gasped.

Confused, she stood up hastily and almost ran from the dining-salon. Back in their cabin, Valerie was still asleep, clutching the pillow with both arms, her glorious red hair spread out fan-wise on the white pillow. Elinor went quietly to the mirror and frowned at her reflection. She did look 'pathetic' . . . she made herself smile, and she still looked miserable. What was wrong with her?

She was wearing a pink and white striped frock. Now, she swung a white cardigan over her shoulders before going up in the lift to the deck. She stepped outside and stood, gasping, at the sheer beauty of the blue sea which seemed to rise and fall before her as the ship gently rolled. She went to the rail, gazing down at the small white waves, feeling the sudden excitement fill her. This was her chance to enjoy herself—to forget responsibilities, to stop worrying about the future. She turned, leaning against the rail, surveying the broad deck, a friendly smile on her mouth, ready to speak to anyone . . . But no one seemed interested. Couples strode by her, mostly middle-aged, sombre-looking men and women striding round the deck solemnly as if they had a certain number of miles to be walked in a limited time. Children were racing round the empty swimming pool. Parents were grabbing the chairs available and arranging them in the sunshine. Groups of young people were playing deck games. But no one paid any attention to Elinor.

She hesitated, knowing well that Valerie would have found a way of making friends. She would join a group casually, asking, 'What gives?' in her friendly voice. This was something Elinor could never do.

She began to walk alone. At least she knew Kit was safely in his cabin writing letters. Why did a farmer have to write so many letters? She began to enjoy her walk, learning to balance herself as she corrected the roll of the ship. Kit certainly did not look like a business executive—he looked like a man who spent most of his life out of doors.

But then Hugh didn't look like a business man, either. He looked gentle, more like a young Professor. What did he do? There was something of a mystery. Or maybe it had just been Alison being catty the night before when she accused Hugh of being a lazy good-for-nothing, preying off his cousin. How furious Kit had been—swinging round to tell Alison crossly that Hugh was invaluable to him, and Alison had merely smiled nastily. It had been an ugly awkward moment saved by Hugh himself, who had made a joke of it.

What had Hugh meant, too, when he said that Alison was afraid Kit's mother would fight the marriage? Somehow you could not imagine a man like Kit asking his mother for permission to marry? He was a man accustomed to making his own decisions. He would not care what others thought. He was afraid of no one—he would know exactly what he wanted from life and go ahead like a bulldozer and get it . . .

She paused by the rail to stare down at the blue sea. She had to smile as she tried to imagine Kit's reaction if she told him he was like a bulldozer. Would he be flattered—or insulted? He was so sure of himself . . . so conceited . . . No, that was not true. Kit was not conceited—it was just his self-assurance. He knew that he could get anything he wanted—no wonder he had that arrogant air . . .

And yet—could he always get what he wanted? What was it he had said the night before? That money could not buy happiness? Was he unhappy, then? He was so good at hiding his feelings that it was hard to tell . . .

She began walking again. She simply must stop thinking about Kit. Yet everywhere she looked, she seemed to see him. Tall, impressive, his vitality making the air throb with electricity for her. It was nonsense . . . in fact, it was worse. She was asking to be hurt . . .

Was Kit in love with Alison? He did not treat her as you would expect a man in love to do . . . yet how could you tell? How would Kit behave if he was in love? He was so different from other men.

There had been substance in the remarks Hugh had made at breakfast. Ever since her father's death, Elinor had been aware of a lack in her life. She had done the loving, the protecting, for her mother had made it so obvious that no one could replace their father in her life. She had leaned on Elinor, craved her company but only to talk about the wonderful man she had lost. She had never been interested in the girls' lives. Valerie had bitterly resented that but Elinor had learned to accept it.

'Elinor . . .' a gay voice called, and Elinor looked up to see Valerie walking towards her, her hand tucked through Kit's arm. Kit was wearing white shorts and shirt. He was looking genial and almost human, she thought, and then realised it was because Valerie was saying something to him. 'They're choosing the Sports Committee, Elinor . . . come along, we must vote for them . . .' She brushed aside Elinor's half-audible protest and tucked her free hand through Elinor's arm. 'Come on . . .'

Elinor had no choice and inwardly she was rather pleased to find herself in the group again, for Alison and Hugh were waiting, and almost at once proceedings were under way to form the committee. No one except Valerie seemed very willing to serve on the committee, but her gay spirits made the little meeting amusing and Elinor found herself strenuously fighting the proposal that she should be on it and was more than chagrined to have Valerie say with affectionate exasperation:

'Oh, don't let's bother poor Elinor. She prefers to sit and watch . . .'

'While we do all the hard work?' Kit drawled, lifting those thick eyebrows of his quizzically as he glanced at Elinor. He and Hugh had been elected but Alison, too, had declined rather frostily.

Valerie glanced at her mischievously. 'I don't really blame you,' she said cheerfully. 'It means hard work as Kit says, and I expect you like to rest a lot . . .'

Before Alison could speak, Hugh was seized with such a bad fit of coughing that everyone had to clap him on the back or rush to get him water and the moment had passed by the time he had recovered—but there was a twinkle in his blue eyes as he shook his head and said softly to Elinor: 'That sister of yours!'

Elinor's cheeks were hot. 'Wasn't it rather rude?'

'Do Alison the world of good—and of course, to you and Val she is an older woman. How she must hate it . . .' Hugh said quietly in

Elinor's ear and then more loudly, 'Now you and Alison must run along—we members of the committee have work to do . . .'

Elinor almost regretted her decision not to serve on the committee as she followed the stiff back of Alison as they walked out of the room. But then she was glad again. Being on the committee would mean being a lot with Kit and giving him further opportunities to be annoyed by her.

But she still seemed to see a lot of him for Valerie, Hugh and Kit all came in search of her when the meeting was over and insisted that she put her name down for all the different sports.

'I shall be hopeless . . .' Elinor said miserably. 'I'll only make a fool of myself . . .'

For a moment Hugh and Valerie were talking to one another and Kit turned in his chair to look at the young face by his side.

'Look, Elinor . . .' he said in the patient voice of a man dealing with a difficult child. 'You have the wrong outlook entirely. No wonder you are a rabbit at most things. You must have faith in yourself. Faith can move mountains.'

Elinor swallowed. 'But how do you have faith in yourself . . .?'

He considered her gravely, noting the quick way she flushed, the way her eyes would sparkle for a moment if she forgot herself, the sudden vanishing of that light, the retreat into herself. 'Why are you so afraid?' he asked.

'I'm afraid of making a fool of myself,' she confessed.

His eyebrows lifted. Elinor found herself clenching her fists, struggling to talk intelligently, wishing she was not always so tense when she was with him.

'Would that matter so much?' he asked. 'So long as you do your very best, does it matter what others think?'

She gazed at him, staring into his dark eyes, trying to think, trying to find the right words.

'I suppose it oughtn't to matter . . .' she said very slowly.

'But it still does?'

She nodded unhappily. She could see that he despised her. Kit would admire women who were capable, efficient, self-assured. Women like Alison . . . like Valerie . . .

'Maybe it's because Val is so good at everything . . .' Elinor confessed in a quiet voice.

Kit frowned. 'Now don't use Val as a scapegoat for your cowardice . . .' he said sharply.

'Kit . . .' Valerie said in that moment. 'We're going to see if we can have a game of table tennis. Coming?'

Elinor half rose but Kit's hand was suddenly on her arm as he drawled, holding her prisoner. 'We're in the midst of an important discussion, Val. You two go and get some practice. Keep the court for us—Elinor and I are going to play later.'

'Oh no . . .' Elinor murmured miserably.

When they were alone, sitting in the sunshine, Kit turned to look at her. 'Why are you scared of me?' he asked abruptly.

She felt her face flame and was furious when he smiled.

'Go on, Lady Kia . . .' he said. 'I know you can't tell a lie . . .'

'Why do you call me that?' she cried. 'I hate it!'

He chuckled. 'If you knew the original Lady Kia, you would be honoured. But I'm not letting you wriggle out of this. Elinor, why are you scared of me?'

It was a worried little voice that answered him. 'Because I always seem to annoy you.'

Kit leaned forward, his handsome face worried. 'Annoy me?'

Elinor swallowed. 'Yes—on the train and the ship . . . and even before that, at the restaurant in Jo' burg . . .'

His face changed as he looked amused. 'You saw me . . .?'

Blushing painfully, Elinor nodded. What must he think of her? 'You were frowning as if I had angered you.'

'You were rather a noisy crowd . . .' he said slowly.

'They were our friends . . . wishing us goodbye . . .' She was on the defensive at once.

'Would you want us to sit around and weep?'

Kit burst out laughing. 'My dear child!'

'I'm not a child . . . nor your dear . . .' Elinor burst out, unable to bear it any more, getting up and almost running down the deck.

She heard his footsteps close behind her and when his hand closed like a vice round her wrist she stopped dead, unable to control the shiver that went through her. Kit stared down at her, his face suddenly blank.

'You are afraid of me . . .' he said slowly, almost as if he had discovered something terrible.

'You are . . . rather alarming . . .' Elinor said lightly, trying to joke.

'I suppose I am . . .' he said and released her wrist.

Without thinking, she began to rub it, longing for his hand to be on her arm again, remembering the thrill that had shot through her when he touched her.

'Don't dramatise the situation . . .' Kit said coldly and she saw that, again, he was vexed with her. 'I didn't hurt you all that much . . .'

She stared at him in dismay and realised what her instinctive gesture must have looked like. 'I didn't . . . you didn't . . .' she began.

He was not listening. 'I want you to meet my mother . . .' he said and led the way down to a lower deck. Meekly, she followed him.

He led the way to where an elderly woman was sitting in the sunshine in a wheelchair. She turned an eager face as she saw them.

'Why, Kit, my dear boy, and this is . . .' she said warmly and held out a welcoming hand to Elinor.

'This is Elinor, the eldest of Aggie's nieces . . .' Kit said and went to find chairs.

Elinor gazed down curiously at the lined pale face that was smiling up at her. Mrs. Anderson had white hair, beautifully set, but her face was devoid of make-up and her grey eyes were gentle. 'You'll love Aggie, my dear,' she said softly. 'And how happy Aggie will be to have you girls. She leads a lonely life in many ways for her husband is very ill. You'll be a great comfort to her.'

Kit had returned with the chairs. He grinned as he sat down and Elinor saw, with something of a shock, how very much he loved his mother.

'This is the elder sister, as I said, Mother. The sensible one . . .' he began.

Elinor's cheeks burned. 'I didn't know you thought me sensible—' she was stung into saying.

Kit chuckled. 'Somehow I've got you all confused with the way I think.'

Elinor drew a deep breath. Of course he was joking—but oh, if he only knew how very confused she was. She was suddenly aware that Mrs. Anderson was looking puzzled. Perhaps Kit saw it also, for he stood up, patted his mother's hand.

64

'Everything under control, Mother? Hip not hurting too badly?' He waited for her smiling reassurance. 'Good—' he went on. 'Now I'll leave you to get to know Elinor but I'll be back in half-an-hour.' He looked suddenly grim as he gazed at Elinor. 'No running away, mind, for I shall track you down.' He turned to his mother again. 'I'm going to teach Elinor to play table-tennis . . .' he finished and was then gone, striding down the deck with long easy movements.

Mrs. Anderson was quiet for a moment as they both gazed at the sea—and then she turned to the girl who was sitting so quietly, her hands folded tightly together, a strangely unhappy look on her young face.

'Now tell me, dear child, the whole story. I've known Aggie for many years but she had no idea of your existence. I remember her talking sadly about her brother who had died in South Africa and that they had lost touch with the wife and children—that there had been a bad epidemic of diphtheria in Johannesburg and they had always feared the children had died in that. Tell me, why did you get in touch with her?' she asked gently. There was only friendliness in her questioning, Elinor realised, and she began to explain everything.

Mrs. Anderson was a good listener. Elinor felt better by the time she had explained the situation.

'My dear, you must not feel disloyal to your

65

mother,' Mrs. Anderson said gently. 'I am sure you have done the right thing. Aggie is probably like her family—not easy to understand—and your mother was so very young and probably scared . . .'

They had not heard Kit's approach. Now he loomed above them.

'Like her daughter. Somehow we've got to cure that,' he said almost curtly. 'Come on, Elinor—the court, or rather table, is free. I'm going to teach you to play well . . . I'm going to teach you a lot of things,' he added sternly.

Elinor followed him.

CHAPTER FOUR

Kit had said he would teach her to play table tennis well and he was undoubtedly a man of his word. Elinor felt she had never run so much in her life before as he played with her, giving her difficult shots to practise, handing out praise when deserved.

'It was a funny thing,' she remarked later to Hugh. They had put two chairs in front of the gymnasium and near the swimming pool. From the open window, they could hear the light-hearted laugh Valerie kept giving as she played a swift game with Kit. 'I'm afraid I'm inclined to do silly things when I'm playing with Kit,' Elinor said. 'It never seems to worry Val if she does anything wrong . . .'

The sun was beating down on them. The blue sea sparkled. Children were diving into the swimming pool, parents hovering anxiously round the smaller ones who wanted to do the same.

Hugh turned his lean, good-looking face towards Elinor. His smile was kind. 'You try too hard,' he said.

Elinor frowned a little. 'Maybe I do . . . now when I play with you . . .'

'You play a good game,' Hugh told her. 'It's only when you are with Kit that you flap and start doing silly things.'

'I know . . .' Elinor spread out her hands on her lap and stared at them. It was all very well for Hugh to talk.

'Why are you scared of Kit?' Hugh asked abruptly.

Elinor sat up suddenly and stared at him, her eyes wide. Was it so easy to read her thoughts? She saw that Hugh was smiling, as if amused.

'I'm . . .' She began to deny it fiercely, but what was the good? 'He . . . he's . . .' She hunted for the right words. 'I don't know, Hugh,' she admitted miserably and knew that it was not the truth. She knew why she was afraid of Kit. It was because she so badly wanted him to like and admire her . . .

'Lazy good-for-nothings . . .' Valerie teased and Elinor looked up and saw Valerie standing before them, her hand carelessly swinging in Kit's. Valerie was flushed, her red hair disordered, but her face was alight with excitement. 'I beat him . . . just think of that, Elinor,' Valerie said eagerly and accepted, with a quick smile, Hugh's chair. The two men sat down on the deck, clasping their knees.

'And I didn't let her . . .' Kit said suddenly, quirking an eyebrow quizzically at Elinor.

She felt her face flame. It was just what she had been thinking! It seemed as if everyone could read her thoughts.

'Oh, Lady Kia . . .' Kit said in that slow drawl she knew so well, now. 'Don't look like that. One day you'll beat me . . .'

'He's good, Elinor . . .' Valerie put in, 'but he has a weakness . . .'

'Like all men . . .' Kit drawled, laughing as he looked at the excited pretty girl.

Elinor stared down at her fingers, afraid if she met his eyes that he would read her thoughts. It was hard to imagine Kit with any weakness. He always seemed so strong, so self-assured . . .

Valerie jumped to her feet. Sometimes Elinor wondered if Valerie ever sat still these days. She seemed to have been wound up to be so excited and afraid to lose a moment that she could not be still.

'Come on, you two . . .' she said to the men. 'We've got a committee meeting, remember? See you later, Elinor . . .'

Elinor felt rather bleak when they went off together and she was left alone. The children were squealing in excitement as the water was slowly drained out of the pool and even the tiny ones could play in the few inches of water.

She stood up and began to walk along the deck, balancing herself as she walked, adjusting herself to the slight roll. How beautiful it all was—the blue sea sparkling in the sun, stretching away to the far distant horizon. It was her own fault she was not with the others. It was inconsistent and downright stupid to feel they had neglected her. She could have been on the committee. It was her own fault . . .

She found a vacant chair on a quiet part of the deck. She could see the blue water reflected in the lounge window. From the decks above, drifted the laughter of people practising for the sports. She ought to go up and practise . . .

Kit had told her she should not belittle herself. Hc said people judged you on your own valuation. Well, how did she value herself . . .?

First—she knew she was not pretty. Not likc Val . . . nor beautiful with Alison's perfect features. But Hugh had told her that she should wear bright colours because she had a perfect skin and the longest curliest dark lashes he had ever seen. Was he just being kind or . . .?

She stood up abruptly. That was just the sort of thought she must not have. It was a defeatist attitude, as Kit called it. She must believe that she was pretty and then she would be . . . she must believe she could play games well . . .

She hurried up the steep staircase to the upper deck. In a few moments, she found herself part of a group.

'Answer to our prayer—' a fat jolly young man said cheerfully. 'We needed a fourth.'

It was quite a shock to Elinor when the afternoon ended and she realised how swiftly the time had flown. She had thoroughly enjoyed the games, discovering that she could play quite well . . . being part of a group and liking it. It was what she needed, practising— and also mixing with others. She must overcome her shyness, must try to be like Val . . . Valerie was in the cabin when Elinor reached it. Valerie was already changed into a slim green sheath frock. 'Where on earth did you vanish?' she asked Elinor, leaning forward to gaze at her face in the mirror.

'I was playing deck quoits,' Elinor said, looking at her watch, gathering her things for it was nearly time for her bath.

'See you in Kit's room later . . .' Valerie said, her hand on the door. 'We're all meeting there for drinks . . .' and then she was gone.

Again, Elinor had to fight her shyness, as when she had bathed and dressed carefully in a deep carmine-coloured frock, she made her way to Kit's luxurious suite. It was her own fault but she was outside the little group— Valerie, Kit and Hugh made a threesome, into which they kindly admitted Elinor . . .

But the welcome she got reassured her a little. Both Hugh and Kit hurried to greet her, fussed over her until she was settled in a chair.

'Where did you get to this afternoon?' Kit asked.

'She was playing on the boat deck . . .' Valerie said cheerfully. 'We fussed for nothing . . .'

'Fussed?' Elinor repeated slowly, looking puzzled.

Hugh smiled. 'You just vanished. After the committee meeting, we went back to find you and you had gone.'

'You see, Elinor . . .' Valerie said, holding Kit's hand steady as he lighted her cigarette for her, 'Kit was worried about you. He was afraid you'd gone down to your cabin in miserable loneliness . . .' She laughed but the words had a sting for Elinor.

Her cheeks were hot as she answered. 'I thought I needed some practice so I went up on the boat deck. We played quoits most of the time . . .'

'I knew you'd be all right,' Valerie said lightly. 'I said to them, leave Elinor to enjoy herself in her own way—even if we do think it is a rather funny way . . .'

Before Elinor could say anything, the door opened and Mrs. Anderson, in her chair, was wheeled in by a tall, blonde girl in nurse's uniform, who smiled at Kit and then left them. Kit went to greet his mother and wheeled her to a space near Elinor.

In a few moments, Elinor and the older woman were deep in conversation. Elinor liked Mrs. Anderson more each time she met her but, at the same time, her ears vainly sought to overhear what the other three were talking about. Even as she told Mrs. Anderson about life in Johannesburg and how beautiful Pretoria was in jacaranda time, Elinor was wondering what Valerie could have said to make Hugh and Kit laugh so much. It was almost a relief when Alison came to join them, causing the hilarious conversation to die down, bringing her usual dampener on the scene. Elinor noticed how deftly Hugh took control of the conversation, making it more general, including Elinor and Mrs. Anderson in it.

It was quite a relief when the dinner gong sounded and the nurse appeared to fetch Mrs. Anderson who preferred to eat in her own cabin.

'Why does Alison always look so disapproving?' Elinor asked Hugh as they walked down the corridor together. Kit and Valerie had led the way, with Alison walking close behind, talking to Kit, deliberately ignoring Valerie.

Hugh chuckled. 'I think she was born with that expression . . .' he said and tucked his hand under Elinor's arm. 'Don't let it worry you.'

'I won't . . .' Elinor promised, but it was a hard promise to keep.

All through dinner, Alison talked, dominating the conversation, telling them about the trips round the world she had made, about a flight to Central Africa once to go on a big game hunting trip, about the last time she was in London and was presented to the Queen. All the time, she kept making tiny jabs at the other two girls, implying that they had led a very narrow life, that they must envy her. Elinor noticed how very quiet Kit was. How thin his mouth looked, the ominous white line around it. With whom was he angry?

After coffee in the lounge, they all played 'Housey-housey' and Elinor found herself enjoying the game, although at first she had been nervous lest she could not play it. The evening flashed by and when they went down to their cabins, she realised how very much she was enjoying the voyage.

It was like being transported to fairyland. Nothing seemed quite real. Maybe it was the luxury—the wonderful food—the music—the beautiful sea—the friendliness of the people— the amusements . . . Maybe it was the fact that for two weeks they were enclosed in this little world with no outside distractions, no need to set the alarm to call you in the morning, no need to hurry to work, worrying lest it rain and ruin your only decent pair of shoes, no standing in a bus, no eating sandwiches for lunch. She felt like a new person . . .

The days began to slip by—each one as wonderful as the last.

'It's done you good . . .' Kit said one evening, as he strolled along the deck with her. 'I told you I'd teach you to enjoy yourself . . .' he added.

Elinor caught her breath. The moon was reflected in the dark water, a shimmering pathway. Distant music made a perfect backgound—a romantic background, she thought wistfully.

'I am enjoying myself,' she said rather flatly, aware that he was staring down at her curiously.

'There's still something wrong . . .' Kit said very slowly. 'Something worrying you, Elinor. What is it?'

She turned her head away so that he should not see her face. Wrong with her? There was only one little thing that was wrong with her. He would be horrified if he knew. But it was not his fault that she had fallen hopelessly in love with this big impressive man.

'There is nothing wrong . . .' she said softly, tightening her mouth.

'You can be as stubborn as a mule . . .' Kit said, but he sounded amused rather than cross.

'You and Mother get on well, don't you?'

This was a safe topic of conversation so she snatched at it.

'I think she is a darling . . .' They stood by the rail, watching the water dancing.

There was silence. Apart from the distant sounds of music and laughter, it was very still. They might have been completely alone. Kit's arm brushed hers as they stood side by side and she wondered if he could hear the pounding of her heart. It was wonderful to be out here alone with him, and yet so fruitless. For she knew that, to Kit, she was just a girl he had been asked to look after, a girl he was sorry for and intended to help. He never saw her as a pretty girl—nor had he the affection for her that he plainly showed to Valerie. Yet she had tried so hard to make him like her, Elinor thought unhappily. She had sat, happily listening for hours, as his mother told her about him, about his youth, his favourite colours—and then Elinor had worn those colours, buying fresh cardigans from the ship's shop. She had learned what subjects he liked to discuss, had even got his mother to tell her about the large sheep station he owned and had gathered a little knowledge about sheep so that she could talk to him intelligently.

But he never gave her a chance to do so. If she tried to be serious, he would look amused and she would find herself losing the words, saying stupid things, and that tolerant, exasperated look would come on his face and she would give up, knowing it was hopeless trying to impress him.

Now it suddenly seemed to her that she must be boring him, that he was longing for an excuse to return to the dancing . . .

'Will your mother ever walk again?' she asked, saying the first thing that came into her head.

'Of course she will—' he said, almost curtly, and she sighed inwardly, for again she had said the wrong thing.

'She says . . . she says that the doctors believe she will be better once she is at home . . .' Elinor struggled on.

'Of course she will,' Kit said, still curtly, as if it was a stupid remark to have made.

They were silent again. Mrs. Anderson had told her how she had fallen while visiting friends in South Africa, how she had lain months in hospital, had seen specialist after specialist, and no one seemed to know why the hip bone would not heal. In the end, they had decided she should go home to Australia. It might be that she was unhappy, there . . . that in Australia, she would feel more relaxed. Mrs. Anderson had told Elinor how lonely and unhappy she had been, how she fussed herself over making the long journey alone—for she was not allowed to travel by air—and how thankful she had been when Kit had cabled that he was flying across to fetch her and had booked their passages. Apparently Hugh had come out from England on this ship and it was purely by chance that he had joined them—but Alison . . . that had been quite different. Alison had learned that Kit was fetching his mother and had flown to Zanzibar to visit an old school friend and neither Kit nor his mother had known of her whereabouts until they had discovered she was returning on the same ship with them. Mrs. Anderson did not like Alison, Elinor had learned, but she seemed resigned to the fact that eventually Alison and Kit would marry. As Mrs. Anderson said, they had known one another all their lives, shared the same interests. In addition, Alison owned a large sheep station nearby and she would undoubtedly make him a good wife. The trouble was that Kit was a man who liked to take his time and Alison was impatient. Nearly thirty-four, Alison wanted to get married as soon as possible. Natural enough, but . . . and Mrs. Anderson had sighed. She supposed it was all right if Kit loved Alison, but he was a man not given to confidences and it was hard to tell. If only she could be sure Alison would make him happy . . .

Elinor gave a quick sideways glance at Kit's grave profile. He was staring at the water, his mouth composed, his face relaxed.

'You like Hugh, don't you?' Kit asked abruptly.

'Oh yes . . .' Elinor said quickly. 'He's so kind and . . .'

'I'm not?' His hands were on her shoulders. She shivered for a moment as he turned her to face him and then she looked up at him. 'Is that it?' Kit asked sternly.

She was glad it was too dark for him to see her eyes. 'You can be kind, too,' she said.

'H'm . . .' he grunted and abruptly released her. 'I'm glad to hear that. I must be improving . . .' There was an oddly bitter note in his voice. Unexpectedly he explained, 'It's not very pleasant, Elinor, to know that I frighten you.'

'Oh, you don't . . .' she told him earnestly. 'Not any more.'

'Really?' he sounded amused for a moment. 'Why ever not?'

'I think,' she said slowly, 'that I have learned that Hugh is right—and that your bark is worse than your bite . . .'

'Hugh said that, did he?' There was a strange note in Kit's voice. 'Kind of him. So I bark a lot?'

Elinor laughed uneasily. It was difficult to know how to take Kit's moods. 'Well, you do rather jump down people's throats, especially if they do something silly.'

'Surely the remedy is not to do anything silly . . .' Kit said and now his voice was cool with displeasure. 'We'd better go back inside . . .'

She found herself following him meekly, aware that once again she had annoyed him.

Everyone was dancing as they went inside, and Kit turned to her, but Elinor pretended she had not noticed and deliberately walked past him, going back to their table close to the window. The music ceased and as Valerie and Hugh came off the floor, Elinor smiled up at Hugh and indicated the chair by her side.

Obediently Hugh sat down, his eyes a little curious as she began to talk to him in an unusually animated manner, but if he was surprised, he hid it well and, for the rest of the evening, Elinor devoted herself to Hugh, being polite but distant to Kit, hardening her heart as she noticed the way Valerie seized the opportunity to have Kit to herself and made him dance every dance. Alison had found herself a tall, good-looking man who was, she had told them haughtily, a diplomat visiting Australia. He was handsome in a dark foreign way, Elinor thought, and he had the same cold smile and hard eyes that she saw in Alison's face.

Dancing with Hugh, Elinor asked abruptly, 'Is Kit in love with Alison?'

Hugh held her a little way away from him and stared down at her. 'Not to my knowledge. Why?'

She hesitated. 'Only . . . only his mother seems to think they will marry.'

Hugh looked amused. 'Kit's mother is aware of Alison's ruthless determination to marry Kit—what Kit thinks about it is no one's

79

business. Personally I don't think Kit will marry Alison—I think he has other ideas . . .' There was a strange smile on Hugh's mouth.

Something made Elinor glance across the crowded floor. Valerie was dancing with Kit and he was smiling down at her . . . His usually stern face had a new expression on it—a tender expression. A loving expression?

Down in their cabin, as the two girls undressed for the night, Elinor was startled when Valerie suddenly said in an oddly strained voice:

'What was the idea tonight, Elinor?'

'Idea?' Elinor said, bewildered, as she slipped into shortie pyjamas.

'Yes—making a beeline for him, like that. It was pretty obvious,' she added rather scornfully.

'Obvious . . .?' Elinor echoed, still puzzled.

She saw that Valerie's eyes were accusing. 'You're in love with Hugh,' Valerie said.

'I am not . . .' Elinor began indignantly. She paused. She was afraid that Valerie's sharp eyes might recognise that she was in love with Kit. Valerie had a queer sense of humour—if she knew the truth, she was quite capable of making a joke of it, of even blurting it out one day to Kit himself. 'I like Hugh very much . . .' Elinor said firmly, getting into her bed, pulling the clothes up to her chin. 'He is a very kind man.'

'Kind . . .?' Valerie said as she switched off

the light. 'He can be very cruel . . .' she said and then there was silence.

It was a strange thing for Valerie to say.

CHAPTER FIVE

As the great liner moved majestically on its journey of six thousand miles, those aboard seemed to be shuffled about until they fell into small groups and settled down. It was a strangely unreal life, Elinor felt, and yet an exciting one. Or it would have been had it not been for her love for Kit, which she was trying so hard to overcome.

Ever since the night when Valerie had accused her of chasing Hugh, the little party had seemed to move around and find fresh partners. Where, before, Kit had divided his attention between the two sisters, and his cousin Hugh had done the same, now it seemed automatically to fall into place that Hugh and Elinor were paired off while Kit and Valerie seemed content to be together. No longer did Kit insist on Elinor practising for long hours; now, he seemed almost indifferent. Now it was Hugh who practised with Elinor, Hugh who praised her, taught her to mix easily and have a good time. Now it was Hugh who was always looking for Elinor, always looking after her, too. It would have been very

81

pleasant for she was not only fond of Hugh but completely at ease with him. The great difficulty was that her feelings for Kit were not so easy to kill.

She tried everything. She listened to his mother talking about his life, hunting for something to dislike Kit for . . . She watched him, trying to find something she could pounce on and feel that he was someone just not worth becoming involved with.

She tried being logical. After all, she knew nothing about him—and yet she felt that she knew all about him. You didn't just meet a man and automatically fall in love. (Didn't you? her other self enquired sarcastically.) There were lots of things about Kit to be disliked—his arrogance . . . only it wasn't real arrogance, it was because he was so sure of himself. His quick temper, habit of jumping to conclusions . . . but was she any better herself? His air of amused tolerance when one did something stupid—no matter how hard she tried, she would still find herself dreaming about him, picturing his great sheep station, the sun blazing down, the groups of huge trees throwing pools of dark shade on the green grass—the long white house Mrs. Anderson had described so well—his fiery red stallion that no one else could ride—his red sports car—his garden where, hard as it was to believe, Kit spent many hours, even showing his flowers at the local Agricultural Show each year. It was a thrilling wonderful Kit that grew in Elinor's mind as every day she sat talking to Mrs. Anderson. But more than that was the fact that he was always there—how could you stop thinking about a man you saw all the time? She found it almost impossible not to look at him, the stern profile, the sudden softening of his whole face when he smiled—those dark eyes that could suddenly blaze—the deep drawling voice that could make her heart seem to turn over . . .

Alison and her diplomat had joined the small circle and Elinor found him pleasant with a rather dry humour. When Kit danced with Alison, Elinor usually found herself dancing with Alison's diplomat and he seemed a pleasant friendly man—so much so that she began to be ashamed of the quick judgement she had made of him.

One morning Elinor was on deck watching the children playing with the pink and green balloons that had been left over from the dance the night before. The balloons floated out over the sea and Elinor was laughing at the children's faces as they watched their precious trophies float away from them.

'Come and have a game of table tennis . . .' a deep drawling voice said in Elinor's ear.

Her face was hot as she swung round to see Kit smiling down at her. She had not heard him approach. For a big man, he was very light on his feet. He was wearing blue shorts and a white shirt. Whatever Kit wore, she thought, looked right on him. Now she noticed that a tiny wisp of hair was standing up on the top of his head. Her hand ached to smooth it down. What would he say if she did? She could imagine his amazement—his irritation. She could think of no reason to refuse so she followed him.

The young gym instructor in a white jersey and black trousers was helping Valerie vault. Valerie's flushed face was alight with happiness as she welcomed them.

'I'm going . . . to be . . . just so fit . . .' she said breathlessly.

Kit smiled. 'You're determined to beat me in the finals!'

'Too right I am . . .' Valerie said gaily and put her head on one side cheekily. 'See, I'm practising my Australian.'

Kit was handing Elinor a bat but he smiled. 'My word, you are . . .' he said.

'Discovered Kit's weakness yet, Elinor?' Valerie called laughingly.

'Not yet . . .' Elinor said, gripping the handle of the bat firmly.

'I wonder if you ever will . . .' Kit said quietly as he passed her the balls, for she had won the toss.

Startled, she looked up at him and straight into his eyes. For a moment, their eyes seemed to cling. Was there a challenge in his? If so, why was he challenging her?

'I'm not sure that I want to . . .' she said in as casual a voice as she could muster.

'You're a very bad liar, Elinor,' Kit told her quietly and his face was amused. 'Your service . . .'

She was trembling a little as she served two faults. The next serve was a perfect one and, as she concentrated on the game and forced herself to forget Kit, Elinor began to play well. It was a close game. Even though she lost the set, she saw the respect in Kit's eyes as they finished.

'You really have improved . . .' he said.

Defiantly she looked at him. 'Hugh has been coaching me,' she told him.

His mouth seemed to harden. 'Hugh is an excellent coach,' he said almost curtly.

They went outside to sip iced bouillon as they sat on green and white striped chairs outside in the sun. The swimming pool was crowded, the chairs round it filled with parents keeping an eye on offspring.

'It can't be much of a holiday . . .' Kit said thoughtfully, 'bringing children for a voyage like this. Of course, a lot of people are emigrating to Australia. I wonder what you will think of my country.'

'I like what your mother tells me about it,' Elinor said.

Kit gave her an amused glance. 'I'm afraid your life with Aggie won't be much like that. They live just outside a city whereas we live

85

miles from anywhere or anyone.'

'Alison is your nearest neighbour, isn't she?' Elinor asked him, watching his face carefully, wondering if he would betray anything.

'Alison? Oh yes, when she's at home, which isn't often, and when she is, she is usually over at our place . . .' he said.

He said it as if it was only natural that Alison should practically live on his station. She reminded herself that they had been brought up more or less together. 'Does she like country life?' Elinor asked.

Kit chuckled. 'She pretends she does. Actually Alison is only really happy in a big city like Paris or New York. She cannot stand Sydney, and she calls it a small-town-trying-to-be-a-city, much to Hugh's annoyance. He thinks Sydney is the finest place in the world.'

'And you . . .?' Elinor asked.

'I like the country,' Kit said simply.

'I've . . . we've never lived in the country,' she admitted slowly.

Kit chuckled again. 'So I gather from Val. She was greatly relieved when she found your Aunt Aggie didn't live on a station . . . Country life is the best—the only life. Room to breathe, to move around. In cities there are always so many people, all rushing about madly trying to earn money.'

'Money can be important . . .' Elinor told him, frowning a little. 'It's easy enough to despise it when you've got plenty.'

86

He looked startled. Perhaps he was surprised at her taking him up, she thought. 'You may have something there,' he said slowly in his deep drawling voice. 'I've always had enough.'

And we never have, Elinor thought quickly, remembering the long years of careful living, of trying to balance an unbalanceable budget, trying to make a pound stretch, trying to . . . Oh, why think about it? Those days were over.

'It was awful when my mother died and we had nothing,' she told him.

'Valerie doesn't seem to have worried about it,' Kit said unexpectedly. 'She said you got into what she calls a "flap".'

Elinor's cheeks burned suddenly. 'I was the one who had to flap . . .' she said indignantly. 'One of us had to worry . . .'

'You are the elder . . .' Kit pointed out smoothly. Why was he staring at her like that so oddly? 'And Val was the one who thought of writing to your father's family.'

'I . . .' Suddenly Elinor felt very tired. To Kit, it seemed, Valerie was perfect. She might be young and foolish, she might be catty, at times, but Kit could forgive it all. For a moment, her eyes stung with unshed tears. 'Yes, she did. I would never have thought of it,' she admitted. 'Even then, I didn't like it.'

'You know . . .' Kit said slowly, 'I think you did the right thing. Even if you had been able to keep yourselves comfortably, I still think it was right to get in touch with them. After all, Elinor, supposing you had a son who went overseas and married, wouldn't you long to hear about him and his children? And if he died, wouldn't that make his children even more precious to you? I don't blame your mother for not writing, though I think it was a pity . . .' He paused. Elinor's eyes were blazing with anger.

'That's generous of you,' she said, her voice shaking. 'What right have you to judge? So my mother was jealous and possessive and she didn't want to share us—but what right have we to judge her? You're far too fond of doing that . . . you don't know the whole story . . . we shall never know it, but Mother must have had a reason for hating them so and . . . and . . . Anyhow it's none of your business . . .' Her voice trembled. 'You're so . . . so beastly smug . . .' she said almost violently and, feeling the tears horribly near, hastily got up and almost ran down the deck and down to her cabin.

She flung herself down on her bed and let the tears have their way.

The gong chimed for the Second Lunch and she had to bathe her eyes hastily in cold water to hide their redness. Even so, she felt very conspicuous as she slipped into her seat, the last at her table. She felt every eye was on her but no one commented as she ordered her lunch.

That evening the Captain invited them to

88

a cocktail party. He was a heavily-built, charming man who spoke politely to everyone but who was obviously only doing his duty and to Elinor, at least, it was a relief when they could leave him. She wondered why Valerie was so excited, hanging on to Kit's arm, talking eagerly. As they walked away, Elinor met Alison's cool thoughtful gaze and, for no reason at all, felt her cheeks burning.

'Now what's wrong, Lady Kia?' Hugh asked in her ear.

Startled, Elinor stared at him. No one but Kit had ever called her that. 'N-nothing . . .'

'Yes, there is,' he said. 'Alison looked at you and you went bright red. Why?'

'I don't know . . .' Elinor said.

As if he saw she would not tell him, Hugh went on: 'How are you getting on in your heats? Soon be the finals for the sports.'

'I've got two to play tomorrow . . .' Elinor told him.

He smiled at her approvingly. 'You've done very well. Aren't you pleased with yourself?'

Impulsively, Elinor laid her hand on his sleeve. 'I owe it all to your coaching and encouragement,' she said warmly, her small pale face suddenly glowing, her eyes bright.

Hugh put his hand over hers and held it tightly for a moment. 'You have been a delightful pupil . . .' he said smilingly.

Something made Elinor turn her head and she saw Kit staring at them, a strange look on

89

his face. And then the tall man with the arrogant walk looked away, speaking to Valerie, but not before Elinor had seen the ominous white line of anger round Kit's mouth.

They were dancing that evening when Alison stopped Elinor on her way back to the table with Hugh. 'Where is your sister?' Alison demanded.

She looked very beautiful, her classic features cold and unfriendly, but her slim body elegant in a softly-pleated white silk frock.

'Val . . .?' Elinor was taken aback. She looked round vaguely. 'She was around just now . . .'

Hugh's hand was warm on her arm. 'She and Kit went out on deck,' he said, something mischievous in his voice.

'I know,' Alison said coldly. 'But that was three-quarters of an hour ago.'

'There is a full moon—maybe they find it attractive . . .' Hugh suggested, a smile flickering round his mouth.

Alison frowned and turned away. Alone, Hugh and Elinor sat down and he offered her a cigarette. Elinor managed to talk but every nerve in her body felt tense, as if she was waiting for something. It was silly to feel like this but . . . Hadn't she often gone on deck with Kit while they talked? It meant nothing. Why, then, was Alison so angry? Why had she looked almost frightened?

It was nearly twenty minutes later and Elinor, still watching for Valerie and Kit but trying to hide the fact from Hugh, was quite relieved when he left her, murmuring an excuse about getting cigarettes. Almost as if she had been waiting for the moment, Alison walked across the room and sat in Hugh's place.

Her face was cold as she stared at Elinor, her voice low and tense.

'Is your sister aware that Kit and I are going to be married?' she asked.

Elinor caught her breath. So it was true! 'I . . .' she began but Alison gave her no chance.

Alison's icy-cold fingers closed round Elinor's wrist like a clamp as she said in a low fierce voice. 'Your sister is a child and Kit is being kind to her, but I don't want her to get hurt. He forgets that, even at seventeen, a girl today is a woman. You have had such drab unhappy lives that he enjoys making Valerie happy—he has told me so and I understand perfectly, but . . . and this is up to you—will you make sure that your sister does not get any stupid ideas about Kit falling in love with her?'

Elinor's mouth was dry. 'I . . . I don't think Val would . . .'

Alison laughed—a harsh unamused sound. 'I'm quite certain she would. Your sister may be young but her head is screwed on all right. She is looking for a rich husband and here is

Kit, all ready and waiting, so she thinks. But she is wrong. He is mine. Make no mistake . . .' Her violent voice was suddenly quieter. 'You don't want your sister to be hurt, do you? Then make it plain to her that Kit is mine . . .'

At that moment, Hugh and the diplomat walked up and Alison's face changed instantly. 'Ah . . . Nicholas . . . I've been wondering where you were . . .'

Elinor was dancing with Hugh when they saw Kit and Valerie returning. Valerie's face was flushed with excitement, she was talking to Kit, who was listening with a tolerant smile.

When they went back to their table, Hugh and Elinor were greeted by Val's excited voice. 'Just think—we have been up on the bridge with the Captain . . . it was just too wonderful, and Kit . . .'

Elinor heard little more. A wave of relief was flooding her. So Valerie and Kit had not been out on the deck . . . She paused in her thoughts. Her mind boggled at the thought of Valerie in Kit's arms . . . of Kit's mouth closing over Valerie's . . . Yet Alison had thought . . .

'Dance this with me, Elinor. . .' Kit said, in his usual arrogant way.

Elinor, jolted abruptly from her thoughts, looked up into his face and found herself, the next moment, circling the floor in his arms. She half-closed her eyes. Kit danced beautifully. She liked to enjoy it whole-heartedly—she hated to talk to him when they danced, for she had to watch her words, guard her expression.

'Must you always look so bored when you dance with me?' Kit asked explosively.

Startled, Elinor opened her eyes very wide—her pale face suddenly red with embarrassment. 'I'm not bored . . .'

'Then why go to sleep?' he demanded.

'I . . . I . . .' Elinor wondered how to tell him without giving herself away. 'I love dancing and . . . and I hate talking when I dance.'

'You talk to Hugh when you dance with him . . .' Kit pointed out.

'I . . .' She did not know what to say.

Suddenly he had stopped dancing, had her firmly by the arm, was opening the door to the deck. ' I want to talk to you . . .' he said grimly.

She had no choice. Out on the dark deck, she waited for what he was going to say.

CHAPTER SIX

Elinor did not know what she expected Kit to say. She thought vaguely that he must be going to scold her for speaking so rudely to him—for daring to call him smug, but she was completely amazed when he abruptly said to her:

'Have you forgotten Max?'

She turned to face him, startled. The great

expanse of ocean shimmered in the moonlight. They were standing in a corner, sheltered from the wind, not very brightly lighted and she could not see the expression on his face.

'Max?' she echoed.

'Yes—Max . . .' Kit said sternly. 'You promised not to forget him—remember?'

Elinor gripped the rail with her hands, still puzzled. And then she remembered and felt ashamed because she had so soon forgotten him. Max—the journalist who was in love with Valerie, Max who had brought Val the lovely flowers at which she had barely looked; Max with whom Valerie was so impatient because he would not take *No* for an answer.

'Your memory appears to be conveniently short . . .' Kit was saying, his drawl intensified. 'I was on the train and chanced to see Max giving you those flowers and I also heard you promise him that you would not forget him . . .'

Elinor began to speak and then paused. 'I didn't see you.'

'Of course not,' Kit said coldly. 'You were engrossed in the young man. He seemed to be very upset about something . . . The same man with whom you were sitting in the restaurant the night before we left Johannesburg . . . Don't,' he said impatiently. 'try to deny it. Valerie was telling me about him—that he is desperately in love with you and that you are, unofficially, engaged.'

'Val said . . .' Elinor gasped. 'Val . . .' It could not be true. Why, Valerie would not lie like that . . . There must be some mistake.

'Yes. Look, Elinor . . .' Kit continued, his voice warmer. 'I know you are very young and that this strange unnatural life on board ship encourages romances, but do you think it is fair . . . now, be honest . . . is it fair to encourage Hugh as you are doing when you are already promised to another man?'

Elinor drew a long breath. 'Hugh . . .? Why . . . wh-what . . .?'

Kit's hand was warm on hers for a moment. 'Hugh is not only my cousin but . . . Look, Hugh and I are very close to one another and I don't want him to get hurt. You are deliberately encouraging him and yet you . . .'

With a quick furious movement, Elinor withdrew her hand from his clasp. 'Are you mad?' she said, her voice shaking. 'Hugh is not in love with me nor am I encouraging him. Besides Max is . . .'

'Six thousand miles away,' Kit commented drily.

A door opened and a shaft of light shone out. 'Kit . . . Kit!' Valerie called excitedly. 'They're having a dancing competition right away—you promised to be my partner . . .'

'We're coming . . .' Kit called. In a lower voice, he spoke to Elinor. 'You're a sensible girl. Please think about what I've said. Hugh is too nice to be wilfully hurt . . .'

Elinor was still shivering with anger as she followed him indoors. In a moment, she was with Hugh who insisted that they, also, enter the competition.

'We might get the booby prize . . .' he said, his lean good-looking face alight with amusement, 'But it'll be fun.'

Fun! It was sheer purgatory to Elinor, as she danced in his arms. How dared Kit . . . how . . . The tears were horribly near for a moment. How he must despise her. Why had Valerie led him to believe that it was Elinor Max loved . . . ? How could he think that she was encouraging Hugh? Elinor wondered miserably. She looked up into his lean face and he smiled at her . . . but she was sure there was nothing but friendship in that smile. He never held her hand, never tried to kiss her . . . Kit must be wrong, be imagining things . . .

It was a gay party with lots of laughter, and finally ended up with a sing song, but all the time Elinor was unhappily conscious of Kit's watchful eyes and it made her feel very self-conscious with Hugh. Watching Valerie dancing with Kit, Elinor was suddenly afraid for her. Was Val in love with him? Was that why she had pretended that Max was in love with Elinor? If so, then poor Val was going to be badly hurt. Somehow she must warn her . . . tell her that Kit and Alison were going to be married one day.

They were very late going down to their

cabin and Valerie was not in the mood to talk.

'Oh, Elinor—there's always tomorrow . . .' she said in the middle of a yawn as she undressed.

'I never see you alone in the day,' Elinor said. Suddenly she lost her patience. 'Why did you tell Kit I was engaged to Max?' she demanded.

Valerie yawned again, stretching slim arms above her red head.

'I didn't . . . he jumped to conclusions and I didn't bother to correct him,' she said, smiling sleepily.

'But . . . but . . .' Elinor drew a deep breath. Valerie was always so maddeningly plausible. 'Look, it isn't true . . .'

'So what?' Valerie slid into bed. 'I didn't want Kit to think I was tied up at all with Max . . . Kit is a frightful stickler for conventions, you know, and loyalty and all that sort of thing. I knew it didn't matter to you what Kit thought—for you can't bear the sight of him. That's obvious.'

Elinor stared at her quickly. Was Valerie being sarcastic? Surely anyone could see the truth? She was suddenly relieved. Valerie really meant it. Then no one, least of all Kit, could have guessed her secret.

'Don't look like that—so smug . . .' Valerie said crossly. 'Just like a cat with a plate of cream. We all see what you are going to do . . . you're going to marry Hugh, aren't you . . . ?

97

Don't deny it . . . I can see it on your face, Elinor . . .' Her voice rose angrily. Then she slid into the bed still deeper, pulling the sheet up over her head. 'Well, if you're going to marry Hugh, I shall marry Kit. He's quite nice and very wealthy—not many girls can manage to grab a man like that . . .'

Elinor pulled back the sheet quickly and looked down at her sister, startled to see tears in Valerie's eyes. 'Val—Kit is going to marry Alison . . .'

'That'll be the day . . .' Val began angrily.

'No—I mean it. His mother told me so . . .' Elinor went on. She sat on the edge of her bed, her face anxious. 'Val dear. Don't fall in love with Kit . . .'

'Who said anything about love?' Valerie said. 'I'm going to marry him.'

'Val . . . Alison spoke to me tonight. She is afraid you'll fall in love with him and get hurt. She told me definitely that they are going to be married,' Elinor said earnestly.

There was a strange look on Valerie's face. 'They don't behave like a . . . well, I'm sure they're not in love . . .' she said, her voice hesitant.

'They've known one another all their lives—their sheep stations are next door to one another . . .' Elinor went on.

Valerie sat up, hugging her knees, resting her chin on them, her eyes very green. 'You mean, it's a sort of marriage of convenience?'

'I don't know,' Elinor said wearily. 'I only know that Kit's mother doesn't like Alison but she seems to accept the fact that Kit will marry whom he likes, and if he has chosen Alison . . . Apparently Alison has all the right qualities for a wealthy pastoralist's wife and . . .'

'Their sheep stations will be combined and both will benefit . . .' Valerie finished bitterly. 'What hope have girls like us to grab rich husbands, Elinor, when there are women like Alison who can buy a man?'

Elinor's cheeks burned. 'Kit would never be bought . . .'

Valerie laughed, a short hard bitter sound. 'I wonder. He wouldn't put it like that—probably call it *expansion* or some such word, but it all boils down to the same thing. Rich marries rich—if you have money, you get more.'

'Val . . . in any case, you wouldn't marry Kit if you didn't love him, would you?' Elinor asked worriedly. She looked at her sister. Why had Val that unhappy bitter look on her face, why was her mouth so sad? It wasn't like Val . . .

'Wouldn't I?' Valerie asked and put out a hand to switch off the light. 'I'm tired . . .'

Elinor lay in bed, wide awake. The suppressed roar of the air conditioning filled the cabin. The ship was still rolling very slightly and it was a strange sensation. Was poor Val already head over heels in love with Kit? It would not be surprising. How could any girl resist him? Elinor closed her eyes tightly—

99

seeing in her mind that tall, broad-shouldered, powerfully-built man with the stern mouth and the suddenly kind eyes. Kit was everything a girl dreamed about. Strong, handsome, strange, tender, exciting . . . and yet so comforting. It would be wonderful to be loved by a man like that—someone on whom you could lean, someone you could trust implicitly, someone who would understand. What a wonderful life you could have . . . Mrs. Anderson had told her enough about the homestead for her to be able to imagine it . . . the long white building with the verandah that ran round three sides of it, the lofty cool rooms, the beautiful gardens. Funny to imagine Kit in a garden—his powerful brown hands tenderly handling seedlings, pruning roses. It was roses that were his favourite flowers, Mrs. Anderson had said. Imagine being married to Kit—having, say, four children. They would be able to afford ponies for the children. What fun it would be. Kit was talking of having a swimming-pool built, his mother had said. He entertained a lot—took a prominent part in local politics.

Elinor let out a long sigh and buried the dream. Kit needed the right kind of wife; a girl who knew the local customs, was friends with everyone. No wonder he had chosen Alison.

In the morning, Elinor was late for breakfast on purpose. She wanted to work out for herself how she was to treat Hugh. She

100

could not bear to encourage him—though she was sure both Kit and Valerie were quite wrong. Hugh looked upon her as a friend and nothing else. Valerie was still asleep when Elinor left the cabin, her gorgeous red hair a cloud of colour on the white pillow, her relaxed face very young.

Hurrying down to the dining salon, Elinor found herself praying that Valerie would not get hurt. Unrequited love was such pain. And no matter how hard you tried to be sensible, how you fought to overcome it, it seemed almost impossible to cure yourself of loving the wrong man.

Hugh had finished so she had the table to herself. It seemed funny to be sitting alone at the table which was usually so alive with talk and laughter. There was a dark pretty girl alone at the next table and somehow they drifted into conversation.

'My husband and I take it in turns to eat . . .' she told Elinor cheerfully. 'We've two small brats and it's quite impossible to leave them.'

'It must be very difficult,' Elinor sympathised. 'Spoil a lot of your fun . . .'

The girl—she must have been about Elinor's age—laughed.

'Oh, well, if you will have children you have to expect your life to be different. It's just that—sometimes . . .' A cloud came over her pretty face. 'Sometimes it spoils things . . .'

They parted at the door, the girl to go to her

cabin presumably, and Elinor to take the lift up to the boat deck. She found a quiet corner in a sort of V-shaped alcove, sheltered on one side by a canvas sheet and under the shadow of one of the huge striped fawn and black funnels. She clutched the book that was to be her camouflage if anyone came looking for her—but she hoped no one would. She had played the last of the heats for the sports and was not in the finals, but Hugh had said she had done very well. Alison was in the finals and so was Valerie, and Elinor was hoping that everyone that morning would be far too busy to miss her.

It was all so very, very beautiful. Perhaps it was too much to ask for happiness, too. Yet she was happy, in a way—apart from this hopeless emotional involvement with Kit. She did not think she was really the kind of girl a man like Kit loved. She could well imagine him admiring Alison's cool beauty, appreciating her poise, her elegant charm—or even falling for Valerie's young vivacity, her naturalness, her gaiety. But as to falling for a *pathetic-looking . . . afraid-of-men, dignified* girl of twenty . . . Valerie's casual words still stung. It was funny how many things Valerie said hurt—and yet Valerie would be shocked if she knew it.

She heard voices and ducked down behind her book. How stupid could she be! She had forgotten that they would be coming to play deck croquet just in front of her. She looked round the book and saw with relief that none of their party was there and she quickly got up and slipped down the stairs and joined the crowded deck chairs round the swimming pool. She was lucky enough to find a chair and she put it in the middle of a crowd of people, hoping that if she was looked for, they would not find her.

It was very hot here for it was sheltered. Girls lay around in swimsuits—men were sprawled lazily, their brown bodies glistening from swimming. Two people had brightly striped sunshades attached to their chairs. It was a gay scene and yet noisy with the children screaming with excitement or squabbling with one another.

A small two-year-old trotted in front of Elinor, wearing a minute white bikini—she tripped and fell flat, letting out a howl of anguish. As Elinor picked her up, she recognised a voice.

'Oh, Sally girl, will you never learn?'

Elinor looked round and found herself gazing at the pretty girl she had talked to at breakfast.

'This one of yours?' Elinor asked.

The girl laughed. 'The eldest . . . and most trouble. She won't keep still . . .'

Elinor took her chair and sat next to the girl, whose name was Petula Keet. She met the husband, a pleasant, very young man with a harassed look and gleaming black hair. It was rather nice, Elinor thought, to sit and talk to them and she would be safe if Hugh came to look for her.

Petula laughed in answer to a question as to where they were going.

'Australia—to discover a grand new life . . .' she said, a note of bitterness in her voice.

Sam Keet spoke quickly. 'Petula is feeling a bit glum—we lived near her family and she's missing them.'

The pretty girl gave him a quick look. 'I'll be all right once we get there, Sam. It's just that we had such a lovely life and . . .'

'I know—but we'll get that in Australia,' Sam said slowly. 'There's sure to be a lot of dancing there . . .'

They told Elinor that, before the babies arrived, they had been professional ballroom dancers. 'I had the loveliest dresses . . .' Petula said, her eyes shining. 'We could afford them, then . . .' The baby in the pram beside her began to cry and Petula with a quick murmur of apology to Elinor lifted the baby out and hurried away with her.

'Time for feeding . . .' Sam explained with a friendly grin. He had the small Sally standing between his knees, playing with the thin bracelet round his wrist. 'I'm afraid this is rather tough for Petula . . .' he went on. 'She's only just twenty and when we first decided to come out here, we were both thrilled with the thought of the voyage. The trouble is we have to stay with the kids at night or else we take it in turns to go up, but that's not much fun. I think Petula misses the dancing, too. I know I do . . .' he said wistfully.

Elinor had a wonderful idea. Impulsively she put her hand on his arm. 'Sam . . . look. There'll be a dance tomorrow night. You and Petula go and I'll baby-sit for you.'

He stared at her, his face excited and then it sobered. 'I couldn't let you. You want to have fun, too.'

'No . . . no, I don't,' Elinor assured him quickly. 'I . . . I . . .' She could feel her cheeks burning. 'Look, I'd be glad of the chance to avoid some . . . someone . . .' She blushed still more as he looked at her with an understanding smile.

'A lover's tiff . . .?' he teased.

'In a way,' she admitted.

'Well . . . I . . . I don't know what to say . . .' Sam told her. 'It's most frightfully good of you. The kids won't wake up—they rarely do . . . we won't be late.'

'Be as late as you like,' Elinor told him cheerfully. 'Enjoy yourselves . . .'

She looked up, feeling a strange sensation and saw that Kit was standing outside the gymnasium, gazing at her, frowning a little. Immediately she turned to Sam and began to talk to him eagerly—sure she was talking a lot of nonsense because of the bewildered look on

105

his face, but determined to show Kit that she would talk to whom she liked . . .

Kit had gone before Petula and the now sleepy baby returned. Petula's delight and gratitude when she heard Elinor's offer made Elinor feel a little ashamed, for it would be no hardship to skip the dance. Somehow she must avoid Hugh without making it too conspicuous. As soon as she could, she left the couple and found her way to the deck where she knew Mrs. Anderson always sat in the sunshine in her chair.

Mrs. Anderson laid down her book and smiled warmly. 'Nice to see you, child. It is good of you to spare me so much time . . .' she said.

Elinor blushed. 'I like talking to you,' she said, again a little ashamed because people would read good intentions into her selfish actions. 'I love to hear about your home and what it's like in Australia.'

'Do you think you are going to like it, living there?' Mrs. Anderson asked, her faded blue eyes interested.

'I think . . . so,' Elinor said slowly. 'At first I didn't want to come at all but now . . . I'm beginning to see I shouldn't have let myself be prejudiced.'

'That's a long word for a very young woman . . .' a drawling, amused voice interrupted.

'Oh . . .' Elinor cried, startled, turning to stare up at the tall man who had come to join

106

them so quietly. 'I didn't hear you.'

'Should I blow a whistle or sound a horn to announce my arrival?' Kit asked slowly, fetching himself a chair and joining them. 'You jumped like a startled rabbit.'

'Well . . . well, I wasn't thinking about you and . . .' Elinor began.

Kit's thick fair eyebrows were lifted quizzically. 'Indeed? I am hurt. What have you been up to this morning? We couldn't find you anywhere and then . . .'

'You saw me . . .' Elinor said, meeting his eyes defiantly.

'I have other friends, you know,' she said stiffly, clenching her hands tightly.

'Children . . . children!' Mrs. Anderson interrupted, laughing at them. 'Are you both trying to pick a quarrel? We were talking about Australia, Kit darling. I was asking Elinor if she thought she would be happy.'

Kit's eyes were hard as he gazed at Elinor. 'I doubt if she'll stay there long . . .' he said, and then, as if in answer to Elinor's startled look, added: 'She'll probably be going back to South Africa before long . . .'

She caught her breath. What did he mean? And then she remembered Max—and his belief that she was unofficially engaged to Max. Now was the time to put him right.

'I'm not . . .' she began and then stopped. It was a little difficult. As good as calling Valerie a liar. He would be sure to ask why Valerie had

107

let him believe it in the first place and then . . .
'I'm sure I shall love Australia . . .' she said
firmly.

'That is a typically foolish remark to make,'
Kit told her coldly, bending to tuck his
mother's rug in more firmly round her. 'Cool
wind this side of the ship.' He turned to Elinor,
his face cold. 'How can you know that you will
love a country you have never seen?'

Elinor could see that Mrs. Anderson was
puzzled and a little distressed. Could she, too,
sense the tension between them? Elinor
wondered. For a moment, she hated Kit. Why
was he so quick to judge others, to expect
them to conform to the pattern he believed in?

Mrs. Anderson plunged into the breach,
obviously trying to avert a quarrel. 'I think
Elinor will make some lucky man a very good
wife, Kit . . .' She laughed but there was a
thread of gravity in her voice as she went on.
'Why don't you marry her, Kit? I'd love her for
a daughter-in-law.'

There was an appalled silence. Elinor,
startled into silence, hardly dared to breathe.
She could feel her cheeks flaming as Kit gazed
at her, a strange smile on his mouth.

'That's quite an idea, Mother. What do you
say, Lady Kia . . .?' he asked quietly, just as the
uniformed nurse suddenly appeared and said
that it was nearly time for lunch.

Left alone for a moment, Elinor gazed up
into Kit's amused face. She knew what he was

thinking and she hated him for it. He was thinking she was looking for a wealthy husband.

'If you were the last man in the world, Kit . . .' she said, her voice trembling with anger and pain, 'I would not marry you.'

CHAPTER SEVEN

As soon as she had spoken, she regretted the words. It was a lie, too. She turned and hurried away, only to have Kit follow close behind her, saying in an amused voice:

'Chance is a fine thing, you know.'

She could not bear it. She turned to go to the lift, forgot the high step, tripped and fell flat on her face. For a moment she lay there, stunned, and then she felt Kit's powerful but gentle hands lifting her up and she gazed up at him through tear-filled eyes.

'Tut . . . tut . . .' he drawled. 'Temper always meets its own reward.'

'Oh, you . . . you . . .' She found herself stuttering. Somehow she wrenched herself free and hurried to the lift and down to the shelter of her cabin.

Suddenly the great ship was like a prison. There was no way to avoid Kit—and to add to the difficulties, lately he had seemed to be deliberately baiting her, trying to make her angry, amused when he succeeded. If only he would leave her alone.

Kit was very formal and polite during lunch, but several times Elinor caught him staring at her, a strange look in his dark eyes. Was he amused? If only . . . if only . . . She must try to forget those useless words and find a plan. She would just be very formal herself and pretend not to notice the way he was watching her. Deliberately she set out to be friendly to Alison, asking about life in Australia, Alison's hobbies. Rather to her surprise, Alison was friendly in turn and so it was quite simple when the meal was over and they went up to the lounge for coffee, for Elinor to walk by Alison's side and even sit by her, and the others were soon engrossed in a conversation of their own.

'Australia is very beautiful,' Alison told her, 'but it is an entirely different way of life. Whether you will settle down happily or not depends on how well you adjust yourself. Aggie—with whom you will live—is near a city and so you will not have the loneliness many girls hate so much on a station.'

'You don't mind it?' Elinor asked, trying not to crane to listen to what the others were discussing so animatedly.

Alison laughed. It was a strange laugh, Elinor thought. It had no amusement in it, no happiness. What was it Kit had said that first day? That Alison was the unhappiest woman he knew, that she never enjoyed or praised anything.

'I don't stay there long enough to get bored or lonely,' Alison said. 'My ideal way of living is just to go back for short holidays. Kit and I have a stud of racehorses, which is a sideline of course—sheep are our mainstay—but the horses are interesting and often pay good dividends . . .' She smiled thinly. 'In Australia, you know, we are keen racegoers. I don't suppose you have ever been to one . . .'

'No,' Elinor admitted.

A warm hand touched her shoulder and stayed there. It was Hugh.

'Then stay away, Elinor . . .' he said in his friendly manner. 'It becomes like a drug. You should just see Alison during a race . . . it's quite a sight.'

Two flags of colour waved in Alison's cheeks. 'What do you mean—a sight?' she asked icily.

Hugh chuckled. 'My dear Alison—you have eyes and ears for nothing but the race and if you lose any money on it . . . whew . . . one daren't speak to you for hours!'

'It's not true . . .' Alison said indignantly.

'Isn't it?' Kit chimed in, his voice amused. 'Be honest, Alison. You're a menace on the racecourse, isn't she, Hugh?'

'My word! and how,' Hugh chuckled. 'She loses all her money and then proceeds to lose ours . . .'

Elinor sat very quietly in the chair, tense under Hugh's hand that remained on her shoulder. What a little group they were—what memories they shared. Racecourses, training horses . . . the very way Alison spoke about Kit and the station proved that she was certain that it was almost her home already.

'What shall we do . . . .?' Valerie said suddenly, impatient because she was out of the conversation, Elinor thought. So Valerie also noticed how naturally the three—Kit, Hugh and Alison—mixed, with experiences no one else could share. 'Let's play deck quoits . . .'

'I don't think Elinor is speaking to me . . .' Kit drawled, his eyes amused as he watched the colour flame up in Elinor's pale cheeks. How frail she looked at times and yet she had a quick temper. 'Are you, Lady Kia?' he asked.

Elinor looked at him very quickly. 'Of course I am . . .' she said lightly. 'I was mad with you but not mad enough to send you to Coventry.' She was proud of the laugh she managed. 'But count me out for quoits. I've a headache and am going down to my cabin . . .'

'Then how about you, Alison, or are you still talking politics with your pet diplomat?' Hugh asked.

'He is a very interesting man,' Alison returned with dignity. 'It is pleasant, sometimes, to have an opportunity to talk to an intellectual.'

'I bet it is . . .' Hugh chuckled. 'After boring

112

pastoralists and stockbrokers . . . Come on, Al . . .' he said suddenly. 'Climb down from your high horse—it must be cold way up there—and mix with the *hoi polloi*. Do you good to play with rabbits, for a change . . .'

Elinor left them hurriedly while they still argued whether or not it was too hot to play. They had not tried to stop her going—they would not miss her. Alone in her cabin, she stared bleakly before her. She could have been up in the sunshine, close to Kit, hearing his voice, watching every now and then the way his dark eyes changed colour, just . . .

That night she had her dinner sent to the cabin. She was so mixed-up that she felt she could not face Kit's amused eyes.

The days were slipping by, she realised the next morning, as she and Hugh stood on the deck watching a great white albatross wheeling over the ship, swooping down to float for a while on the waves, then flying low across the water.

'An albatross . . .' she said excitedly. 'Isn't that good luck?'

Hugh laughed. 'It's supposed to be bad luck if you kill it, so maybe it's good luck if you don't . . .'

She was conscious that he had turned to stare at her. She stared at the deep aquamarine-blue sea that stretched away into the distance, flecked with Chinese-white waves. There were small clouds in the great blue sky. From behind them drifted the laughter of children, voices.

'Not much longer—we're more than half-way to Australia . . .' Hugh said and there was a wistful note in his voice.

Elinor was startled. 'Are we really?' She turned to stare in dismay. That meant that soon—very soon—Kit would go out of her life. Oh, no doubt they would meet again, but how differently. When he visited her Aunt Aggie—or when the two sisters went to his wedding, because Alison had told her the day before that they must come and stay with them when she and Kit were married, it would be quite different from here—here, where they were sort of marooned . . . sort of away from the world and its various distractions. Here there was nothing to do but eat and enjoy yourself. Once ashore, Kit would be working hard, would forget this voyage. She herself would never forget it.

'Elinor, you're an honest little soul,' Hugh began, his voice teasing but his eyes, she saw, grave. 'What have I done to offend you two girls?'

'Offend us . . .?' Elinor repeated. 'I don't understand . . .'

He smiled ruefully. 'I'm no Adonis like Kit but I do have a way with girls . . .' He smiled again. 'At least, I like to think so, but somewhere or other, I seem to have stepped off with the wrong foot. Val is very friendly and all that in public but when she is alone with me, she is positively . . .' He hesitated. 'Well, off-hand. She acts as if she couldn't get away fast enough. As if she can't bear to be with me.'

'Oh, Hugh . . . aren't you imagining it?' Elinor said quickly. 'I think she likes you . . . we've never discussed you . . .'

'You're not much better yourself, Elinor,' he went on. 'The last few days you've behaved as if I might be poison ivy. You run away all the time . . . hide.' He laughed but he didn't sound as if he meant it. 'Not playing hard to get, are you?' he teased.

'Why, Hugh . . .' Elinor stared at him in dismay. 'I . . . I . . .' She could see that while he was making a joke of it, he was actually hurt. Impulsively she put her hand on his warm brown arm. 'Hugh—I'll tell you the truth. I don't know about Val but I like you very much indeed.' Her cheeks were hot as she paused. 'The reason I . . . why these last few days I've . . .'

'Go on . . .' he said gently.

'I don't know how to tell you . . .' Elinor tried again. 'You see, Hugh, Kit told me to stop encouraging you . . .'

Her cheeks flamed again.

Hugh frowned. 'Kit said . . . that?'

She nodded unhappily. 'He said you were too nice to be hurt wilfully. Those were his very words. He said I was encouraging you . . .'

115

'You were not,' Hugh said indignantly. 'You were just being a nice friendly girl . . .'

Relief flooded her. 'Oh, Hugh, I'm so glad. I've been so worried . . .' she gasped.

His hand closed over hers. 'Kit must be . . . mad.' He looked suddenly thoughtful. 'Now I understand. Look, Elinor, just go on being your natural self. I promise I won't be hurt by you. In any case . . .' he added ruefully, 'it's too late . . .'

Elinor's eyes searched his face. Her soft, dark-brown, curly hair was blown about by the wind. In her pale face, her eyes looked enormous.

'Oh, Hugh, you're in love . . .' she said. 'And . . . and have things gone wrong?'

He smiled at her, squeezing her fingers. 'No—not really. I think they just appear to have gone wrong, but actually, I'm feeling a great deal more hopeful . . . Ah, here they come . . .' he added hastily, leaving his hand on hers, as Kit and Valerie joined them. Elinor often wondered how it happened that Valerie always made her first appearance in the morning accompanied by Kit—and somehow she had always thought it happened by chance. Now, for the first time, she wondered. Did Valerie go to his suite and literally drag him away from his business letters? Or had they an arrangement whereby they met at the same time each morning? She felt suddenly desolate, and wondered how she would bear it if Kit became her brother-in-law.

The day passed like all the others. There was nothing to do and yet plenty to do. In the wonderful sunshine they swam and sun-bathed, and then either chatted idly or summoned enough energy to play quoits or croquet on the boat deck. The hours floated by, seemingly endless, but always it came as a shock to Elinor when it was time to go to dress for dinner.

That evening as she left the drawing-room where they had all been having tea, she was startled when Kit suddenly said: 'Don't forget there's dancing tonight, Elinor. Save me the first dance . . .'

It was the first time he had said anything like that to her. She stood very still, staring at him, feeling as usual the colour mounting in her cheeks, waiting tensely to hear him call her 'Lady Kia'. But for once he looked at her gravely, no glint of teasing or anger in his eyes. She was about to accept when she remembered that she had promised to baby-sit.

In her disappointment and embarrassment, she was abrupt.

'I'm sorry but I'm not dancing tonight. I have other plans . . .' she said and turned away quickly, not waiting for his reply.

All through dinner, Valerie teased her. 'What other plans, Elinor?' she kept asking. 'Found yourself a new boy friend?'

Very aware that the others were looking at her, Elinor refused to answer, merely saying: 'It's my own affair.'

Half-way through dinner, Sam Keet stopped by their table. He smiled at Elinor and bent down over her shoulder, saying quietly—and yet loud enough for the others to hear: 'Okay about tonight?'

Elinor nodded and smiled into his eyes. 'Yes—quite okay,' she said.

Sam hesitated, his eyes roving over the others. 'Look, if you regret your promise it's not too late . . .'

Elinor laughed. 'Oh, Sam, a promise is a promise and I'm not regretting it . . .'

There was a stillness about the table after he had gone. Elinor was aware that everyone was waiting for her to explain. Why should she? Cheeks hot, she solemnly ate, determined to make someone ask her a question if they could not control their curiosity.

'Who's the handsome one, Elinor?' Valerie asked at last.

Elinor smiled at her very sweetly. 'A friend of mine. His name's Sam Keet.'

'Where did you meet him?' Kit asked, his voice stern.

Elinor laughed outright. 'My dear Kit . . .' she said airily. 'Where do we meet everyone on the ship? At the swimming-pool, of course. Don't you remember . . .' she went on, half-scared and yet determined to stand up to him.

118

'You saw me talking to him yesterday . . .'

'He's smooth,' Valerie said excitedly. 'Why didn't you tell me about him?'

Elinor might have said 'Because he is happily married' but she decided to say nothing. It wouldn't hurt Kit to know that she could be independent and look after herself. He was inclined to be a great deal too bossy . . .

As they went up to coffee in the lounge, Kit caught her by the arm and held her back so that he could speak to her quietly.

'Elinor . . . won't you introduce that man to us?'

Startled, she looked up at him. 'Why, if you want me to . . .' she began meekly and then drew a deep breath. Kit was not her lord and master, he had no right to judge her friends. She thrust out her small chin defiantly and glared at him. 'I'll ask Sam if he'd like to meet you . . .' she told him.

Kit's mouth was a thin line. 'I think it would be best, Elinor. After all, I am responsible for your well-being . . .'

'Oh, for . . .' Elinor began and controlled herself with an effort. 'Look, Kit,' she said very patiently, 'I'm not a child. I know just what I am doing . . .'

He gave her a queer look. 'I sincerely hope you do . . .' he said, releasing her arm and walking away from her.

CHAPTER EIGHT

It seemed a long endless evening to Elinor, curled up on Petula's bed, pretending to read but all the time thinking about the dancing up in the verandah café. She wondered what had made Kit ask her for the first dance like that. Usually he danced first with Val or with Alison. If only she had not promised Sam and Petula that she would baby-sit for them . . . but she had promised and it meant so much to them.

The babies were sweet and as good as gold. Sally, looking so angelic, was curled up into a ball, her thumb in her mouth; the baby had the faint flush of sleep on her cheek.

She must have dozed off, for she awoke suddenly when the door opened and there was Petula beaming down on her.

'Have they been good?' Petula whispered as Elinor hastily stood up, smoothing her crumpled blue frock.

'Not a sound . . .' Elinor whispered. 'Enjoy yourself?'

'Oh, it was just heavenly,' Petula whispered back. 'Just like old times. I can't thank you enough . . .'

'That's all right. I'll . . . I'll baby-sit another time if you like . . .' Elinor volunteered, moved by the happiness on the other girl's face.

120

'You really are an angel . . .' Petula said softly.

Back in her cabin Elinor had just undressed and got into bed when the door flew open and in came Valerie. Valerie's eyes were shining excitedly.

'Oh, Elinor—you've missed so much fun,' she said eagerly.

Elinor's heart sank. 'The dance was good . . .?'

Valerie waved an airy hand. 'Oh, we didn't dance. One can dance any night. No—we had a party. It was terrific, Elinor . . .' She was stripping off her tight sheath frock as she spoke, rolling down her stockings, tossing them in the air and catching them. 'Oh, Elinor, it was fun. We acted charades and had a grand time. Even Alison managed to unbend and played one of Cinderella's ugly sisters . . .' Valerie laughed. 'I wish you could have seen her . . . she really can act.'

'I take it you were Cinderella . . .?' Elinor asked.

Valerie exploded with laughter. 'That's the fun of it . . . Kit was Cinderella and Hugh the Prince.'

'And you?'

'Oh, I was on the other side. There was that nice Third Officer and Alison's stuffy diplomat, who is really fun when he gets going . . .' Valerie said, sliding into bed, switching off the light. 'The best evening of the voyage so far . . .'

121

A little pang of misery shot through Elinor. Yet what alternative had she had? And they hadn't even missed her.

From the darkness came Valerie's chuckle. 'Really, Elinor, Kit was fussing like a mother hen about you. He kept going back to the dancing to see where you were, but he couldn't find you. Where have you been?'

'Reading . . .' Elinor said truthfully.

Valerie laughed. 'Reading! Tell that to the marines!'

They were silent for a while and then Valerie said: 'Could you guarantee to wake me at half-past five, Elinor?'

'Half-past five!' Elinor echoed. 'What on earth . . .'

'I'm watching the sunrise with someone . . .' Valerie told her airily. She switched on the bedside light. 'Lend me your alarm clock, Elinor. This is a very important date . . .' she finished and chuckled as she wound and set the clock. ' 'Night . . .'

Again in the darkness, Elinor lay and pondered. Val, who loved her bed and who, when given her chance as on this trip, never got up before ten o'clock, was getting up at five-thirty. Was it for Kit . . .?

When Elinor awoke in the morning, she saw Valerie's empty bed and knew that either she herself must have been sleeping heavily when the alarm went off or Valerie must have switched it off very quickly, for she had heard

122

nothing.

She was alone at breakfast. There was no sign even of Hugh. She wandered round the decks, wondering where everyone had vanished, and then she saw Kit . . . he was standing, feet apart, hands clasped loosely behind his back as he gazed, frowning, at the beautiful blue water. Elinor's hand flew to her mouth for he turned round suddenly as if feeling her eyes upon him.

'Good morning . . .' he drawled with that touch of formality he occasionally used. He was wearing a white sports shirt and white shorts and his brown face under the bleached sun-kissed hair was grave. 'I wondered where you girls had got to . . .'

'I thought . . .' Elinor said, moving to his side, 'Val was with you.'

Kit lifted one fair eyebrow in that maddening way he had. 'Indeed . . . what made you think that?'

'Well . . .' Elinor hesitated. She did not like to point out that Val and Kit usually appeared on deck together in the mornings as though they had met by arrangement. 'She set the alarm for five-thirty . . .' Elinor went on, gazing up into his stern face, 'and said she was getting up to see the sunrise . . .'

'A most laudable desire . . .' Kit drawled sarcastically, 'but not with me. The sunrises here are nothing compared to ours in Australia.'

'You told me not to be narrow-minded about my country . . .' Elinor pointed out, 'but you and Hugh are always talking of Australia as if it is the only country worth living in . . .'

Kit's stern face relaxed and his eyes twinkled. 'Well, it is, Lady Kia . . .' He paused to watch the effect of his teasing words as the pretty colour flooded her cheeks. 'But I stand corrected. Doubtless you have wonderful sunrises in South Africa.'

'We certainly do . . .' Elinor told him warmly. 'Wonderful ones . . . only . . .' she went on with her usual honesty, 'I haven't seen many of them for I never got up very early.'

'I see the sunrise every day,' Kit said. 'I never grow tired of looking at it. Well . . .' He looked at his watch. 'I've some work to do. You quite happy?'

'Of course . . .' Elinor said, but she watched him walk down the deck with his deceptively slow strides that yet covered the ground with considerable speed and thought miserably that she could not even keep him by her side for ten minutes.

Where was Valerie, then? And Hugh? Could they be together?

But Valerie wasn't with Hugh for, looking into the writing-room where golden squirrels nibbled away at nuts on the silver-panelled walls, Elinor saw Hugh engrossed in writing letters. He looked up and smiled at her so she went quietly to his side and asked him if he

124

had seen Valerie.

He shook his head. 'No, I came straight here after breakfast.' He looked at his watch and his lean face was amused. 'Is she up yet?'

Elinor nodded. 'She got up at five-thirty to watch the sunrise.'

Hugh whistled softly and earned a disapproving look from a plump white-haired woman sitting opposite him. 'Doesn't sound like Val . . .' Hugh said. He looked into Elinor's troubled eyes. 'Why, you're worried . . .'

She blushed. 'I know it's silly—Kit says I fuss, but . . .'

Hugh nodded. 'I know, but I don't think there's anything to worry about, Elinor. I've three more letters to get off and then I'll come and help you look for her. Just relax meanwhile . . .'

She tried to obey him, but it wasn't easy. For no rhyme or reason she was worried. She wandered all over the decks, looking for Valerie, but there was no sign of her at all.

'She must be somewhere—' Kit pointed out impatiently when he met her wandering around and asked her why she looked so worried. He frowned. 'You really do fuss about her, Elinor. Try to leave her alone.'

'It's easy enough for you to talk . . .' Elinor said, furious with him. 'She isn't your sister.'

Kit smiled. 'I'd be proud of such a pretty sister . . .' He looked grave. 'You're not thinking she might have fallen overboard?'

Elinor had not been thinking that but now that Kit had suggested it, Elinor was afraid. Her hand flew to her mouth agitatedly. 'Oh, Kit . . .'

'Oh, really, Elinor . . .' he said. 'Be your age. You'll probably find her down in your cabin.'

'I never thought of looking there . . .' Elinor said, startled.

Kit smiled. 'Why not simply say you never thought . . .' he drawled. 'You just get into a panic and flap wildly.'

'I am not flapping wildly . . .' Elinor said indignantly and turned and hurried down to her cabin.

Valerie was there, curled up on her bed, sobbing her heart out.

'Val . . .' Elinor said in dismay. 'What's happened?'

At first Valerie would not talk. She sobbed noisily into a damp hankie. But at last she looked at Elinor, her mouth trembling.

'I . . . I owe thirty-five pounds,' she said and burst into tears again.

'Thirty-five pounds!' Elinor echoed, horrified. 'But Val—how did you . . .'

'Oh, it all began as fun and then . . .' Val dabbed at her eyes vainly. 'Oh, Elinor, I am sorry, really I am, but I only have seven pounds left and . . . and I've simply got to pay it and . . .'

Valerie made a great effort, blew her nose and dried her eyes, and stared at Elinor

126

unhappily. 'I simply must have the money . . .'

'But . . . but we haven't got it . . .' Elinor said. She unlocked the suitcase where she kept her passport and travellers' cheques and riffled through them. 'I can let you have twenty pounds, Val, but . . . but I must keep something for tips and . . . and suppose Aunt Aggie wasn't at the ship to meet us, we must have some money in hand.'

'We need another eight pounds . . .' Val said, wringing her hands together miserably.

'But Val—you must tell me . . .' Elinor said. 'How can you owe all that money?'

Valerie's face changed. It became sullen, her mouth pouting. 'Now I suppose you'll go all big-sister and lecture me . . .' she said rebelliously. 'The truth is I was an absolute idiot, Elinor. This—this morning, we watched the sunrise and then . . . then we went along to someone's cabin and had coffee and they suggested a game of cards and when I tried to get out of it, well . . .' She laughed uneasily. 'Elinor—you know how one hates to look . . . I said I hadn't the money and they said it didn't matter, play for fun . . . they'd stake me and then . . .'

'Then when you lost, they didn't,' Elinor said dryly.

'You're not mad?' Valerie asked, her voice surprised.

Elinor bent and kissed her quickly. 'Of course not,' she said reassuringly. 'I know what

127

you mean. One hates to . . . to . . .' She laughed uneasily. 'But Val darling, I just don't know where to get the money.'

Valerie was washing her eyes in cold water. 'We only need eight pounds,' she said almost cheerfully.

'Only!' Elinor echoed.

Valerie was making-up her face now. 'You'll find a way, Elinor,' she said happily. 'I know you will. Kit will lend it to you . . .'

'Kit!' Elinor cried in horror. 'I couldn't ask him . . .'

'Who else?' Valerie asked. 'He can afford it.'

Elinor drew a long deep breath. 'You ask him.'

'Me?' Valerie said. 'I couldn't . . . I mean, he'd be furious with . . . with those people. He'd probably go to the captain and make a scene. You are nearly of age, darling . . .' Valerie suddenly smiled. 'I know you'll find a way . . .' she said and opened the door, closing it behind her.

Elinor sat on the edge of the bed and stared at the place where, such a short time before, Valerie had lain, sobbing her heart out. And already Valerie had shelved her problem on to someone else's shoulders, and lost her misery and gone off to enjoy herself, leaving Elinor to worry at the thought of asking Kit . . .

It was easy to understand why Valerie could not ask Kit—if she loved him. Kit would be angry; Valerie was right. And Kit angry was rather terrifying.

The lunch gong sounded. Elinor dragged reluctant legs down to the dining salon. Valerie was already there with Kit and Hugh, chattering away.

'So you found her?' Kit said. 'Was she in the cabin?'

Elinor looked at him miserably. 'Yes.'

'So I was right?' he said cheerfully.

'As usual—' she said bitterly and saw the quick, annoyed look on his face. Well, perhaps it was rude, but you got tired of Kit always being right—and knowing it.

She ate in sullen silence, hearing Valerie's bird-like voice chattering away. How could Valerie be so cheerful—so completely free from the despair and fear that had chilled her? Was it simply because she knew she no longer had to solve the problem? Yet was it good for Valerie always to be able to hand her troubles to her sister? Elinor wondered if she ought to make Valerie ask Kit herself . . .

She looked at them quickly. Kit was smiling indulgently at Valerie, who was being very silly, teasing him, fluttering her lashes, and then Valerie looked at Elinor and smiled.

'You missed a lot of fun last night, Elinor. Where were you really?' She turned to Kit, laying her hand on his. 'What do you think, Kit—' she said, laughing. 'Elinor swears she was reading . . .'

Elinor felt her cheeks burn. 'I was reading,' she said stubbornly.

'Well, you weren't in our cabin . . .' Valerie told her. 'I went down several times to see, for Kit was worried about you.'

'I was reading,' Elinor said again and, looking at Kit, saw that he did not believe her.

She wondered how she was going to ask Kit for the money. How could she make an opportunity? It would not be easy. They would have to be somewhere alone—where no one could interrupt.

Her chance came that evening. They were dancing and Kit asked her to dance. Once round the room, she allowed herself to enjoy being in his arms and then she looked up at him, unaware of the fear and unhappiness that showed so plainly in her eyes. 'Kit—I must talk to you . . .' she said desperately.

He hid any surprise he might have felt. 'On deck? It's a bit chilly—for the wind has got up . . .'

So he didn't want to be alone with her, she thought. 'I'm sorry, Kit,' she said again, 'but it's urgent.'

Dressing for dinner, Valerie had been suddenly very white-faced. 'Elinor,' she had said miserably, 'I simply must pay that money soon. He . . . he keeps pestering me.'

'Who is *he*?' Elinor had asked, but Valerie had refused to tell her.

'I'll have nothing more to do with him,'

130

Valerie had said almost violently. 'He seemed so nice and he's so . . . so . . .'

'It's urgent . . .' Elinor said desperately, looking at Kit.

'We'll go to my suite and have some coffee . . .' he said, taking her arm and walking with her.

They passed Valerie, dancing in Hugh's arms. Valerie's eyes met Elinor's . . . Elinor saw how frightened Valerie was, for all her show of gaiety.

Kit waited for Elinor to speak. They sat silently, sipping hot coffee, while Elinor rehearsed words and phrases and discarded them.

Finally she blurted out. 'Could you lend me ten pounds? I'll pay you back as soon as I get a job and . . .'

Kit's wallet was in his hand. Slowly he counted out ten pound notes.

'Spending money at the shop?' he teased and watched the colour in her cheeks rising. 'Didn't Aggie give you any money for such things? Not like her to be mingy.'

'She's . . . she's been terribly generous . . .' Elinor said quickly. 'It . . . it's just that I need the money and . . .'

Kit's face changed. It became stern. 'You've been gambling . . .' he accused. Her cheeks burned painfully as she stared at him. 'You young idiot . . .' he said slowly. 'You think you're so capable, you fuss about Val and she's got ten times more sense than you . . .'

Elinor buttoned her mouth. The words longed to be spilled. Why should she always be blamed? But if Val loved him . . .

'I've supposed you'd have sense enough not to play with the crowd that gamble,' Kit drawled on. 'I suppose it started with cards and you were told it was just a game—and then you put on a pound and so on. How much did you lose?' he suddenly rapped at her.

'Thirty-five pounds . . .' she said miserably.

'My word . . .' he drawled. 'Of all the idiots!'

The crass injustice of it stung her. She faced him. 'Is it any worse than betting on horses?' she said defiantly.

To her amazement, Kit's face relaxed. 'Touché . . .' he said almost gaily. 'All right, Elinor, just write it off as experience gained. I'm willing to bet you'll never play cards again.'

'Never . . .' Elinor said with feeling. She thrust the notes in her bag. 'Kit—I can't thank you enough . . .'

'Forget it . . .' he said cheerfully and stood up.

Elinor felt as if she had been dismissed. 'I'll pay you back . . .' she promised.

He smiled at it. 'All right—if it'll make you feel any better but if you don't, it won't break me . . .'

He took her back to the verandah café. Valerie was talking very fast to Hugh. Her eyes sought Elinor's and there was a look of desperation in them. Elinor very slightly nodded her head and caught Hugh staring at her, and then saw the relief in Val's eyes.

It was near the end of the evening that Kit, who had left them for some time to talk to an old friend travelling on the ship, suddenly stood in front of Elinor. 'Dance,' he said curtly.

Startled by his reappearance, a little guilty, for she had just—surreptitiously, under the table—handed Val the rest of the money she needed, Elinor stood up.

They danced in silence for a while and then Kit drawled:

'I hate to have to tell you this, Elinor, but it's something you ought to know. You remember that man . . .'

'What man?' Elinor asked, wondering why he looked so stern.

'Last night—the man you were with, I presume, though you insist you were reading . . .' Kit said sarcastically.

'Oh—' Elinor understood. 'You mean Sam . . .'

'Is that his name? Well, Elinor, that man is married,' Kit told her, looking down at her gravely.

'I know he is,' Elinor said, a little puzzled.

'You . . . know . . . he . . . is,' Kit drawled.

She saw the thin white line she dreaded so much appearing round his mouth and she wondered what she had done to offend him, this time.

'Of course I know Sam is married . . .' she said, staring anxiously at Kit. 'Does it matter?'

CHAPTER NINE

Before Kit could speak, someone tapped him on the shoulder and, with barely-hidden annoyance, he gave way to Elinor's next partner, Val's jolly Third Officer.

The plump cheerful young man twirled Elinor round until she was quite giddy and then he slowed up. 'Did I rescue you in time?' he asked.

Puzzled, she looked at him. 'Did I need rescuing?' she asked.

He grinned. 'Your sister seemed to think so. Val said Kit was probably tearing a strip off you and you needed help. He looked a bit grim,' he said cheerfully, as the music stopped. As he walked back to the table with her, he grinned again. 'Anyhow the ogre seems to have vanished.'

It was true, and for the rest of the evening, Kit did not appear again.

In bed that night, Valerie demanded to be told *all*.

'Was Kit very mad—what did he say?' she asked.

Elinor described the scene as carefully as

she could. 'He said I was an idiot but he didn't seem to be really mad,' she admitted. 'Not as mad as I expected him to be. He said I needn't pay him back . . .'

'Good-oh . . .' Valerie said cheerfully. 'Now I'm out of *that* mess . . .'

Elinor was startled by Valerie's emphasis on the one word.

'You're not in another mess, are you?' she asked anxiously.

'Of course not . . .' Valerie said quickly. With just a little *too much* emphasis? Elinor wondered worriedly. Valerie went on pettishly: 'I suppose I'll never live this down. You'll always be reminding me of what a silly thing I did. You should have been a school marm, Elinor. You never let sleeping dogs lie.'

'I'm sorry but . . .' Elinor began, really worried now as she gazed at her sister's angry face. What other mess could Valerie be in? 'Val . . .' Elinor began again, more firmly this time. 'I absolutely refuse—and I mean it this time—to ask Kit for more money . . .'

Val laughed unsteadily. 'Money . . . we won't need any more money once we get to Aunt Aggie's. Hugh was telling me she has even more money than Kit and we shall be her heirs . . . or heiresses, I suppose . . .' She yawned and got into bed. 'Why do you always want to talk at night when I'm tired?' she asked crossly.

Feeling that Valerie had somehow neatly side-stepped any awkward questions, Elinor got into bed, switched off her light and shut her eyes.

But sleep was far away. Why had Kit looked like that? Why had he repeated her words with that strange look round his mouth? What did it matter if Sam was married . . .

But of course, it would matter, to Kit, she realised with a shock. He thought she was friends with Sam—might even be having a little romance with him. Of course, Kit did not know she was merely baby-sitting . . .

She wanted to laugh and cry at the same time. She seemed fated to appear at her worst in Kit's eyes. Flirting with a married man and being so off-hand about it; gambling away thirty-five pounds and expecting help to repay it . . . What must he think of her?

Dreading another lecture and afraid she might lose her temper and tell him the truth, thus involving Valerie and proving her to be a liar, she decided to keep out of Kit's way the next day.

It proved easier than she had expected and with her usual inconsistency where Kit was concerned, she felt out of things and vaguely hurt, and even resentful as a result. It must have been arranged the night of the charades when she had been baby-sitting, but Kit, Hugh, Alison and Val were all part of a group who were going to dress up as Henry the Eighth and his wives for the Fancy Dress Ball soon to be held. They all disappeared in Kit's suite and they were laughing a lot, buying masses of crêpe paper, and it was all very hush-hush and Elinor was obviously not wanted.

Rather downcast, she sought out Mrs. Anderson and, as usual, got a warm welcome. Mrs. Anderson's cheeks were no longer so pale; she seemed much more cheerful.

'Yes, my dear,' she said in answer to Elinor's enquiry about her health. 'I feel a different woman. I even stood for a little while today . . .' She beamed. 'I hear you are all having a wonderful time. Kit was telling me last night how much he liked you . . .'

'Kit said that?' Elinor almost gasped. A warm glow of happiness spread through her.

Mrs. Anderson smiled. 'Yes, my dear. He said that you were two of the nicest girls he had met and he was sure Aggie will be very happy to have you . . .'

Some of Elinor's elation left her. She was just one of *the girls*.

Mrs. Anderson's long thin white hands were folded idly in her lap.

'This is a strange life, isn't it, my dear? All day long in which to do nothing. So very different from our life at home,' she said thoughtfully. 'Kit was saying the same thing last night. I sleep badly and he often drops in to see how I am in the small hours when life seems so very depressing. He is longing to get back to the station and down to work. He works very hard . . .' she went on proudly. She frowned suddenly. 'You know, Elinor, I was rather troubled last night. When Kit came in, he was in a bad temper. I can always tell. After a while, he seemed to get over it but then he said to me that he thought it was time he settled down and got married and what did I think. I told him it was a matter he must decide . . . that all I wanted was for him to be happy.'

'And what did he say?' Elinor asked, her eyes enormous in her small pale face.

'He told me that he had chosen the girl he was to marry—that I knew and approved of her—that he had thought very carefully . . .' Mrs. Anderson said.

'And . . . and the girl's name?' Elinor asked breathlessly.

Mrs. Anderson shook her head. 'He refused to tell me. He said I would know all in good time. That when we got back to the station, I would know. Elinor . . .' she went on and her voice was troubled. 'I'm afraid he means Alison . . .'

Elinor swallowed. 'I think he does . . . She . . . she will make him a good wife . . .'

'Good wife!' Mrs. Anderson snorted a little. 'What man wants a good wife? He wants a woman, warm, loving, a woman who thinks he is wonderful. Alison has no heart, no warmth. I pray that Kit will not marry her, but I am very afraid he will. He always was one to choose the practical solution and she is the practical answer . . .'

When she left Mrs. Anderson, Elinor bumped into Alison on the promenade deck. The chairs were all on the sheltered side of the ship, which was rolling slightly in the rough seas. Alison hesitated and then paused.

'You'll wear fancy dress, won't you?' she asked.

'I . . . I haven't thought about it . . .' Elinor admitted.

'I've left them all sewing. You should see Kit . . .' Alison said, laughing. 'He is going to be Henry the Eighth and will need his clothes padded. I'm glad he is enjoying himself . . .' Alison went on in her cool voice. 'He gets little recreation on the station, works much too hard, and it may be a long time before we go on a voyage again.' She turned away and then looked back. 'If you don't want the bother of making a costume, Elinor, I've got one you might like. You'll need to shorten it a lot . . . you're very short, aren't you, but it would suit you perfectly.'

'That's kind of you, Alison . . .' Elinor began, not wanting to wear anything of Alison's and yet not sure how to refuse. 'What is it?'

Alison smiled. 'A Quaker's costume. I've never worn it. Somehow it didn't look right on me . . .' She smiled again and walked on.

Elinor drew a long deep breath. A Quaker. It would suit her, would it . . .? Doubtless, it was Kit's idea—or even Valerie's. Why should she wear a drab unexciting costume when the others . . .

Walking rapidly, she bumped into someone and saw it was Petula Keet, holding small Sally by the hand. It gave her an idea.

'Petula,' Elinor said before she could regret it, 'I could baby-sit tonight if you like . . . They'll be dancing . . .' She was rewarded by the radiance of Petula's smile.

'You are a darling. Sam will be thrilled . . .' Petula said excitedly.

Elinor decided to tell no one what she was going to do. After coffee in the lounge that night, she disappeared quietly. Perhaps no one noticed her going but she was settled in the Keets' cabin at last, with several packages of bright scarlet crêpe paper on her lap and an old black blouse. She had a whole evening in which to sew—not even Valerie would know she was going to the Fancy Dress Ball as a gipsy. Why should she go as a drab Quaker . . .?

The dress was finished and she was trying it on when Petula returned.

'It suits you beautifully . . .' Petula hissed in her usual whisper when the babies were sleeping. 'Look—I've got some nice chunky necklaces and bracelets.'

'I don't want my sister to know . . .' Elinor explained. 'Could I leave the costume here?'

'Of course . . .' Petula told her warmly. 'We

140

had a lovely evening, thanks to you . . .'

Hurrying back to her cabin, Elinor felt absurdly elated. For a whole evening she had been engrossed in something and had not thought about Kit. At least, not much. Just to wonder now and then what sort of married life he would have with Alison. Alison had stated plainly that she did not intend to be buried alive on the station, she would expect an overseas trip every other year and frequent visits to Melbourne for the races. Perhaps that was what Kit would like . . .

'Elinor, where have you been . . .' a deep voice demanded angrily.

Kit was outside Elinor's cabin door as she got there.

He caught her arm roughly. 'I've been looking everywhere for you . . .'

'You haven't got to keep tabs on me . . .' she told him. 'I've been with . . .'

'Not Sam Keet this time . . .' Kit said significantly. 'I saw him dancing with his wife. Who was it this time . . . and why didn't you tell us? We've been searching the ship for you . . .'

'Oh, please, Kit. As you once said to me about Valerie, be your age. What harm could come to me?' Elinor said crossly. 'I wish you would stop snooping . . .'

'Look,' he said angrily. 'Listen to me, young woman. Your aunt asked me to look after you and I intend to do so. Tomorrow I shall expect an explanation and an apology . . .' With that he strode off.

Quivering with anger, Elinor went into her cabin and saw that Valerie was just starting to undress. Valerie looked up, smiling.

'You just missed Kit. He walked down with me to see if you were here. He's pretty mad . . .' she said cheerfully.

'I know,' Elinor said grimly. 'I saw him.' An apology, if you please, she thought angrily. For what?

'You had him really worried,' Valerie went on. 'I think he thought you might have been gambling again . . .' She chuckled. 'Poor Elinor. I have given you a bad name in Kit's eyes, haven't I? Just as well you didn't fall for him . . .'

If only she hadn't fallen for him, Elinor thought miserably, as she went to bed. If only she could hate him wholeheartedly—or despise him. Anything but this helpless love— this breathlessness she felt when he was near— this longing to touch him, to smooth down that wisp of hair, to love him. If only . . .

But the following day, the only person who referred to her absence was Hugh. 'We were a bit worried.' he admitted as they walked round the deck, doing their daily 'mile'. 'By the way,' he went on, 'I'm terribly sorry you're out of the Henry the Eighth group. It was all arranged that night of the charades, but I hate you being out of it.'

142

Elinor smiled at him. 'It's all right, Hugh, really it is. I've got a costume.'

'So Alison said. She's lent you one, hasn't she? She said it was most suitable for you,' Hugh went on.

Elinor's cheeks burned for a moment. 'Did she? Yes, I think it will be,' she added, smiling—a little aware of Hugh's curious glance but refusing to allay his curiosity.

'It's the children's Fancy Dress party this afternoon,' Hugh remarked as they completed another circle of the deck. They paused to look at the water. Small black objects were diving and jumping out of the water.

'Hugh . . . look!' Elinor cried.

'Porpoises . . .' Hugh said.

They watched them in silence as the sleek black animals cavorted in the water. Standing side by side, their shoulders touching, they were not aware of Kit and Valerie until they were standing beside them. Then both Hugh and Elinor were startled. Perhaps they showed it, for on both Kit's as well as Valerie's face was a look of apology.

'I didn't mean to break up anything . . .' Kit drawled, his eyes cold as he looked at Elinor. 'But we've got to have a dress rehearsal, Hugh. Mrs. Pomfret—she's being kind enough to do the sewing of the costumes—' Kit explained formally to Elinor, 'is afraid they may not fit . . .'

'Sorry I've got to go . . .' Hugh said, smiling

143

at Elinor, patting her hand lightly.

Alone, Elinor turned back to watch the porpoises. What a lovely time they were having in that beautiful blue sea.

Later she went down to her cabin to tidy up before lunch. As she opened the door, she saw Valerie sprawled out over her bed, sobbing bitterly.

For a frightened second, Elinor was afraid. How could she ask Kit for more money . . . and then she went inside and closed the door.

'Val . . . Val darling, what is it?' she asked.

Val shook her head. Her voice came through her hair that was untidily rumpled, hanging over her face. 'I'm in love with someone . . .' Valerie sobbed, 'and he doesn't know I exist . . .'

The relief that flooded Elinor was breathtaking. If that was all. Her legs feeling weak, Elinor sat down on her bed and leaned forward.

'But Val darling, you knew all along that he was going to marry Alison . . .'

'He is not . . .' Valerie began and then sat up, her face flushed and wet. 'It's Kit who is going to marry Alison.'

Elinor caught her breath. 'I thought we were talking about Kit. Isn't it Kit you're in love with?'

'Kit?' Valerie's voice was scornful. 'Kit is good fun but he's much too stuffy. Nothing romantic about Kit . . .'

Elinor stared at her. Valerie must be mad. To Elinor, Kit was the most romantic . . .

'Then who do you love, Val?' Elinor asked slowly.

Valerie threw her a look of hatred. 'You know very well. You knew I liked him from the beginning and you've deliberately stolen him . . .'

'Val—what are you talking about? Who do you mean . . .?' Elinor asked, thinking for a wild moment that perhaps Valerie meant the ship's Third Officer.

'Hugh . . .' Valerie said dramatically. 'I love Hugh and you know what you've done to me? You've broken my heart. You stole him and now he has eyes only for you . . .'

'Val—you're wrong . . . Hugh and I are just friends. Honestly,' Elinor said.

Valerie stared at her. 'And you don't want to marry him?'

Elinor tried to laugh. 'Of course not!'

'Lift your hand and swear . . .' Valerie was half laughing, half crying.

Smiling, Elinor obeyed. 'I swear that I am not in love with Hugh—nor is Hugh in love with me . . .'

She was nearly knocked over by Valerie's bear-hug. 'Oh, how wonderful!' Valerie gasped. 'I was sure he was in love with you. Oh, Elinor, you're so sweet to me. First you get that money I had to have and now you . . .'

'Say that Hugh doesn't love me . . .?' Elinor

said, laughing. 'Oh, Val—what a child you are. First it was Max and then . . .'

'It was never Max—' Valerie said. 'It was Hugh from the first moment.'

'Then why are you always so cool and casual with him?' Elinor asked.

Valerie drew a long breath. 'Because . . . because . . . I couldn't bear to have him think I was chasing him and then . . . then when I thought he and you . . .'

She jumped up, stretching her arms high above her head. 'Oh, isn't life wonderful . . . absolutely wonderful . . .'

She began to sing as she washed her face and made-up. Elinor watched her, amused, tender, thinking for the thousandth time how quickly Valerie's moods changed. Now she was so sure she would win Hugh's love . . .

But would she?

At lunch time, Elinor seized her chance to study Hugh's face. It was a mobile face, lean, handsome, full of humour. His face was amused when he spoke to Valerie, carefully composed if he spoke to Alison, and warm and friendly when he spoke to Elinor herself. She noticed also that Valerie was not behaving any differently, still very gay, making Kit laugh, ignoring Hugh. What did Valerie propose to do, Elinor wondered. Perhaps she could learn a few things from her young sister!

They watched the children parading for the Fancy Dress competition. All sorts of

146

ingenious costumes, tiny angels, ballerinas, Hawaiian dancers with string skirts. Then came a small snowball, holding Petula Keet's hand. Sam followed close behind, the baby on his shoulder, another little white snowball. Seeing Elinor standing with her friends, Sam waved and called: 'Thanks a lot, Elinor . . .'

'What is he thanking you for?' Valerie asked at once.

Without thinking, Elinor told the truth. 'I baby-sat for them twice . . .'

'You what?' Kit asked.

Startled, Elinor looked up at him and realised she had given away her secret. She gave a little shrug. 'They were professional ballroom dancers before they had the babies and settled down,' she explained. 'They missed dancing terribly because they couldn't leave the children so . . . so I said I'd baby-sit for them.'

'And I thought . . .' Kit drawled slowly.

Elinor smiled at him and could not resist the opportunity. 'You always jump to conclusions, don't you, Kit?'

She watched the white line form around his mouth and waited for his reply. When it came it was devastating.

'Rather childish to be so mysterious about it . . .' he drawled. 'And not your style. You're the quiet simple type.'

147

CHAPTER TEN

Elinor remembered the unkind words as she dressed in Petula's cabin for the Fancy Dress Ball. She wondered whether Kit would say the costume was unsuitable, that she would make a better Quaker than a gipsy . . . would perhaps make one of his typical remarks . . .

She put her hands worriedly to her hair which she brushed vigorously so that it stood out round her face. It seemed that, in the last weeks, she had meekly accepted more insults than she had ever had in her life. Though, to be honest, they had not been meant as such. But to be told you are pathetic-looking, that you are dignified—a quiet simple girl—afraid of men . . .

Elinor gazed at her reflection. The black bodice fitted her slim form closely, the layers of scarlet pleated paper stood out around her. Petula had lent her black stockings and high-heeled shoes. Great chunky gold jewellery adorned Elinor's neck and arms. Her eyes shone excitedly, her cheeks glowed.

'I don't look like me at all . . .' she said in a surprised voice.

Petula laughed. 'You look very nice indeed . . .' she said reassuringly.

Elinor took her place in the procession that had to march past the judges. The dining-room had been gaily decorated with red, white and blue streamers and paper decorations hanging from the ceiling. Everyone had been given a funny cap. Kit looked comical in a policeman's helmet. They had had a hilarious dinner, Kit and Elinor being very formal and polite to one another.

No one had changed until after dinner, for most of the costumes were carefully-kept secrets. In the lounge there was a wonderful buffet table decorated in red and white with a crown in the centre above a swan. How hard the staff must have worked to prepare everything, she had thought.

Now, as the procession formed, everyone was laughing and joking and staring at one another curiously. They would have to march past the judges as they sat in a gaily decorated verandah café, balloons hanging from the ceiling.

Looking round her, Elinor found it hard to recognise faces. There was a man in a white toga with a gold belt and sandals . . . There were three witches—a huge pink elephant formed obviously by a husband and wife who were quarrelling softly, Nell Gwyn, charwomen galore, and then Elinor, her eyes hidden by the black mask she had made, saw the Henry the Eighth group. She gasped a little. How well the costumes had been made . . . Kit, enormous in his costume, his cheeks puffed out, his face made-up, moved heavily, followed by his wives, one of them bearing her 'head' on her arm.

They were quite close to Elinor and it was amusing to hear them talking about her.

'I don't see her anywhere . . .' Alison was saying, looking very regal indeed.

'I suppose she is coming . . .' Hugh said worriedly. He made a quite presentable-looking 'queen'.

Elinor could see the quick look Valerie gave him. 'She said she was,' Valerie said.

'I lent her a costume . . .' Alison put in. 'A very pretty one . . .'

Oh, it had been pretty enough. A demure grey dress, a great white collar. Something that would suit her, Elinor thought rebelliously.

As the procession began slowly to move, Elinor kept close behind a Sheikh in flowing white robes. The six judges were seated behind a table, making notes. As Elinor walked by the table, she rattled the small tambourine Petula had lent her, and swirled her full skirts . . .

Much later when the prizes were announced, Elinor was amazed to find she had won third prize. The Henry the Eighth group had won first group prize and, as the names were called out, and Elinor took off her mask, she smiled at the astonished faces of her friends.

'I thought you were coming as a Quaker . . .' Kit said, his face looking strange and almost frightening in its disguise. Elinor lifted her

150

small chin and smiled at him. 'I thought I would surprise you!'

'You might have told me,' Alison put in coldly. 'Someone else might have liked to borrow my costume . . .'

'You look lovely, Elinor darling,' Valerie said eagerly. 'I think you were clever to make it. I hadn't an idea. When did you do it . . .?'

'When I was baby-sitting . . .' Elinor said.

'Good for you,' Hugh told her and took her arm. Elinor saw the quick shadow flit across Valerie's face and felt sorry for her. She smiled at her sister and tried to reassure her, but Valerie turned away, her shoulders drooping a little.

It was a very gay, enjoyable evening. Most of the uncomfortable costumes were soon discarded and Kit returned, his handsome self, immaculate in his white jacket and black trousers, his face ironical as he saw that Elinor had kept her costume on.

'You look . . . quite different . . .' he told her as they danced.

It might have been the glass of champagne Hugh had insisted on her drinking to celebrate their prize winning, or the knowledge that she looked pretty for once, but she had courage enough to smile up into his dark eyes and say: 'Is it an improvement?' saucily.

He danced for a moment in silence and then drawled: 'In some ways, yes. You look . . . alive.'

151

She tried to hide her dismay. 'Don't I always look alive?' she asked in a voice that was meant to be gay.

'No . . .' he said, after he had considered the question. 'You usually look either scared or confused or worried about something. Tonight you look as if you are enjoying life . . .'

'I am,' she told him, and her gaiety was real this time. She let herself relax in his arms, giving herself up to the joy of dancing with him, pushing aside her worries about Val's happiness, her own unhappiness at knowing the wonderful voyage was drawing to an end and soon she would be thousands of miles away from Kit. Would he ever remember her, she wondered.

When they joined the others, Elinor noticed that Valerie, sitting next to Hugh, was looking rather bleak. Alison was speaking in her clear arrogant voice, looking as elegant and regal as the queen she represented:

'Of course Hugh is right . . . gambling is a mug's game . . .' she said.

Hugh was putting out his cigarette, leaning forward to do it.

'It seems so senseless to me—but then betting on horses does, too . . .' he said slowly.

'That is quite different,' Alison told him. 'You breed horses to race—you know their ancestry, you train them . . . It's not just like throwing down cards—there is skill attached . . .'

'So there is in playing cards,' Kit drawled. He glanced at Elinor and, for a moment, a warm, sweet smile flashed across his face. 'I'm sure we've all, at some time or other, lost money at cards until we became wise enough to leave them alone.'

Elinor realised with a shock that Kit was trying to reassure her, comfort her, 'save her face'. She flashed him a quick grateful smile for, after all, he believed she was the one to be so foolish as to lose all that money—and then she looked at Valerie's unusually downcast features and, for a moment, felt sick with anxiety. Was Val going to be hurt . . . badly hurt?

Now Hugh was dancing with Valerie—he was always very pleasant to her sister, but he did treat her as a very young girl, Elinor realised. Was that all Valerie was to him, she wondered. What hope had Valerie of making Hugh love her . . .? Probably Hugh had a girl he loved in Sydney . . .

'Shall we dance?' Kit asked and Elinor came back to her surroundings with a start, seeing that Alison was dancing with her diplomat. Elinor met Kit's amused eyes. 'Where were you?' he asked.

She blushed. 'I was thinking about Val . . .' she admitted.

As they circled the floor, he frowned down at her. 'Don't you think you fuss about Val too much?' he asked in what was, for him, a gentle

voice. 'Val is well able to take care of herself
. . .'

Elinor looked away quickly, unable to hide
the little smile that came before she could stop
it. If only Kit knew . . . He was always praising
Val's common sense and ability to take care of
herself. If he knew that it was Val who had lost
thirty-five pounds, Val who was in another
'mess' but would not talk about it.

'Your mother is much better . . .' Elinor
said, trying to steer Kit away from the subject
of Valerie. 'She tells me she can stand, now.'

'Yes, the voyage has done her good—'
Again the little note of formality had crept
into Kit's voice, putting a great distance
between them, even though she was in his
arms, held close to his heart, his chin brushing
her hair. 'I want to thank you, Elinor . . .' he
went on stiffly, 'for being so good to her,
spending so much of your time talking to her.
It is very good of you . . .'

Startled, she looked up at him, her pale face
with its shining dark eyes and gentle mouth.
'But I enjoy it, Kit,' she said earnestly. 'She's
given me a wonderful impression of your home
life and . . .'

'Bored you to tears with details of my past
. . .?' he drawled, looking down at her with
amused eyes.

'I wasn't in the least bored . . .' she began
indignantly and then stopped, uncomfortably
aware that her cheeks must be scarlet. Had she

154

given herself away?

'That's kind of you, Lady Kia . . .' he said softly.

Her eyes sparkled. 'Why must you call me that?' she said angrily.

'It's a compliment,' he told her, laughing at her. 'Suits you down to the ground.'

'Who is this Lady Kia?' she asked.

'A lady I am extremely fond of . . . a lady who has won me fame . . . in a small way,' Kit told her, his face even more amused. 'One day I'll introduce you to her . . .' he promised. 'My mother is very fond of you . . .' he went on, his voice changing again.

'I am very fond of her,' Elinor told him.

'Good . . . so it's mutual,' he said and she saw that he was laughing at her.

Elinor had been in bed for nearly an hour before Valerie joined her in the cabin. 'We lost you, Val . . .' Elinor said, putting down her book, for she had been trying to read and not worry about Val's disappearance.

Valerie's face was desperate. 'Oh, Elinor, I'm in trouble . . .' she said, going to sit on Elinor's bed, twisting her hankie between nervous fingers. 'That man . . . the one I . . . I lost the money, too . . . he's . . . he's been pestering me to play again and . . .'

'You haven't!' Elinor said in a horrified voice.

The ship was rolling a little and the air conditioning suddenly seemed very loud. It was as if they were boxed up together and fear filled the cabin. She couldn't ask Kit again . . . she wouldn't . . .

'Of course I haven't . . .' Valerie said crossly. 'Do let me finish . . .'

Elinor felt the relief flooding her. She relaxed. 'I'm sorry. Go on . . .'

'Well, he thinks it a sort of joke. He knows Hugh and . . . he says he'll tell him I was the one to lose the money and not you and then . . .' Valerie's eyes were suddenly huge with misery, 'Hugh will despise me. Not only for losing the money but for letting you do my dirty work. He's always saying people should shoulder their own responsibilities and stand on their own feet . . . and he says you spoil me shockingly and . . . I can't bear it if Tim . . .'

'Tim?' Elinor said quietly. 'Is that the man's name?'

Valerie nodded miserably. 'Tim Harcourt . . . he's very handsome and smooth and I was flattered . . . he asked me to watch the sunrise with him and it seemed quite an adventure somehow . . . he's the kind of man that makes you feel he thinks you are wonderful . . . but I hate him . . .' she ended fiercely.

Elinor was trying to think. 'But how did he know I got the money?'

'I told him . . .' Valerie said unhappily. 'At first I was quite desperate—I told him I couldn't possibly pay him . . . and he said that I could get the money from Kit but that maybe

156

it wouldn't be a wise thing, for Kit might cut up rough—on account of my age and . . . and he said it might be unpleasant and I would look an awful fool and . . . and then I said I'd ask you to get it . . . and he . . . he said that was a good idea . . .'

'Having planted the idea in your mind,' Elinor said.

Valerie stared at her. 'Of course . . . that's what he did . . .'

Elinor sighed. 'Not a very nice type, obviously. So what is he trying to do, now?'

Valerie shivered. 'He thinks it's terribly funny . . . he says he'll tell Hugh that you got the money for me and then . . . Hugh will despise me and . . .' Her lower lip began to quiver.

Elinor put her hand on her sister's. 'But Val—Hugh isn't like that. Hugh would understand. We all do silly things when we're young. Kit understood . . .'

'You don't know Hugh . . .' Valerie said desperately. 'He's got ideals and hc's terribly conventional and . . . It won't be the losing the money so much as my being a coward . . .' She covered her face with her hands and rocked herself. 'I can't bear it . . . to have Hugh despise me . . .'

It all seemed very melodramatic but Elinor knew herself how easy it was for things to get out of their proper perspective when one loves someone. On an impulse, she said:

'Suppose I speak to Tim . . .?'

Valerie lowered her hands and stared at her. 'Elinor . . . would you?' she breathed. And then her face clouded again. 'But what would you say?'

'I don't know . . .' Elinor confessed, suddenly regretting her impulsive words. 'I'll think of something but . . . but I still think it would be better to tell Hugh yourself, and then Tim can't hurt you.'

'Oh, I couldn't . . .' Valerie said with a terrible earnestness. 'You see, he's just beginning to *see* me, Elinor. I've been talking to him tonight—about Sydney and his life there and . . . and for once, he treated me like an adult and not a spoilt brat and . . . and if he finds out . . .' Her eyes filled with tears.

'All right,' Elinor said, stifling a sigh. 'I'll speak to Tim tomorrow.'

It was easier said than done. Although she kept an eye out for Mr. Harcourt the following day, it was not until the evening when they were all dancing that Elinor saw him. Still not sure what she was going to say to him, yet feeling she must seize her opportunity, Elinor managed to pass him by casually and pause and say, rather nervously: 'You are Mr. Harcourt?'

The handsome, dark-haired man with the narrow shifty-looking eyes stared at her. 'Yes, I am Tim Harcourt, Miss Johnson.'

'I want to speak to you . . . alone,' Elinor

said and went scarlet as he looked at her with a smile and said significantly:

'That will be a pleasure.'

'Shall we go to the drawing-room?' Elinor suggested. 'At this time, it is usually empty.'

'I am at your disposal . . .' he said with another unpleasant smile.

As he followed her to the drawing-room, a small but luxuriously-furnished room, with light beige wooden panelling and fawn carpet, Elinor racked her brains as to what to say to him. He spoke first.

'You want me to arrange a game for you?' he asked. His voice, to her, was very insolent.

She felt her cheeks grow hot. 'I most certainly do not,' she said indignantly, anger giving her the necessary courage. 'I want you to stop persecuting my sister.'

'Persecuting?' he said. 'That's a strong word. She has no sense of humour.'

'You have a strange one if you call it that . . .' Elinor said angrily. 'First of all you rob her of all that money . . .'

'Please . . .' he said, his voice sharp, his hand on her arm. 'That is a lie. There was no cheating. You should thank me for teaching your sister a lesson. She will never gamble again . . .' His smile was unkind.

'You . . . you knew we couldn't afford it . . .' Elinor said. 'It was wrong of you to encourage her.'

'My dear girl, she needed no encouragement

159

. . .' Tim Harcourt said smoothly. 'As for being able to afford it—I already knew about your wealthy aunt . . .'

It was a waste of time talking to him. She only felt grubby and humiliated as a result. 'Please . . .' she said earnestly. 'Please don't tell anyone that it was Valerie who lost that money . . .'

'Why not? I think it's a good joke. Of course if it was made worth my while to keep my mouth shut . . .' he said, still smiling. She was not sure if he was serious or teasing her.

'Is . . . is this blackmail?' she asked, her voice unsteady.

He put his arms round her suddenly, tilted back her chin with a rough hand. 'Not in money, my dear girl, but there are other ways . . .' he said, and kissed her.

The next moment he had been jerked away from her and thrown back on to a couch. Elinor stood there, shivering, staring at Kit . . . a Kit who was angrier than she had ever seen him.

'Go down to your cabin, Elinor . . .' he said curtly. 'I'll deal with this.'

Tim Harcourt was standing up—rubbing his shoulder gingerly, an ugly look on his face. Elinor was suddenly frightened.

'Please . . . please, Kit . . .' she said, clutching his arm, hanging on to it. 'He didn't hurt me . . .'

She could feel him shivering as he tried to

control his anger.

'Haven't you caused trouble enough?' he asked Tim Harcourt. 'Do you know that this girl is a minor? That she is only just twenty? I could make trouble for you if I liked to . . . already people are beginning to know about your methods . . .'

'Kit . . . it's all right, honestly, it is . . .' Elinor pleaded, still afraid as the two men stood, glaring at one another, Kit, legs apart, head lowered like a bull about to charge; Tim Harcourt, still rubbing his shoulder, his eyes suddenly wary.

'I was only trying to kiss her . . .' Tim Harcourt said in a sulky voice.

'A likely story—' Kit drawled. He had stopped shivering and Elinor could see he had himself under control now. 'Are you sure you were not persuading her to play cards?'

'It wasn't . . .' Tim began and Elinor, seeing that he meant to tell Kit the truth, tugged at Kit's arm . . .

'Please . . . Kit . . . I don't feel too well . . .' she said, leaning against him, half-closing her eyes.

She felt him put his arm around her, help her out of the room and out on to the cool deck. The moonlit sea met the starlit sky and as she sat down, the horizon seemed to vanish and then appear again. The roar of wind down the ventilators filled the air—they could hear the distant strains of music . . .

'Are you all right now?' Kit asked sharply.

Elinor opened her eyes and stared at him.

'You're not a very good actress,' he drawled. 'What was that man about to tell me? Something I'm not to know?'

His hands were hard on her shoulders, gripping them, as he shook her none too gently. 'I'm tired of your extraordinary behaviour, Elinor . . .' he told her as he released her. 'I must say I am disappointed in you. I thought you were a nice girl—decent, honest. Instead you lie to me—you gamble money that isn't yours—you break your word to a decent young man who loves you—and get involved with that kind of tyke I nearly thrashed.'

He pulled her to her feet, gripping her arms, so that she was very close to him, very aware of his anger.

'Now . . .' he said, his mouth a thin line. 'You're not leaving this deck until you tell me the truth.'

CHAPTER ELEVEN

How long they stood there, glaring at one another, Elinor never knew, for at that moment, there came the click-clack of high heels along the deck and suddenly Valerie was there, holding Kit's arm, her pretty face flushed and apologetic. Hugh came along behind her, an inscrutable look on his handsome face.

'Kit . . . it wasn't Elinor,' Valerie said.

Kit's hands fell away from Elinor's arms. He turned to look down at Valerie—Valerie, who, Elinor thought as she stared at her, looked prettier than ever with her flushed cheeks and shining eyes, and the corn-yellow frock that swirled as she walked.

'Kit . . .' Valerie said. 'I was the one who gambled . . .'

There was a sudden silence. Elinor caught her breath and then Valerie turned to her. 'It's all right, Elinor . . .' Valerie said. 'When I saw your face when you spoke to . . . to Tim, and I knew you hated doing it then . . . then I grew up . . . When Kit followed you, I knew I had to tell the truth so . . .'

'She told me,' Hugh said and his voice was indulgent. 'The poor kid was scared to tell you, Kit.'

Kit rubbed his hand over his face as if suddenly weary. 'Afraid of me?' he said slowly. 'I thought only Elinor saw me as an ogre. I wasn't cross, Val . . . I understood. We all do silly things when we are young—that's the way we learn.'

'I know . . .' Val said eagerly. 'That's what Elinor said. She said you were wonderfully understanding. But I was scared. You see . . . you see . . . Aunt Aggie asked you to look after

163

us and I knew you'd be mad at me . . . and I am rather young in your eyes, and I was afraid . . . afraid you'd go all grown-up and stern and stop me from having fun . . .' Her voice died out unhappily.

It was all Elinor could do to hide a smile. What a little actress Val was—the plain truth being, of course, that she had not wanted Hugh to have a poor opinion of her.

'So Elinor took the blame . . .' Kit said slowly. He turned to look at the slight girl standing so quietly by his side, her face calm. 'You certainly fooled me . . .' he said bitterly.

'Anyhow it's all over now . . .' Hugh said calmly, 'so we can forget it. Valerie has owned up and been forgiven . . . let's go back and enjoy ourselves. Coming, Valerie . . .?' he said, turning to the girl with a smile.

Valerie smiled back and Elinor wondered that Hugh was too blind to see the love in her eyes. At least, he did not seem to be angry or disillusioned. Indeed, his voice was warmer to Valerie than it had ever been before.

'We'll follow you . . .' Kit said curtly, his hand suddenly round Elinor's wrist. In silence, they watched Hugh and Valerie walk down the deck, going through the door into the verandah café. Then Kit turned to her, still holding her hand. 'It seems I owe you an apology, Elinor . . .' he said gravely. 'I wonder in how many other ways I have misjudged you.'

She was trembling suddenly—breathless

because he was so near to her, because of the feel of his hand on hers, because it seemed to her that never had they been so close.

'It's all right, Kit . . .' she said, unaware that her voice was listless and unhappy. 'It wasn't your fault.'

He let go of her wrist and they walked silently back to the dancing. Valerie and Hugh were dancing and laughing . . . and Elinor was conscious that Kit was staring down at her worriedly. She suddenly wanted to laugh hysterically—to tell him the truth. He always believed the worst of her. That was what he thought of her—that she was capable of anything. Did he think now that she was jealous of her own sister—simply because Hugh was dancing with Val?

She was sound asleep that night when Valerie crept into the cabin, but Elinor awoke and asked sleepily how she was.

'Oh, fine . . . just fine . . .' Valerie's voice lilted happily. 'I'm making progress, Elinor darling. Hugh's been absolutely sweet to me tonight. Maybe confessing my foolishness made him respect me and see that I am really grown-up . . .'

In the darkness, Elinor smiled. Would Valerie ever really grow up?

The days were slipping by so fast. Very soon they would reach Perth and the end of the voyage as far as Kit was concerned, for he and his mother were landing there, together with

165

Alison, and would fly home. Once again it was as if the great ship had shaken herself and reshuffled the small groups of people. Now Valerie and Hugh were together all the time— Elinor found herself dancing mostly with the Third Officer, and somehow Kit and Alison seemed drawn together.

There was nothing definite about it—the group still was a group, but it seemed to Elinor as if she was rarely alone with Kit these days, and whenever she saw him he was usually with Alison. And one afternoon, when she was sitting alone on the boat-deck, it was a shock when Alison came along, pulling a chair and sitting down by her side with a smile.

'Everyone seems to have vanished,' Alison said in a friendly voice. She looked very beautiful—her gleaming golden hair immaculate under an invisible net—her skin glowing with health, her eyes bright as she smiled at Elinor. 'I expect most people are starting to pack. Luckily my aunt's nurse kindly offered to pack for me so I'm let off that horrible job . . .'

There was a long silence. The roar of the ventilators filled the air. A few seagulls came swooping down out of the blue sky. The sea was rough—flecked with white waves, and the ship rolled slightly.

Alison stretched her arms above her head and then folded them behind it, her golden hair lovely on the green sleeves of her loose jersey. She wore a beautifully pleated white skirt that even Elinor recognised as being very expensive. 'I see you spoke to your sister about Kit . . .' Alison went on, tilting her head as if to watch the white seagulls overhead. 'For she has transferred her affections to Hugh . . .' Elinor stiffened but Alison went on, her voice indulgent. 'What a child she is—pretty but oh, so vulnerable. I hope Hugh won't hurt her. If ever there was a confirmed bachelor, Hugh is one,' she said slowly.

'I can imagine it . . .' Elinor said guardedly.

'Rather,' Alison went on cheerfully. 'He has a wonderful penthouse in Sydney, scores of beautiful girl friends, and a good time. He spends quite a lot of time with us—on the station. He handles all Kit's book work. You might not think it to look at Hugh, but he is a very clever accountant. He works—when he feels like it . . .' she said with a smile, 'for a big firm of stockbrokers in Sydney. Actually he is a partner so he is more or less his own master. He has a very good life—why get married?' she asked lightly.

'I suppose . . .' Elinor said very slowly, 'if he fell in love . . .'

'My dear . . .' Alison said, 'he does that with monotonous regularity, but he's never serious. Now he is so very different from Kit . . .' her voice changed, taking on a proud, almost possessive note. 'Kit will marry when the right time comes. I've always known that and have been prepared to wait for him.' She moved, sitting upright, turning to stare at Elinor, her hands clasped in her lap. 'You know, Elinor, we've loved one another for years but the right time has only just come. I'm restless and Kit is devoted to his work, but somehow things have dovetailed now and it's the right moment. Isn't it wonderful?' she said, her voice serene. 'I was wondering if you and Valerie would like to be my bridesmaids?'

'How nice of you to ask us . . .' Elinor said a little stiffly. 'Have you fixed the date yet?'

'It will be the first thing we do when we get home . . .' Alison said happily. 'Probably marry in three months' time. I've got some of my trousseau already. There will be crowds of people at the wedding, of course. Kit is very well-known. I'd prefer a city wedding, but I know he will want us to go to the funny little church near the station that we have always attended.'

'And . . . when you are married,' Elinor said, 'will you be able to settle down on the station?'

Alison's laugh rang out. 'Of course not. I don't intend to . . .' she added complacently. 'It's time Kit had a manager for the station—he can well afford a dozen managers—so that we can lead our own life. I know I'll be able to make Kit understand my point of view. We'll go to other countries and study their methods of sheep and horse-rearing and Kit will be happy and I will enjoy myself . . .'

'If you have children . . .' Elinor said with difficulty, 'it won't be so easy.'

Alison laughed. 'Oh, we shan't have any for a few years and then I intend to have two, a boy and a girl. We'll have a good nurse—probably a Norland nurse sent out from England—and I'll still be free . . .' Her voice changed. 'I suppose when you marry your Max, you'll settle down in a small suburban villa in England and do all your own work and manage a horde of babies, too. You're the type of girl who has a big family and enjoys being a martyr . . .'

'I am not . . .' Elinor began indignantly. But it was partly true. She wanted at least four children.

Alison stood up. 'You've as little sense of humour as your sister,' she told Elinor. She paused, staring down at her. 'By the way, don't go spreading the news around about Kit and me, will you? We want to keep it a secret until the engagement is announced.'

'I won't tell anyone,' Elinor promised.

When Alison left her and she was alone, Elinor held up the book as a shield and stared at the blurred print. Would Kit be happy if he married Alison? Alison's idea of a marriage was a selfish one. The other girl had never once said anything about Kit's happiness. Would Kit enjoy a life rushing round the world with Alison?

But would he do it if he didn't want to?

Somehow it was impossible to imagine a man like Kit meekly obeying his wife's whims. Why, there was something about him so strong, so vital . . . you felt his strength when he just entered a room. He would not obey any woman . . . Then what would happen? Would Alison nag him . . . or leave him . . .?

Elinor stood up, the wind tugging at her hair, wrapping her blue skirt round her legs as she battled her way against it, down the steep staircase and along to Mrs. Anderson's cabin.

There were trunks on the bed, suitcases on the floor, all half-packed. The warm welcoming smile Elinor got from the woman sitting in an armchair made it easier for Elinor to go in for a chat.

'My dear, I am glad to see you. Patricia . . . that's the nice girl who is nursing me, or rather . . .' she laughed, 'has been looking after me, has gone to meet her boy friend. Romance is in the air . . .' Mrs. Anderson went on. 'Pat came with me from South Africa, because she wanted a chance to see the world, and now she has fallen in love and got engaged. Such a nice boy, too . . .' Mrs. Anderson's face was quite excited, her eyes bright. 'I do love a good romance, dear, and Pat has told me about this so that I have followed it every step of the way. She'll be settling in Australia so I'm very happy for her . . .'

Mrs. Anderson fingered the pearls around her neck and gazed at the quiet girl. 'What have you been doing this morning, Elinor?' she asked. 'You don't need to start packing yet for you're going on to Melbourne, of course.'

'No, I don't need to start yet . . .' Elinor said dully. Not that it would take long, in any case, for she and Valerie had not got very much. 'Mrs Anderson . . .' she said suddenly, finding courage at last. 'Do you think Alison loves Kit?'

Mrs. Anderson looked at her thoughtfully. 'I think she loves him as much as she is capable of loving anyone.'

Elinor's eyes widened. 'But is that enough?' she asked.

'I imagine Kit thinks so,' Mrs. Anderson said drily. 'He has known her all his life—he knows just how egotistical and selfish she is. I suppose he's prepared to accept this . . . what made you ask?'

'Well . . . I . . . we . . . Alison has just been talking to me. About their marriage . . .' Elinor began, her hand flying in dismay to her mouth. 'Oh, I promised not to mention it,' she said, really distressed.

Mrs. Anderson looked suddenly tired. 'I won't repeat it, Elinor. What did she say?'

'Just that Kit and she had . . . had an understanding for years that when the right time came, they would marry. She says it has come now, that when they get home, they would probably marry in three months' time . . .' Elinor said.

Mrs. Anderson sighed. 'And Kit has said nothing to me . . .'

'They want to keep it a secret until the engagement is announced officially,' Elinor said quickly.

'I see . . .' Mrs. Anderson said slowly. 'Go on.'

'Well . . .' Elinor hesitated. 'She asked us to be her bridesmaids and said she'd prefer a city wedding but Kit would want it in the little church near by . . .'

'She is right there. Kit would,' Mrs. Anderson said.

'Then . . . she was talking about their life afterwards,' Elinor went on. 'She said Kit would get a manager and they would travel all over the world, studying other methods of sheep-rearing and . . .'

'Subjects in which she is so very interested,' Mrs. Anderson said with the first sarcasm Elinor had ever heard from her.

'She wants to travel, she said . . .' Elinor went on. 'But would Kit be happy?' she asked earnestly, leaning forward, her rumpled hair falling round her small flushed earn est face. 'Kit is a fine man, Mrs. Anderson. He deserves happiness. I don't think Alison loves him at all—she just wants a husband . . .'

'Alison is an ambitious young woman, Elinor,' Mrs. Anderson told her. 'Kit has a great future. Apart from his wealth, he is highly thought of in our own district, interested in politics, in expanding the local industries. Alison's land adjoins us and the two combined would make a very wealthy station indeed. I don't think for a moment that she wants to marry Kit, the man . . . but she does want to marry Kit, the important wealthy pastoralist, if you know what I mean?'

'In other words, if Kit went broke tomorrow, Alison wouldn't be interested?' Elinor asked, shocked. 'But that isn't love. Now if I loved . . .'

Mrs. Anderson leant forward and touched Elinor's hand lightly.

'My dear, lucky the man you love. Kit has told me about your young man, Max . . .' she went on gently. 'Dear, why not encourage him to come out to Australia to settle? It would make Aggie so very happy to have you near her and you could visit us and . . .'

Perish the thought, Elinor thought unhappily. This wretched Max—how he dogged her footsteps.

'I don't know . . .' she said evasively. 'I just don't know . . .'

'My dear,' Mrs. Anderson said gently. 'Don't let yourself be muddled by the atmosphere on board ship. Here you have so many other things to think of that probably Max seems very vague and remote, someone in the dim past. But ship-board flirtations rarely mean anything. It is an unnatural atmosphere—you are apt to make ordinary men into heroes . . . see them through rose-coloured glasses . . .' she went on kindly. 'Once you are ashore and far from them, you'll remember your Max and realise how much you love him . . .'

Before she could answer, Elinor was relieved to see the nurse, Pat, come hurrying in, her eyes shining like stars. 'Sorry I was so long, Mrs. Anderson. Time for your medicine . . .' she said.

Elinor seized her opportunity, murmuring goodbye and going out to the deserted windy deck. Already the atmosphere on the ship was changing. The old carefree intimate relationship was gone. Now people were packing, thinking about their homes and other things.

She leant against the railing, watching the sea . . . feeling the cold wind on her cheeks. Had that been a tactful reminder from Mrs. Anderson that she had made it obvious that she was in love with Kit . . .?

'Cable for you . . .' Kit said as he approached and she, startled, looked up to see him holding out something for her. 'From England,' he said, his voice significant.

Elinor held it as if it might bite her. 'It might not be for me . . .'

'It says Miss Johnson . . . and if it was for Valerie, it would say Miss V. Johnson . . .' Kit said, his voice cool and amused. 'I must say you behave very strangely when you get cables.

Do you always look so scared?'

She flung him an annoyed glance. 'I am not scared. Just wondering who could be cabling me from England.'

'Then open it and find out,' he suggested.

She obeyed and stared at the words.

GOT WONDERFUL JOB LONDON AND ROUND WORLD SUGGEST YOU COME WITH ME DARLING NO MATTER WHAT HAPPENS WILL ALWAYS LOVE AND ADORE YOU MAX.

'It's from Max . . .' Elinor said weakly. The paper fluttered in her hand and a sudden gust of wind tore it from her fingers and blew it along the deck.

As Kit chased it, Elinor was thinking fast. She must tell Valerie . . . Valerie had always wanted to see the world. Maybe this would make her realise that she loved Max . . .

Kit gave her back the cable, his face stern. 'What does he want?'

Elinor stood, her back to the rail, the wind blowing her hair over her face. 'He has a job going round the world . . . he's a journalist . . .'

'And wants you to go with him?' Kit asked. 'Why not?'

'Because . . . because . . .' Elinor turned and faced the great expanse of ocean blindly. 'I don't . . .'

'Look, Elinor,' Kit said slowly. 'Don't be confused by this voyage. The impossible seems possible on board . . .' He sounded almost wistful. 'But in a few days we shall land and then all these fantastic dreams will vanish and your feet will be firmly on the earth. If you love Max . . .'

'But I don't,' Elinor said violently, unable to bear any more, turning to look up at him.

'Then why did you encourage him?' Kit asked, his voice cold. 'A man needs some encouragement . . .'

It was true. Valerie had certainly made use of Max and his small sports car and his company. Valerie's gay manner and friendly intimate way could easily have made him believe she loved him.

'How can you know if you love anyone unless you see a lot of them?' Elinor said desperately. 'If you're going to call that encouragement . . .'

'It depends on how you behave,' Kit told her sternly. 'You've only changed since you've been on board. Hugh . . .'

'Has nothing at all to do with it . . .' Elinor told him, her eyes shining with tears of frustration. 'I was never for a moment in love with Hugh, nor was he with me. We were simply good friends. He's a dear and so very easy to get on with. He isn't conceited and arrogant and bossy and . . .' she paused for a breath.

'Like me?' Kit asked in an ominously quiet tone.

She glared at him. 'Yes, like you. You're so

176

sure of yourself that you think you can kick other people around. You're smug . . . smug . . .' She stopped, biting her lip, trying not to cry. In a moment, she had her voice under control. 'Kit . . .' she went on, her voice shaking very slightly. 'Marriage is most terribly important. It's for keeps. You've got to be sure. It's not enough to marry a person because you share the same interests, because it seems sensible . . .' This was her chance, she realised, and she was seizing it. She gazed up at him, her flushed face earnest, her wind-tossed curls in pretty confusion, her eyes brave. 'You must be sure that you can make that person happy. It isn't enough to be happy yourself—loving someone means caring for them, wanting them to . . . to . . .'

'Be happy,' Kit supplied the words coldly. 'What is all this leading up to, Elinor?'

For a moment she was tempted to tell him the truth. That she was terribly worried about him—that all she cared about was his happiness—that she knew he could never be happy with a selfish woman like Alison. She longed to tell him that she loved him—that if they hadn't a penny or a sheep in the world, she would still love him. That if he was her husband, she would spend her days loving him, caring for him, cooking his favourite dishes, darning his socks . . .

'Elinor . . .' Valerie cried excitedly. She came running down the deck, her hand in

177

Hugh's. 'I hear you've had a cable . . . Is it from Max?'

Elinor swallowed back all her words she had so nearly said—words that perhaps it were better left unsaid, for poor Kit would have been horribly embarrassed to learn that she was so hopelessly in love with him.

'Yes,' she said simply, holding out the cable to Valerie.

Valerie read it quickly—her face changing, her eyes excited. She looked up. 'But how wonderful, Elinor . . .' she said. And added, 'For you.'

CHAPTER TWELVE

It was the 'Derby' that night and everyone was very gay. Valerie was Hugh's jockey and Alison was Kit's. In the verandah café, a green 'field' was laid. There were wooden horses and the jockeys wore coloured hats.

Elinor had not time to feel left out for she had plenty of partners. But inside her, she felt dead. The voyage was nearly over. Soon they would reach Perth, and Kit and his mother would go ashore, and the next time she saw him, it would probably be at his wedding.

Again, Valerie was much later than Elinor in going down to the cabin; again, Elinor awoke to see Valerie's eyes shining, and hear her say how happy she was, that Hugh was quite different, now . . .

Elinor was afraid all the same. Alison's words about Hugh's frequent falling in and out of love worried her. She tried to warn Valerie but was laughed at.

'Hugh isn't like that,' Valerie said with complete assurance. 'When Hugh falls in love, it will be for ever. I'm just trying to make him fall for me.'

'Val . . .' Elinor said earnestly. 'Why did you say that . . . about me? I mean, when you read Max's cable, why did you say it would be wonderful for me?'

Valerie looked at her surprised. 'I mean it, Elinor. You're going to feel rather out of things if I marry Hugh, and I was wondering why you didn't take over Max . . .' She looked even more surprised at Elinor's gasp of dismay. 'I'm serious, Elinor. You always did like Max a lot. Why, you met him first—it was only through you that I met him at all. I know he admired you—tremendously. And you do like him . . . look how you used to praise him to me, tell me what a kind person he was . . .'

'But, Val . . . that's not reason enough for marrying a man,' Elinor said.

'Look, Elinor . . .' Valerie said earnestly. 'You'll write to Max for me, won't you? Tell him I'm glad about his job but . . .'

'No, I will not,' Elinor said violently, turning to escape from the cabin. 'Do your own dirty work for once,' she said before she slammed the door.

And then it was suddenly the last day. That night there was to be a wonderful party—a party to out-party all others, the ship's Third Officer told Elinor. Already the rooms were being decorated in readiness for this party, which was called 'Landfall Night.'

Elinor wandered over the ship miserably. You could feel the excitement in the air as land approached. People were exchanging names and addresses, vowing they would keep in touch with one another, talking of the future, what they planned to do. The weather was chilly, the water rough, the ship rolling. For the first time since they had left South Africa, Elinor dreaded the future. Supposing she and Aunt Aggie did not like one another, supposing Hugh broke Valerie's heart . . .

It was funny how, if you think of a person, you often hear from them, for suddenly Hugh was there, by her side, leaning over the rail, watching the flying fish round the sides of the ship.

'Elinor . . . I want to talk to you,' Hugh said gravely. His handsome face looked worried. He took her arm and led her away to a secluded corner of the deck, pulling two chairs close together, settling her in one. 'Elinor—I want your opinion. Your honest opinion . . .'

Puzzled, she stared at him. 'Yes . . .?'

'Do you think I'm too old to marry Val?' he

asked earnestly. Even as Elinor was gasping, as she tried to grasp the wonderful fact that he loved Valerie, he went on. 'I'm nearly thirty-five, Elinor, and she is only seventeen. I'm afraid I'm too old . . . She says I'm not . . . that age isn't important. But she is so very young, Elinor.' He leaned forward and took her hands in his, holding them tightly. 'I love her very much, Elinor. I won't rush her. Are you very surprised?'

She was honest. 'I am rather. You see, I had been told you fall in and out of love rather often and . . . and it seemed too wonderful to be true that you could love Val . . .'

He stared at her. 'You don't mind?'

She smiled. 'I'm absolutely thrilled, Hugh. I know Val loves you very much—she was afraid you . . .'

'Didn't?' Hugh said. He laughed. 'I'm afraid I deliberately kept her guessing. Val is a difficult girl, Elinor. I needn't tell you that. Things she gets too easily, she doesn't want. That's why I always treated her as a rather sweet child while she wanted me to treat her as a woman.'

'Hugh—how clever of you . . .' Elinor gasped.

'I wanted to be quite, quite sure . . . I'm not rushing her into this, Elinor. I shall insist on a six months' engagement and give us both time to know one another . . .' he told her. 'How are you going to like having me for a brother-in-law?' he teased.

'I couldn't ask for a nicer one,' Elinor told him, her eyes shining. 'Oh, Hugh, I am so happy,' she said earnestly. 'Val needs someone like you—someone old enough to guide her but young enough to have fun with . . .'

'We're announcing it tonight—if that is all right with you?' Hugh went on. 'And . . .' He hesitated. 'Would you be very hurt if I steal Val from you tomorrow? I want to take her home to meet my people. We can fly quite quickly from Perth—it seems silly to waste time going on to Sydney by ship and then flying back.'

'Of course I don't mind,' Elinor said stoutly, but inwardly she felt a great desolation, knowing that she was to be really and truly alone for the last part of the journey.

Down in the cabin, however, she hugged Valerie warmly.

'Darling, I'm so glad for you,' Elinor said. 'It's wonderful . . .'

'Isn't it?' Valerie said, her face radiant. Then she thought of something and put her hand on Elinor's arm. 'Elinor—you will be an angel and write to Max for me, won't you?' she said appealingly.

What could Elinor say to such a question at such a time?

Up in the pretty little writing-room with its unusual walls, she wrote the difficult letter.

'I am most terribly sorry, Max,' she

finished. 'I know how hurt you must be. Valerie asks me to tell you how sorry she is, but she is sure you will understand. It would be a terrible thing to marry a man you did not love, simply because he asked you to . . . Hugh is a good man and kind, Max, and they will be engaged six months so that Val can be really sure, this time.'

It was with great relief that she sealed the envelope and went down to the purser's office to post it.

The Landfall Party was a great success and if some of the gay revellers were hiding sore hearts, they were well hidden. Elinor danced with Hugh and Kit and the diplomat and the ship's Third Officer and with many others. She laughed and joined in the singing and it seemed as if the evening would pass off all right and without any unpleasantness at all, until the moment when Kit led her out of the verandah café and on to the wind-blown deck.

Elinor's hands flew to her hair instantly. It had become a mop. His arm round her, he guided her to a corner, sheltered from the wind. It was dark and chilly and his arm stayed round her shoulders.

'Elinor . . . I must know,' he said urgently. 'In a moment, Hugh and Valerie are going to announce their engagement. You are sure you don't mind? You weren't in love with Hugh?'

She could not see his face but the warmth of

his arm seemed to burn her back. She let herself lean against it for one moment. Then she drew herself away stiffly.

'What good can you do if I *was* in love with him?' she asked defiantly. 'In any case, Kit, I keep telling you that I was never in love with Hugh.'

'If only I could believe that . . .' From the darkness, Kit's voice came. He sounded worried. 'I don't want you to be hurt,' he said simply.

'Nothing that Hugh can do could hurt me . . .' she managed to say.

'And Max . . .?' he asked.

'Oh, please, Kit . . . why must you always harp on Max?' she said irritably. She was suddenly very near to tears. What would happen if she told him the truth? If she said that he himself was the only man she loved . . .

She could bear it no longer. 'We'll miss the announcement if we don't go back . . .' she said and turned towards the café door. Kit was close behind her. As the door opened and a wave of bright lights, noise and music hit them, she glanced up into his face and wondered at the strained unhappy look she saw there—and then she forgot it as she saw Valerie waving to them excitedly.

After Hugh had made the announcement, there was champagne all round. Mrs. Anderson had been brought up for the occasion and she smiled and beat time to the music with her hand.

'The doctor says I'll soon be dancing again . . .' she said, laughing, to Elinor. 'Imagine it, at my age!'

'I bags the first dance, Mother . . .' Kit said, smiling at her.

'And I the second,' Hugh chimed in. 'What do you think of my future bride?' he asked proudly, holding Valerie's hand tightly.

'I think she's charming,' Mrs. Anderson said warmly. 'And that you are a very lucky man. I only wish . . .' she added wistfully, 'Valerie, that your nice sister could have fallen in love with my son. I should have loved her for a daughter-in-law . . .'

For a moment there was an appalled silence and Elinor's cheeks were the colour of red peonies as she looked wildly round her for escape.

'Unfortunately she didn't . . .' Kit said smoothly and the music began so that he could hold out his arms to Elinor and sweep her out on to the floor.

'I am sorry Mother had to make such a remark,' he said stiffly as they danced. 'I'm afraid it cmbarrassed you.'

Elinor kept her eyes downcast, unaware that her long dark curly lashes on her now pale cheeks were very lovely. Her mouth trembled a little. She looked very young and vulnerable. 'I'm afraid it embarrassed you . . .' she murmured.

185

'I'm used to my mother . . .' he said and tried to laugh.

'Kit . . .' Elinor looked up at him, her eyes wide and appealing. 'Please don't talk . . . let's just dance . . .'

He looked first startled and then annoyed. 'All right,' he said.

In silence they danced. Elinor kept her eyes closed, giving herself up entirely to the dance, knowing that this might be the last time she would ever be in his arms . . . there was a choking lump in her throat as she faced the truth.

As soon as it was over, she slipped away down below to her cabin, hastily undressing, sliding into bed. The ship was rolling rather heavily and she wondered if, after they left Perth, it would be rough as she had been told it sometimes was. She was awake when Valerie came to bed but she pretended to be asleep. She felt that she could not bear it if Valerie wanted to talk about Hugh and how wonderful he was . . .

In the morning, they had to be up early. At six-thirty in the lounge, they queued to go through to the immigration officials who sat in the verandah café to stamp passports and take the cards. Valerie and Elinor had gazed at the big freighters they were passing as the ship moved majestically in towards Fremantle. The sun was very bright in the blue sky, the water calm and peaceful-looking. The town itself

186

looked very white and clean.

At breakfast, Hugh, Valerie and Elinor were alone.

'I hate to leave you like this, Elinor,' Valerie said worriedly.

Elinor smiled at her. Even the dining-salon felt cold and unfriendly; an atmosphere of departure hung in the air. 'I'll be all right.'

'You could have come with us,' Hugh said. 'Mother would love to see you but . . .'

'Aunt Aggie . . .' Elinor finished for him with a smile. 'She'll be expecting us and . . . and we couldn't disappoint her . . .'

'You will be all right?' Valerie persisted.

Elinor laughed. 'Of course I'll be all right. Haven't I got your Third Officer?'

They were still laughing when Kit appeared. He looked stern and aloof. 'Elinor—we're just leaving. Do you want to say goodbye to my mother?'

'Of course.' Elinor was on her feet, dismayed with the realisation that in moments Kit would have gone . . .

She kissed Mrs. Anderson warmly. The rather wistful-eyed woman was in her wheelchair, clutching her handbag. 'Dear girl,' she said, 'I do hope you'll be all right. I hate to think of you all alone on the ship . . . You know what I mean . . .' Mrs. Anderson looked as if she wanted to say something more and then gave a quick nervous glance at Kit's cold face as he waited. 'So this is goodbye, Elinor . . .

No, au revoir . . .' she said hastily. 'So soon as
Aggie can spare you, you must come and visit
us . . .'

'Thank you, I'd love to . . .' Elinor said
stiffly. 'Where is Alison? I didn't say goodbye
to her.'

'She's gone on . . . We're meeting her at the
airport,' Kit said curtly.

Pat, the nurse, began to push the
wheelchair. Kit held out his hand to Elinor. All
round them there were people. The dock was
crowded with cars and people and already the
great cranes were moving slowly.

Elinor's hand felt very small in Kit's firm
grasp.

'Goodbye, Elinor,' he said gravely. 'I hope
things will sort themselves out all right for
you.'

'Goodbye, Kit . . .' she said solemnly and
heard her voice thicken perilously. 'I hope . . .
hope you and Alison are very happy . . .' she
said and wrenched her hand free, turning
blindly and almost falling down the staircase to
the safety of her cabin.

But she was not alone for long, for Valerie
and Hugh arrived, to collect Valerie's luggage,
to insist that Elinor must go ashore, Hugh
buying her a ticket for a bus trip round the
city, and there was only time for one last
bear-hug from Valerie, and a warm kiss from
Hugh . . .

'We'll be seeing you soon. I can only keep

Valerie for two weeks at home for I have to be back in Sydney at my job,' Hugh explained. 'See you soon, Elinor . . .'

Elinor stood on the ship's deck, watching them run down the gangway, seeing the way Hugh looked after Valerie, how he helped her into the taxi—and a cold desolation swept over her.

Now she was really alone . . .

Rather than spend a day by herself on board, she went on the bus trip, trying to find interest in the town, admiring the great beaches, the beautiful river, the very white clean-looking houses. She was back on board soon after lunch, having seen the Swan River, the beautiful, unusual War Memorial and the truly amazing University. It was a lovely town, but she was not in the mood to enjoy anything at that moment.

Alone in her cabin, it seemed empty. All signs of Val's untidiness had gone, and with them the warmth of her companionship. Elinor tried to read but her eyes smarted with unshed tears and so, in the end, she let herself lie there, gazing miserably at the ceiling, trying to face the lonely life that lay ahead of her . . .

There was a knock on the door and, as it opened, Elinor hastily sat up, her hands smoothing her rumpled hair.

It was the stewardess, carrying a large cellophane sheaf of flowers.

'For you,' the short plump woman said with

a smile.

Surprised, Elinor took the flowers in her arms. Who would send her flowers? There were a dozen roses—a most beautiful shade of red. Could they be from Hugh? It was the sort of kind, nice thought he would have—especially as he had felt rather guilty because she was being left on her own.

And then she saw that there was an envelope attached to the sheaf and her heart seemed to stand still as she recognised the large sprawling writing.

Kit!

Her hands trembling, she opened the envelope and drew out a single strip of paper.

Kit wrote without any conventional opening.

'What made you think I was going to marry Alison? I've never heard such nonsense in my life. Your imagination works too hard. What made you dream up such an idiotic idea? Alison and I have grown up together, we're cousins, more like brother and sister. There has never been any talk, or idea, of such a thing . . .'

As she read, Elinor's knees seemed to crumple, so she sank down on the bed, trying to take in the meaning of Kit's words. He wasn't in love with Alison—he was not going to marry her . . . not even for 'practical'

190

reasons.

She read on:

'I hope you like the roses. They are called *Lady Kia*. Now you know why I nicknamed you that! Your cheeks are this colour when you blush—which is quite often! I've won three first prizes at agricultural shows with these roses of mine, so you see, I *was* paying you a compliment and not insulting you as you always thought! You were jumping to conclusions, as usual.'

Elinor was half-laughing, half-crying. How typical of Kit was the letter. She lifted the roses to her cheek and gazed in the mirror at her reflection. Were her cheeks really this lovely shade when she blushed? And why had Kit noticed . . . it meant, then, that he had *seen* her!

There was not much more in the note but she read it hungrily.

'I'm sorry because this is such a short scrawl but I am doing it at the airport and sending it to a friend of mine in Perth, who grows my roses. I wish . . .'

Kit had written something here but he had crossed it out, and crossed it out again, so that, though Elinor tried to read what was written

191

under the thick lines, she could not see. Then he had finished:

'I hope you and Max will be very happy.'

And it was signed simply—Kit.

Elinor's eyes were filled with stupid tears as she read it. So he was still sure that she would—if she was an honourable girl—marry Max. She read—and re-read—the letter again and again. It seemed to bring Kit closer to her.

If only she had known Alison was lying . . . if she had known Kit was free . . .

But what would she have done? Could she have done anything? She so badly lacked Valerie's frank open approach to things.

The gong sounded for the first dinner . . . She would have to bath and change.

The stewardess had brought her a long glass vase and, tenderly, Elinor arranged the beautiful roses in it. The cabin seemed full of their fragrance and somehow it was as if she was dressing to meet Kit . . .

It was something of an anti-climax to go down to the dining-salon and find all strangers at her table. But they were a friendly lot and soon they had all exchanged names. But all the time, Elinor found herself stupidly but hopefully glancing towards the door . . .

There was a dance that evening and Elinor was not short of partners, Valerie's Third Officer being one of them. He said wistfully that life on the ship wasn't the same without the others . . . and Elinor agreed fervently.

She slipped down to her cabin early, thankful that no one had been given Valerie's bed. She had the cabin to herself, so that she could lie on the bed and read Kit's letter again and again.

The weather was getting cold and rough as they had said it might be through the Bight. The cabin seemed to tilt so that she was almost afraid of falling out of bed.

She had a bad night, with recurring nightmares. She did not feel sea-sick, but then, neither did she feel her usual self. She ate little breakfast, hurrying up to the deck, huddled in her warm duffle coat, a red scarf tied over her hair. She lurched as the ship rolled, found herself almost walking up hill one moment and then running down the deck the next. It was the strangest feeling. The sea was rough, spattered with white waves. She could see the coastline clearly. If only the ship would hurry—hurry . . . Every moment on it made her remember Kit so vividly.

How different it all was. Gone was the glamour, the warm sunshine, the holiday spirit. Everyone looked miserable, huddled in warm clothes, crowding the lounge and verandah café for hot drinks.

She stood near the rail, gripping it tightly, the cold wind biting her face. How different the voyage might have been had she known that Kit was free . . . that Alison was lying . . . that there was no marriage planned. Had she known Alison was lying . . .

And then, suddenly, as if a veil had been lifted, she knew something. If Kit had known that she was free . . . if Kit had not thought she was in love with Max . . . promised to him . . . would he have behaved differently?

She drew a long breath, seeing again Kit's stern face as he reminded her of Max and of Max's love for her . . .

If Kit had known that it was Valerie who Max had loved . . .

She turned to hurry below, almost falling down the stairs. She knew what she must do. There had been too many misunderstandings, too much hiding of the truth. Hugh would have to learn in the end that it was Valerie whom Max had loved—but Hugh would understand, and forgive Val's little deception. Probably Val had told him the truth already.

Loyalty to Val had seemed all-important— but wasn't there also loyalty due to Kit? And to herself? Suddenly she knew that she must be as honest as Kit had been. He had told her there was nothing between him and Alison. Now the least she could do in return was to tell him that she was free—the rest depended on Kit. He might not be interested but . . .

It was not easy to find the right words. In the end, she wrote simply:

Max Valerie's stop never mine stop love Elinor.

After she had sent the cable and gone back to her cabin, she was uncertain again. Should she have left out the word *love*? Was that a little too . . .? Should she have cabled at all? Was it just a waste of time? Would Kit merely be amused?

How slowly the days dragged, Elinor thought, as she paced the decks or spent the time with the Keets, who were going on to Sydney. She found some comfort in the sweetness of small Sally and the baby, telling Sam and Petula to leave the infants with her and spend the time enjoying themselves. It helped to see their pleasure in being free for a little while—and it made the long evenings pass when she spent them in the Keets' cabin, watching the sleeping children and letting herself indulge in day dreams . . .

They were her babies and she was just putting them to bed, waiting for the sound of Kit's footsteps in the hall. Then she would leap to her feet, run to welcome him with arms wide open, and then she would find his slippers and make him sit down in the most comfortable chair, and she would pour him out a drink, and put his pouch and pipe by his side and . . .

Then about this stage, she would let out a long sigh and tell herself that she would only get hurt if she went on weaving such foolish, impossible dreams.

195

At last they were near the end of the wearisome lonely days and, as Melbourne approached, she hurried up to be on the deck. She stood in the cold wind, hardly seeing the people around her, gazing at the white buildings that gradually became easier to see. There, ahead of her, lay the background of her new life. Hope dies hard and she wondered if there might be a letter from Kit—or a telegram . . .

The breakfast gong sounded, so she hurried down, though she was not hungry. All the food tasted like sawdust and she was trembling a little. What would Aunt Aggie be like? Would she come on board—or would Elinor have to make her own way to the address Aunt Aggie had sent? Aunt Aggie was a typical Englishwoman, they had said. Elinor was not sure what that meant or what she would look like. Gruff. Blunt. Kind. Surely no woman who could write such a warm loving letter could be anything but nice?

She realised that they must have docked, for the boat was no longer moving. She must go up and see if Aunt Aggie . . .

Hastily she tipped the stewards and walked out of the dining salon into the vestibule beyond and, as she did, a man stood up from where he had been sitting on one of the couches.

It was as if time stood still as she stared at him.

He was just as she had remembered . . . so tall, so broad-shouldered, so very impressive. He was wearing a dark suit and, in his hand, was a wide-brimmed hat. She was surprised to see that his dark eyes were almost anxious as he came to meet her.

'Elinor . . .' he drawled.

'Kit!' she gasped, meeting him half-way, gazing up at him with wide, wondering eyes, as if unable to believe the truth of what she saw.

'Thank you for the cable,' he said awkwardly.

'Thank you for the roses,' she said at the same time.

For a moment they stared at one another silently.

'Maybe . . .' Kit began, and it was the first time she had known him to be unsure of himself. 'Maybe we got off on the wrong foot, as Val would say, but . . . but perhaps we could start all over again?' he asked, almost timidly.

Elinor wanted to laugh and cry at the same time. Dear, darling Kit—that he could be uncertain—that he could fail to know how much she loved him.

'Is it really necessary?' she asked in a whisper, the words rushing out. 'We've wasted so much time already . . .' she added, and felt her cheeks burning.

He laughed suddenly. 'You're right . . .' he drawled in his fascinating way. 'Too much.' And then he was putting his arms round her, drawing her towards him, as he added softly 'Let's not waste any more time, now . . .'

She stood in the warm circle of his arms, lifting her mouth for his first kiss. Her eyes were like stars, her face radiant with happiness. They forgot other people; it was as if they were completely alone in the world. Just the two of them. And that was the wonderful part of it—it would always be like that. Just the two of them . . .

'I love you, Lady Kia . . .' Kit said softly and kissed her again.

'Oh, Kit darling . . .' was all Elinor could say, but her shining eyes finished the sentence for her.

We hope you have enjoyed this Large Print book. Other Chivers Press or Thorndike Press Large Print books are available at your library or directly from the publishers.

For more information about current and forthcoming titles, please call or write, without obligation, to:

Chivers Large Print
published by BBC Audiobooks Ltd
St James House, The Square
Lower Bristol Road
Bath BA2 3SB
UK
email: bbcaudiobooks@bbc.co.uk
www.bbcaudiobooks.co.uk

OR

Thorndike Press
295 Kennedy Memorial Drive
Waterville
Maine 04901
USA
www.gale.com/thorndike
www.gale.com/wheeler

All our Large Print titles are designed for easy reading, and all our books are made to last.

Gwyneth Rees

The Magic Princess Dress

Illustrated by Jessie Eckel

MACMILLAN CHILDREN'S BOOKS

For Eliza and 'Bump',
with love

First published 2010 by Macmillan Children's Books
a division of Macmillan Publishers Limited
20 New Wharf Road, London N1 9RR
Basingstoke and Oxford
Associated companies throughout the world
www.panmacmillan.com

ISBN 978-0-330-46113-9

A CIP catalogue record for this book is available from
the British Library.

Printed and bound in the UK by CPI Mackays, Chatham ME5 8TD

1

It was Ava's mum who had suggested Ava take her fairytale book with her when she went to stay with her dad. Ava's mother had read to her from the book on many occasions and Ava always enjoyed listening to her animated voice bringing to life the entertaining — if unlikely — adventures of the various fairytale characters. Ava found the book extra-comforting now as she curled up on her bed at Dad's house to read her favourite story, about Cinderella. With any luck she would manage to forget for a little while that her mum was so far away.

Of all the storybook's heroines, Ava loved Cinderella the best. She wasn't sure why, but maybe it was because Cinderella seemed more believable at the start of *her* story than some of the other characters did at the starts of theirs. After all, in real life, nobody lived with seven dwarfs like Snow White – or lived in a witch's tower, with hair as long as Rapunzel's. But losing your mother and having her replaced with a cruel stepmother and two horrible stepsisters was something Ava *could* imagine happening in real life. And because of that she always felt more drawn to Cinderella than to any of the other fairytale princesses. Of course the whole story became completely fanciful as soon as Cinderella's fairy godmother appeared and started waving her magic wand about, but by then Ava was always totally captivated. And time and time again she found herself being utterly charmed by Cinderella's magical transformation into the beautiful fairytale princess.

On this occasion, however, Ava found that she couldn't escape into the world of Cinderella as completely as she usually did. She couldn't seem to keep her mind on the story – and it wasn't just because she was missing Mum. The thing that was really bothering her was that Cindy, her cat, whom she had brought with her to Dad's house, had gone missing a few days earlier.

If only *I* had a fairy godmother who could magic Cindy back again, Ava thought, as she put down the book halfway through the story.

Her gaze fell on the little pile of CAT MISSING posters she had made using Dad's computer. There was a description of Cindy printed on each one, together with Ava's mobile-phone number and her dad's address in case anyone found her. Ava had already put up several posters on lamp posts in the streets around Dad's house.

Perhaps now would be a good time to go and see if she could put some up in the windows of the local village shops, she thought. After all, in *real* life there was no such thing as magic to help you out when you had a problem – and that meant that the only thing to do was to try and solve the problem for yourself.

She didn't bother to ask her dad – who was working in his study – if it was OK for her to go to the high street. Instead she wrote him a short note saying that she had gone out to look for Cindy, which she left on the kitchen table. It was Dad who had absent-mindedly left the back door open, letting Cindy escape into the garden. To make matters worse, Cindy's collar had fallen off – they had discovered it in the grass afterwards – so even if somebody had found her by now, they wouldn't know where she belonged. It had happened the day after Ava had arrived, and even though her dad obviously hadn't let Cindy out on purpose, Ava still felt angry with him. Both Ava and her mum had told him Cindy would have to be kept inside for the first few days to give her a chance to get used to her new environment – and he had promised he would be careful.

The trouble with Dad was that he never really listened to what you told him, thought Ava, as she left the house and set off towards the main street in the village. He was always thinking about something else, usually something to do with the books he

wrote – all about historical times.

Just as Ava was stopping to peer over
a wall into an overgrown front garden,
which was just the sort of hiding place
Cindy would like, her mobile phone started
ringing.

'Ava?' It was Dad and he sounded
worried. 'Where are you?'

'On that little side road that leads off
yours – the one that goes towards the high
street,' Ava told him. 'I thought I'd go and
see if any of the shops in the village will
put a poster of Cindy up in their windows.
Oh!' As she looked up she could see a small
corner shop a little further along the road.
'There's a shop on *this* street as well. Maybe I
can put one of my posters up in *its* window.'

There was a sharp intake of breath at the
other end.

'Dad, are you still there?'

'Yes. Listen. I want you to come home right now.'

'No, Dad,' Ava protested, 'I need to stick these leaflets about Cindy in as many shop windows as I can.'

'Ava, you are not to go into the shop on that street. Do you hear me?'

'But why?' Ava was surprised. Generally her father didn't seem to care what she did as long as she kept out of his way when he was busy working.

'Never mind why.' Dad's voice sounded unusually heated now. 'Just do as I say. Come home now and I'll help you with those leaflets later.'

'OK, OK . . .' she grumbled, nearly adding, 'Keep your hair on!' which was what she often said to Mum when she got into a flap unnecessarily about something. But she stopped herself because she wasn't sure how her dad would react if she were to tease him like that. She knew her mum so much better than her dad. After all, until this summer she had spent the whole nine years of her life living with Mum, only seeing her father two or three times a year for the occasional weekend. As she had pointed out to Mum on the way here in the car, Dad felt more like a distant relative than a father.

'Which is why it's great that you're going to stay with him this summer,' her mother had replied.

'I still wish you weren't going away for a whole six weeks,' Ava had said, frowning. 'I'm really going to miss you.'

'And I'll miss you, darling, but this sailing trip is something I've always dreamed of doing. And your dad misses you too, you know. He wants to spend this time with you.'

'No he doesn't,' Ava had said crossly. 'All he has time for are those stupid history books he writes.'

'Ava, that's not true,' Mum had replied gently.

But Ava hadn't been sure if she believed her.

Now, as she slipped the phone back into her pocket, Ava couldn't understand why her father was making such a fuss. She had kept walking as she talked to him and she was already right outside the little corner shop – which looked like it sold second-hand clothes.

On the wooden board above the window

the name of the shop – MARIETTA'S –
was painted in large curly lettering, and
the window display consisted of a solitary
mannequin wearing a fuzzy blonde wig and
an extremely faded, hideously unfashionable
blue sequinned dress. From what Ava could
see through the dirty windowpane, the

clothing inside wasn't much better.

Ava was about to leave when she spotted a little card taped to the glass door just below the 'open' sign.

Printed on the card in large clear lettering were the words: FEMALE TABBY CAT FOUND. ENQUIRE WITHIN.

'Cindy!' Ava gasped, and totally forgetting everything else, she tried the door handle. The door opened at once setting off a little bell inside the shop.

Suddenly feeling sick in case the cat that had been found *wasn't* Cindy, Ava tried to stay calm as she looked around. She was standing in the small front section of the shop, which had a round clothes rack in the centre, full of the sort of second-hand clothes typically found in charity shops. Along one wall another rack was partly filled with dusty-looking old coats and jackets. The shop was half empty of stock, and what there was looked like it had been there for a very long time.

Oh, please let Cindy be here, Ava thought desperately.

In the centre of the back wall was a small archway, which presumably led through to the next room, but Ava wasn't sure if that room was also part of the shop or whether it was private. A multicoloured beaded curtain hung in the arch, preventing Ava from seeing through.

Ava was just wondering whether to call out to let whoever ran the shop know that she was there, when the curtain moved and a smiling young woman appeared.

The woman was slim with pale skin, green eyes and long, wavy, copper-coloured

hair that fell to her waist. She looked ten years or so younger than Ava's parents – in her late twenties maybe – and she wore a long flowing orange dress with big red flowers on it. Her sandals were also orange and she had a stunning necklace made of amber-coloured beads.

'Welcome,' the woman said, smiling at Ava cheerfully. 'I am Marietta. How can I help you?'

'I just read the notice in your window,' Ava mumbled shyly. 'I've

14

lost my cat and I think you might have found her.'

'Really?' The young woman was beaming now. 'What's your name?'

'Ava.'

'Ava! Such a pretty name! How long ago did you lose your cat, Ava?'

'It's been four days. My dad accidently let her out into the garden. I only just came to stay with him and I think she must have got lost. She's a tabby cat with a white bit on her front paw. Does the one you found have a white bit on her front paw?'

'Yes, I think she does.' And Marietta turned and disappeared through the beaded curtain without saying whether Ava should follow her or not.

Feeling curious, Ava followed as far as the archway before hesitating. She could hear

Marietta calling, 'Come here, puss! Oh . . . where *are* you? You were here a minute ago!'

'Maybe she'll come if *I* call her!' Ava suggested through the curtain.

'Of course! Come and help me look! I know she's here somewhere.'

So Ava pushed through the beaded partition and found herself in a very different room indeed.

'Wow!' she burst out, hardly able to believe that she was still in the same shop.

Marietta laughed. 'Do you like it?' she said. As Ava nodded enthusiastically Marietta added, 'I only let *special* customers get to see my *real* shop! First let's find your cat – then I'll show you round!'

2

The room Ava had stepped into seemed
like it belonged in another shop entirely.
Right in the centre there was a small gold
spiral staircase that led both upwards and
downwards. Another door – which was
closed – looked like it led even further back
inside the shop, and in one corner there was
a small changing cubicle with a gold sparkly
curtain pulled across the front.

The walls were beautifully painted
with scenes from fairytales – Rapunzel in
her white tower with her long gold plait
hanging down, a red-lipped Sleeping Beauty

17

lying on a massive four-poster bed, waiting for her prince to come and wake her up, and Prince Charming on a white horse holding a glass slipper on his way to find Cinderella.

Along one wall was a rail filled with exquisite-looking full-length dresses of every fabric, colour and design imaginable. Ava couldn't help staring at them in awe because each one looked fit for a princess to wear. A second wall had shelves from floor to ceiling, each shelf holding a different piece of fairytale costume. The top shelf had velvet hats trimmed with fur and cone-shaped hats with fancy ribbons or flowing scarves attached to the peaks. The shelf below had beautiful bonnets and pretty straw hats trimmed with ribbon. The next shelf down was stacked with different gold, bejewelled crowns and tiaras. Then came

a shelf filled with brightly coloured scarves
and another piled high with pairs of gloves –
black lacy ones, long white ones and
colourful silk ones. The two bottom shelves
contained nothing but footwear. There were
brightly coloured dancing shoes decorated
at the front with bows or silk flowers or

miniature fans, soft slippers with embroidery around the edge, little pointy-toed ankle boots made of shiny red leather, knee-length boots with fur trimming round the top, rainbow-coloured sandals that had little jewels set into the straps, and there was even a pair of solid gold flip-flops (which didn't look very floppy!).

Ava's gaze fell on Marietta, who was crawling on her hands and knees on the floor searching under the skirts of all the dresses, calling, 'Here, kitty!'

'Her name's Cindy,' Ava said, squatting down to help look. 'Are you sure she's in this room?'

'This was the last place I saw her, but I suppose she could have taken herself off into one of the other rooms by now.'

'How many other rooms have you got?'

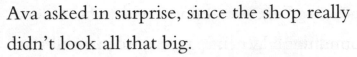

Ava asked in surprise, since the shop really
didn't look all that big.

'Oh – I've lost count,' Marietta replied
vaguely. 'It's a bit like a Tardis, this shop –
much bigger on the inside than it seems
from the outside.' She gave a strange sort of
smile. 'Now . . . where can your little cat
have gone? I haven't had any of the doors or
windows open so she can't have escaped that
way. Of course she might be hiding because
she's trying to catch a mouse. There are an
awful lot of mice in this building.'

Ava looked quickly around the floor,
remembering what her mother had told her
when she'd once asked how you could tell if
a house had mice. 'I don't see any droppings
anywhere,' she pointed out.

'Oh, the mice wouldn't come in here!
This is my fairytale room – they'd be afraid

they might get turned into white horses or something!' When Ava looked puzzled she added, 'You know – like in the story of Cinderella where the fairy godmother turns the pumpkin into a golden carriage and the mice into four white horses.'

Ava didn't know what to say to that, until Marietta smiled to show she had been joking. Ava smiled too then and said, 'It's an amazing shop. Where did you get all these beautiful clothes?'

'Oh, different places.' Marietta got to her feet and started to pull out some of the dresses to show Ava. 'I made these ones,' she said, showing Ava two dresses that were identical apart from one being pink and the other blue. They both had fitted bodices with high waists and long full skirts with underskirts beneath, and wide

sleeves trimmed with gold braid at the cuffs.

'You must be very clever,' Ava said. 'My mum can't sew to save her life, and she says she really envies people who can.'

'I use a special type of thread,' Marietta said. 'That helps a lot.'

'Really?' Ava waited to see if she was going to elaborate, but Marietta seemed to be finished with her explanation.

'Even my Barbie doll hasn't got dresses as beautiful as these,' Ava said as a particularly stunning gold dress with gold beads sewn into the skirt caught her eye. 'And she's a Barbie *princess*, so her clothes are *really* gorgeous!'

Marietta laughed.

Ava was just going to ask her who actually *bought* these dresses when they heard a faint miaow coming from above their heads.

'Cindy!' Ava gasped.

'Come on,' Marietta instructed, leading the way up the gold spiral staircase. 'She must have gone up to my fairytale-wedding section.'

'Fairytale wedding?' Ava queried.

'Yes. You aren't planning to be a bridesmaid any time soon, are you? If so then I've got just the right dress for you.'

Ava shook her head. 'I've never been to a wedding,' she said. 'Except my mum and dad's, but that was when I was a baby so I don't remember it. Mum says it was just a small wedding, which was just as well because they split up a year later.'

Marietta paused on her way up the stairs. 'It is very sad that your parents split up so soon. Do you still see both of them?'

'I live with my mum,' Ava explained, 'and I don't see Dad that often usually, but Mum's just gone away and left me with him for the whole of the school holidays.' She paused and added in a quieter voice, 'This will be the longest time Mum and I have ever been apart.'

'Are you missing her?' Marietta asked sympathetically.

Ava nodded, biting her lip.

'But now you and your father have the opportunity to get to know each other better,' Marietta continued brightly. 'That's a good thing, isn't it?'

'Maybe,' Ava said. Something about Marietta made Ava want to tell her more, and for a few seconds she totally forgot Cindy as she gushed, 'Though I'm not sure he *wants* to get to know me better. Mum's tried to arrange for me to stay with him for longer before, but he's always been too busy. He spends half his time going off on long expeditions to places where he can do research for his books, and the rest of his time *writing* the books. Only I don't reckon any of them can be any good, because none of them are ever for sale in the shops whenever I go with Mum to have a look.'

Marietta looked thoughtful. 'What about you, Ava? Would *you* like to get to know *him* better?'

Ava frowned, thinking about her father, who always seemed so different from her friends' dads, and much more distant.

'Well . . . yes . . .' she admitted. 'The problem is, I'm just not sure *how*.'

'Oh, you'll find a way – don't worry about that,' Marietta said, smiling at Ava

before continuing up the spiral stairs to the
room above. 'Oh, gosh,' she blurted as she
reached the top.

'Wow!' Ava gasped.

There were even more beautiful dresses
in this room than there had been in the one
below, but what really shocked Ava was the
strange golden light bathing the room. It was
as if a multitude of sunbeams were coming
in from all different directions.

'What is it?' Ava whispered.

'It's a . . . well . . . a . . . a *thing* that
happens here sometimes,' Marietta
murmured, 'but I don't know how it can
have —' She suddenly broke off as she noticed
that one of the dresses on a nearby rack had
slipped from its hanger on to the floor. She
bent down to pick up the dress, which was
a child-sized emerald-and-gold-coloured

27

bridesmaid's dress with a pretty beaded bodice and a full skirt decorated with big floppy gold bows. 'Look. One of the bows has been pulled off,' she said, pointing at a piece of loose gold thread on the skirt.

'Cindy is always playing with ribbons and bits of string and things like that,' Ava said excitedly. 'And those bows are quite *dangly*, aren't they?' Forgetting all about the strange golden light, which was fading now anyway, she started to look around the room for her cat.

Over by the window she saw a work-table with a sewing machine on it, and she went across to see if Cindy might be hiding underneath. There was no sign of Cindy, but lying open next to the sewing machine was a rectangular music box. It was very like a music box Ava had at home except that the little plastic figure that twirled round inside hers was a ballerina, whereas this one was a fairytale princess. Hanging up on a stand next to the table was a not-quite-finished, absolutely-to-die-for raspberry-coloured princess's dress with tiny rosebuds sewn on to it, that looked like it was meant for Cinderella herself.

'I'm trying to make a dress exactly like the princess's on that music box,' Marietta explained. 'What do you think?'

'It's beautiful,' Ava murmured, briefly

touching the dress, which was made of the softest, silkiest material she'd ever encountered.

She went back to searching for Cindy, but after several minutes Marietta gently interrupted her.

'Ava, I don't think she's here any more,' she said, still holding the dress that the bow had been torn from.

'But she must be. We just heard her miaow, and I'm sure she pulled the bow off that dress!'

'I know. I can't find that bow and I think it might have got caught in one of her claws, in which case it could be said that she's now *wearing* it.'

Ava frowned. 'So?'

'Well, the dresses in my shop aren't the same as other dresses. Like I said before, they

are made with very special thread – *magic* thread in actual fact.'

Ava gaped at her, wondering if she had heard correctly.

'I know it must sound strange, but you see, the clothes in my shop give a certain magic power to certain people . . . and I'm guessing certain *animals* . . . who put them on,' Marietta continued solemnly.

Ava felt unexpectedly giggly. Marietta had a weird sense of humour – that was for sure. 'Do they make the people and animals invisible?' she joked. 'Like a magic cloak.'

'No, no . . . not invisible,' Marietta replied, completely serious. 'If worn by the right person – a *gifted* sort of person, you understand – it can allow that person to . . . well . . . travel in rather an unusual manner. I've never seen an animal do it before, but

I've heard that most cats – being such free spirits – are in possession of the gift too.'

Ava suddenly saw that Marietta wasn't joking. 'Look, I just want to find my cat,' she blurted, taking a couple of nervous steps backwards. 'If she's not here any more, then where *is* she?'

'That's what I'm trying to tell you! You saw how the room was bathed in golden light just now. Well, that was due to a magic portal opening up.'

'*Magic portal?*' Ava stared in amazement at Marietta because only that morning she had found some books on magic in her dad's bookcase. She had opened up one of them and found a whole chapter on magic portals. According to the book, a magic portal was a kind of invisible magic gateway that linked two parallel worlds – or two different time

periods within the *same* world. She had found it strange that her dad owned such books, but she hadn't yet had a chance to ask him about them.

'That's right,' Marietta was continuing calmly. 'I know it sounds hard to believe, but many of the mirrors in my shop are magic portals. To be able to travel through one of them, a person who is *able* to travel – and very few of us are, Ava – has simply to look at his or her reflection in the correct mirror – the mirror that is the right one for the dress they have on – and the magic reaction will begin. To stop the magic, you simply have to turn away from the mirror . . . it's quite within your control so there's nothing to worry about . . . but of course if you don't *want* to stop it, you must keep looking until the light gets so bright that it

33

forces you to close your eyes. Then you will be transported through the portal.'

'But . . . but . . . that's just . . . it's . . . ridiculous!' Ava burst out.

Marietta shook her head, saying gently, 'I promise you, it's true, Ava. It must have been pure chance that made Cindy look at her reflection in the right mirror while she had the bow from this magic dress caught in her claw. And if you change into this dress, you'll be able to follow her.'

'*Follow* her?' Ava practically choked on the words as she found herself noticing for the first time just how many mirrors there were in this room. As well as several full-length ones, there were about a dozen different wall mirrors – round ones, square ones, oblong ones, oval ones and even a hexagonal one. They were all different sizes and styles, some having antique frames while others looked more modern. And they were all gleaming at her invitingly.

'Yes,' Marietta said encouragingly, 'though there is just one thing that might be a problem. You see, the very *first* time a person travels, they have to choose the correct mirror for themselves or the reaction will not happen. It's a way of ensuring a person is truly ready, I suppose. *I* was ready when I was six years old – but for less . . . shall we say . . . less *sensitive* individuals . . . it can take much longer.' She smiled. 'I have a strong feeling that *you* are ready, Ava, but there's

only one way to know for sure. You must put on this dress and then – with no help from me – you must try and choose the right mirror. If you are successful you can then travel through the magic portal to the place where your cat has gone.'

Ava felt as if her head was starting to spin. 'Stop it! You're scaring me!' she blurted. And without waiting for a response, she turned and fled down the spiral staircase, through the fairytale room and back through the beaded curtain into the front part of the shop.

For one awful, terrifying moment the front door didn't budge when she tried the handle, but then she tugged harder and it did. Half stepping, half falling out into the street, she slammed the door shut behind her. And she didn't look round as she ran as fast as she could back to her dad's.

3

By the time Ava reached Dad's street, she was beginning to think she had been silly to get so freaked out by what Marietta had told her. Marietta was a bit of a weirdo, that was all. Of course Ava couldn't deny that she had seen that strange golden light bathing the upstairs room – but there could easily be another explanation for it besides a cat travelling through a magic portal.

Dad had been very keen for her not to go into that shop and she wondered now if he knew about Marietta and her strange ways, and if he had been worried that Ava might get scared by her. If so, he hadn't been worrying for no reason, Ava thought, frowning. She *had* felt scared, and yet to start with Marietta had seemed totally charming. And the dresses in her shop were without a doubt the most beautiful gowns Ava had ever seen – including all the ones she had ever seen on television or in books.

As Ava let herself into the kitchen through the back door her father appeared immediately to greet her. 'At last!' he exclaimed. 'I've been trying to phone you and I was just about to go looking for you. What took you so long?' His thick dark eyebrows were bunched together in a worried frown and his shock of dark hair looked even bushier than usual – as if he had forgotten to even run his hands through it, let alone use a comb, when

he'd got out of bed that morning.

'Don't know,' Ava grunted, flushing because she knew that was a lie and she wasn't used to lying. She almost always told her mum the truth about things, but she found herself shrinking from telling Dad the truth about this. She just wasn't sure how he would react. Would he understand why she had gone into the shop if she told him about the card she had seen in the window?

'My phone's right here,' she added, slipping her hand into her jacket pocket for it. Her phone hadn't been ringing at all and she reckoned Dad had probably been using the wrong number. Dad was always scrawling down people's phone numbers in a careless manner and not being able to read his own writing afterwards. Since the phone wasn't in her right pocket she tried the left –

only to find that it wasn't there either. She frowned. Where was it?

'Ava, did you disobey me and go round the shops with those posters just now?' Dad asked sternly – and that's when she realized that she didn't have the posters either.

'Oh, no!' she gasped, remembering putting them down – along with her phone – on the counter in Marietta's shop before starting to look for Cindy.

'Oh no – *what*?' Dad demanded.

'I must have left them behind,' she mumbled.

'Left them behind *where*?'

She didn't see how she could avoid telling Dad the truth now – and she just hoped he wouldn't get too angry. 'I think I've left my phone and the posters in that little shop I told you about. I only went inside because they had a card in the window saying they'd found a tabby cat.'

'Ava!' Dad thundered. 'I expressly told you not to go into that shop!'

'I know, but you didn't say why, and . . . and anyway I *had* to when I found out Cindy might be inside. I really have to find her, Dad. Imagine how she must be feeling right now — all scared and lonely.'

'Ava, you know how sorry I am about letting Cindy out . . . but I really can't have you running about on your own in the village, going wherever you please,' Dad said crossly.

'That's not what you said the other day,' she reminded him defensively. 'The other day you said you thought it was terrible the way children don't have any freedom any more. And you said you didn't mind me going to the shops on my own as long as I'm careful.'

'Not to *that* shop!'

'Why not?'

He narrowed his eyes. 'Did you meet Marietta?'

'Yes – she showed me round.'

'She showed you round the *whole* shop?'

'Most of it, I think.' Ava was studying her dad's face closely. 'Dad, do *you* know Marietta? Have *you* been inside her shop?'

Her father immediately flushed – which wasn't like him at all – and instead of answering he asked, 'So what did you make of her?'

'She was really weird,' Ava began slowly. 'She told me she makes the dresses with magic thread and that the mirrors are magic portals.'

'She told you *that*?' Dad sounded outraged.

'Yes, but aren't *you* a bit into magic too, Dad?' Ava asked him quickly. 'I mean, why have you got all those books about it, if you're not?'

'What books?' he snapped.

'The ones on the bottom shelf in your bookcase. I saw them there this morning.'

Her father's face turned an even brighter red as he mumbled vaguely, 'Oh . . . yes . . . well . . . I happen to collect books on many different subjects, Ava. That doesn't mean I am *into* all of them, as you call it.'

'Well, do you *believe* in magic?' Ava asked curiously. 'In magic portals, for instance?'

'Ava, enough of this! As I'm sure you have discovered for yourself, Marietta is a very strange woman, and I don't want you spending any more time with her. Is that clear?'

'But—'

'IS THAT CLEAR?!'

Her father had never shouted at her like that before and Ava was shocked. She felt tears start up in her eyes.

'I wish Mum had taken me with her when she went sailing!' she burst out as she brushed past Dad, out of the kitchen and up the stairs to her room, where she slammed the door shut behind her.

Dad didn't come upstairs to try and comfort her – even though he must have guessed she was crying. It didn't really surprise her, since Dad never knew what to say when anyone cried.

Ava managed to comfort herself a little by sitting on her bed with her laptop balanced on her knees, writing an email to her mum.

She had already written to tell her about
Cindy escaping. Now she told her about
coming across Marietta's shop and about the
weird experience she had had there. She also
told Mum how much she was missing her
and how upset she was with Dad.

She had almost finished her email when she started to feel really thirsty – from crying such a lot, probably – so she decided to go down to the kitchen to get a drink.

She paused on her way down the stairs, hearing voices in the living room.

Her dad sounded cross as he said, 'You should never have shown her the back of the shop.'

A woman's voice replied impatiently, 'I *really* don't see what harm can come of it, Otto.' It was Marietta! And she knew Dad's name!

'You haven't got any children, Marietta, so you can't understand,' Dad snapped.

Ava hurried down the rest of the stairs and entered the living room. 'Understand *what*?' she demanded.

Her father jumped. 'Ava! I thought

you were in your room.'

'I was. I was writing an email to Mum.'
She turned to Marietta and asked bluntly,
'What are *you* doing here?'

If she had been that rude to a guest in
front of her mum she would have got into
trouble. But her dad didn't say anything –
probably because he wasn't that hot on
manners himself – and Marietta just smiled
as if Ava had given a perfectly friendly
greeting.

'Hello, Ava. I'm sorry if I scared you
before,' she said.

Ava didn't respond to that. Instead she
asked, 'How do you know my dad?'

'Oh . . . well . . . you see . . . your father
and I are—'

'Friends!' Ava's father put in before
Marietta could finish. 'We are all friends

47

with each other in this village, Ava. It's small enough to get to know everybody – not like when you live in the city.'

Marietta was giving Ava's father a strange look, and Ava frowned because Dad hadn't *sounded* as though Marietta was his friend when he had called her 'a very strange woman' earlier. But Ava was quickly distracted by another thought. 'Have you found my cat yet?' she asked, suddenly feeling hopeful that that might be the reason Marietta was here.

Marietta shook her head and pointed to the coffee table where Ava's mobile phone and the bundle of Cat Missing posters were sitting. 'I came to have a word with your dad and to return those. You know, you really shouldn't put your address on the leaflets, Ava. You could get any dodgy person turning up on your doorstep claiming to know where your cat is.'

Ava nearly asked what could be more dodgy than Marietta claiming that Cindy had disappeared through a magic portal into a parallel world. But she just managed to stop herself.

Marietta seemed about to say something else when Dad grunted, 'I've put a sandwich out for you on the table, Ava. You'd better go and eat it.'

'But—'

'*Now*, please, Ava.' Ava's dad could sound very stern sometimes and at those times she rarely had the nerve to argue with him.

As Ava took herself through to the kitchen she could hear her father showing Marietta out through the front door.

He came into the kitchen as she was

picking a piece of tomato out of her sandwich. (Dad never remembered that Ava didn't like tomatoes.) 'Have you actually sent that email to your mother?' he asked.

'Not yet,' she replied, looking up at him coolly.

'Did you tell her about Marietta's shop?'

Ava nodded, noticing that he seemed quite agitated.

'Do you think that's wise, Ava? Your mother will only worry – and we don't want to ruin her time away, do we?'

Ava hadn't thought of that. It was true that Mum probably *would* worry when she got Ava's email. But Dad seemed unusually

het-up, and Ava couldn't help thinking
that there was more to his anxiety than just
a desire for Mum to have a trouble-free
holiday.

'I'll delete the bit about the shop before I
send it,' she offered.

'Good,' Dad said, sounding hugely
relieved.

And Ava was certain then that her dad
had his *own* reasons for wanting to keep
Marietta's shop a secret. But what were
they?

4

Two days later Cindy still hadn't come back and Ava found herself thinking more and more about Marietta's shop. Strangely, her father's books on magic had been removed from his bookcase, and when she asked him where they were he told her they were antique books and he didn't want her sticky fingers all over them.

'My fingers *aren't* sticky,' she had snapped at him indignantly, but her father had just ignored her.

He had spent most of the last two days in his study, working on his latest history book.

When Ava had asked him what it was about
he had told her he was researching the life of
children in Victorian times.

Ava had learned a little about this at
school. 'In Victorian times I'd probably have
had a nanny, wouldn't I?' she had said.

'Maybe – if we were rich enough,' Dad
had replied. 'If we weren't, you'd have
been working in a factory or sweeping
chimneys.'

'I thought chimney sweeps were all boys,'
Ava had said, surprised.

'Sometimes they used girls as well,'
Dad had told her, shuddering as if he was
remembering something horrible that he
had seen with his own eyes. 'They were
cruel times. Just be glad *you* didn't live in
them.' And he had cut short any further
conversation by announcing that he had a

lot of work to do and that he needed to get on with it.

Since it was now a lovely sunny afternoon – and Dad was busy in his study yet *again* – Ava decided to go out for a walk by herself and have another look for her missing cat. Dad had already warned her not to assume that the cat in Marietta's shop had *definitely* been Cindy. After all, since Ava had only heard a miaow rather than actually *seen* the cat for herself, how could she be certain? It was important to keep searching for Cindy closer to home, Dad said.

Ava could see the logic in his argument and when she got outside she tried to imagine that *she* was a cat who had just found itself in unfamiliar territory. Where would she go once she had left the garden? A cat would just follow its instinct, she thought.

She allowed herself to do the same, even though letting herself be guided by a *feeling* about where she should go wasn't something that she was very used to doing.

Maybe it was instinct or maybe it wasn't, but she was soon walking in exactly the same direction she had taken two days previously – and it therefore wasn't long before she found herself standing outside Marietta's shop. The card about the cat was gone today and the 'closed' sign was on the door. Nevertheless, she was sure if she rang the bell, Marietta would answer.

She had been waiting several minutes when an upstairs window opened and Marietta's head appeared. 'Oh . . . it's you, Ava! Just a moment. I'll come down.'

Marietta soon arrived on the other side of the door and drew back the bolt. The front room of the shop seemed just as drab and uninviting as it had done previously and it would be impossible to guess what the shop was really like on the other side of the beaded curtain, Ava thought.

'How are you, Ava?' Marietta asked as she invited her inside.

'OK, thanks – but I still haven't found Cindy.'

'If she's gone through one of my magic mirrors, there's no point in looking for her *here* any more,' Marietta said matter-of-factly.

'But we don't know for sure if that cat *was* Cindy,' Ava pointed out. 'It might not have been.' (She decided it was best not to question the authenticity of the magic mirrors again since Marietta clearly believed in them so passionately.)

'I suppose that's true,' Marietta admitted. 'Though I have a very strong *feeling* that it was Cindy. Don't you?'

Ava frowned. 'I don't know,' she said, wanting to add that in any case a strong feeling didn't amount to a fact. But she decided to keep quiet about that too.

'Well, in any case, I'm very glad you've come back because I don't think I made things totally clear to you the other day,' Marietta continued cheerfully. 'Of course, it's quite natural to feel sceptical – frightened even – when you first get told about the magic portals. Especially when nobody has introduced you to the idea of magic until now. But if you can just experience one of my portals for yourself, you'll understand everything. I should have explained to you that there's no need to be scared of going

to find your cat. You see, since the dress
with the missing bow – which your cat
took with it through the mirror – is from
my *fairytale* collection, then we know she
must have been transported to *fairytale* land.
There are many different fairytale lands,
you understand, but we have access to a
particularly nice one in this shop. And it's
a lovely *safe* place for you to visit if you
want to follow Cindy. All you have to do
is choose the right mirror in order to get
there – but that's easy too. There's only one
mirror in this shop that is the true gateway
to fairytale land. I'm sure you'll have no
trouble finding it.'

Ava knew she should have felt as
disbelieving and dismissive as she had done
on her previous visit to the shop, but for
some reason she felt different today. She

had a strange, excited feeling inside, as if lots
of fizzy bubbles had been let off inside her
tummy. Her sensible mind told her that no
one could travel through a magic mirror
into another land, but her imagination
decided to go along with what Marietta was
saying – at least for a little while. After all,
what was the worst thing that could happen?

'You won't tell my dad I was here, will
you?' Ava checked quickly.

'Don't worry, I won't *need* to tell him
anything,' Marietta said, smiling.

Ava thought it was a strange way of
answering but she guessed it was the best she
was going to get.

'Listen, Ava, we can talk about your dad
later,' Marietta added briskly. 'Right now
we must get on with preparing you for your
visit through the mirror. First you must

come and change into that dress. Follow me.'

Ava felt a tingly feeling run through her as she followed Marietta through the beaded curtain into the back room, where Marietta directed her to the changing cubicle. When she pushed back the gold sparkly curtain from the front of the cubicle, she found that the walls inside were a shimmery mother-of-pearl colour. There was a long mirror on one wall, and she briefly wondered if *that* could be a magic one – but it was so plain and ordinary-looking that she quickly dismissed that idea. The gold and emerald coloured bridesmaid's dress was hanging inside, waiting for her to change into. To her amazement it was exactly the right size, and she loved the way the bodice fitted snugly while the ankle-length skirt billowed out at the bottom. As well as fitting her perfectly, the colours seemed just right for her, somehow making her blonde hair look even blonder and her green eyes even greener.

'I look just like a fairytale princess!' Ava exclaimed, when she came out of the cubicle to show Marietta.

Marietta beamed. 'And that is what you shall be when you cross to the other side of the mirror,' she told her.

'I hope you're right,' Ava said, starting to giggle, because whatever else happened, dressing up like this was the most fun she'd had in ages.

'All you need now is some sort of decoration for your hair and some matching shoes,' Marietta said. 'Go to my accessories shelves and choose what you want.'

So Ava went over to the shelves she had spotted on her previous visit and chose a pair of emerald shoes with little gold bows on the front that seemed to have been made to match her dress. 'I can't believe they fit so well,' she said when she tried them on.

'It's just like when Cinderella tried on the glass slipper, isn't it?' Marietta said, with a twinkle in her eye.

Ava grinned, imagining herself as Cinderella offering her foot to the handsome prince. 'Do you think it would be too much to wear a tiara in my hair as well?' she asked

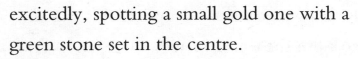

excitedly, spotting a small gold one with a
green stone set in the centre.

'I don't see why not. You're a princess
now, after all,' Marietta replied.

So Ava put on the tiara.

'Now,' said Marietta, 'it's time for you
to choose which mirror is the doorway to
fairytale land.'

'Do *you* know which one it is?' Ava
asked, feeling as if she was taking part in
some sort of thrilling party game.

'Of course, but I can't tell you,' Marietta
said. 'Like I explained before, the wearer of
the dress must find the mirror for themselves
if the magic is to work the very first time
they try it.'

'I think the mirror that belongs with
this dress must be upstairs . . .' Ava began
slowly. 'Because it was *that* room that had

the golden light the other day . . .'

Marietta smiled, pointing encouragingly to the gold spiral staircase. 'You know the way.'

So Ava mounted the twisting staircase for the second time, taking care not to trip on her long gown. At the top she paused and looked around. The room hadn't changed since her last visit. The work-table with the sewing machine was still against the wall under the window, and the rest of the room was crammed full with rail upon rail of beautiful wedding and bridesmaids' dresses.

Ava made up her mind to inspect each mirror before she made her decision. The first was a large oval one with a heavy wooden frame. It looked old but nothing about it reminded Ava of a fairytale. The next two were rectangular with pastel-coloured plastic frames – Ava was sure it

couldn't be either of them. The fairytale
mirror must be one of a kind, she thought.
On the end wall was a huge square mirror
with a very thick gold-painted frame that
had gold ivy leaves set into all four corners.
It was grand enough to belong in a princess's
palace, Ava thought, but somehow she
didn't think that was the one either. Then
she came across a small mirror with a
wooden frame that had animals carved into
it. There were birds, a family of deer, a
hedgehog and some very cute rabbits. Ava
really liked that one, but she still didn't think
it was the one she was looking for.

She began to check out the full-length
mirrors. The first was a plain oblong one
with a wooden frame that swivelled on its
wooden base. The next was similar except
that the glass around the edge had little

coloured flowers on it. Then, half hidden behind a row of bridesmaids' dresses, Ava found a mirror made from stained glass that seemed to contain all the colours of the rainbow. It was the most beautiful of all.

Ava gathered up her courage and stared into the mirror, trying to remember what Marietta had told her about the magic reaction. She stepped forward so that her face was almost touching the mirror, feeling excited as she waited to see what would happen next. Would she really be able to pass through the mirror to the other side? She took a deep breath and another step forward, but all that happened was that she bumped her nose against the glass.

She instantly felt silly – and angry with herself for being taken in by Marietta – and she was about to give up and tell Marietta

that the whole idea was
stupid, when her eyes
fell on the music box
that had been here on
her last visit. It was still
sitting on the work-
table next to the sewing
machine, but its lid was
now closed rather than

open. The picture on the lid was a very
pretty one of Cinderella wearing a raspberry-
coloured dress and a sparkling tiara. Slowly
Ava reached out and opened the box. It
immediately started playing a cheerful
melody, while the little princess figure inside
twirled round, just like the ballerina in Ava's
music box did at home. And just like the
dancing figure in Ava's music box, this one
was reflected in a small rectangular mirror on

the inside of the music-box lid.

As Ava stared at the little dancing princess she found herself remembering how Cindy – who was a very playful cat – sometimes sat in front of her own music box and gave the little ballerina a tap with her paw as it twirled round on its bouncy spring.

Carefully Ava bent down to look at the little mirror more closely. It was so small that she could only see her face and hair and the tiara on top of her head. But as she continued to gaze into the glass, something strange started to happen. The twirling Cinderella's reflection began to glow brighter and brighter. Then Ava saw that her own face had a yellow glow to it and that her tiara was getting more and more dazzling. Finally she found that she couldn't look into the mirror at all any more because

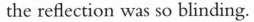

the reflection was so blinding.

After several seconds of keeping her eyes shut against the glare, the brightness seemed to lessen and Ava cautiously opened them again. The little rectangular mirror was still showing her reflection, but incredibly the music box within which it was set had completely changed. The box Ava was staring at now looked as if it had been hand-carved from a very fine goldish wood, and the whole thing was decorated with beautiful hand-painted multicoloured songbirds. Strangest of all, the little dancing princess figure now looked as if she was made of solid gold.

Ava gasped in shock and jumped back from the music box, turning breathlessly to ask Marietta what had just happened. But as she looked round she got an even greater surprise – for she was no longer in the dress shop!

5

Ava rubbed her eyes, hardly able to believe it. Instead of being in Marietta's shop, she was inside the most magnificent room she had ever seen — a room that looked like it belonged in a fairytale palace!

The room was huge, with massive windows framed by very grand gold and green curtains. The walls were also gold and on them hung several old-fashioned paintings and ornate mirrors. Ava looked above her head and saw that the high ceiling had beautiful cornicing around the outside and a dome in the middle with winged cherubs painted on it. A magnificent crystal chandelier was hanging down from the centre of the dome.

The furniture in the room was also very impressive. An enormous grand piano sat in the centre of the floor along with two huge gold harps. Several velvet-covered chairs, and couches with beautifully carved legs, were positioned against the walls, all of them scattered with richly coloured silk cushions. On various little tables around the room stood expensive-looking china ornaments and crystal vases containing beautiful scented flowers.

Ava looked down at her gold and green dress, which was the only thing that seemed to have remained unchanged. Her appearance was now perfectly in keeping with her new surroundings, she realized.

Ava barely had time to take in all of this, before a shrill voice behind her asked, 'Who are *you*?'

A second, equally snooty voice added, 'And who gave *you* permission to enter the palace music room?'

Ava whirled round to see, standing in the doorway, two girls in their late teens dressed in very expensive-looking

gowns. One was blonde, the other dark-haired, and they both had similar sharp features and scowling faces.

'W-where *am* I exactly?' Ava asked, hearing her own voice but feeling as if someone else was speaking the words.

'We just told you. You're in the royal music room. Only family members and special guests are allowed in here.'

'Yes,' said the other girl haughtily. 'So you'd better go back to the guest quarters with all the other princesses.'

Ava blinked. 'Princesses?' Maybe I'm dreaming all this, she thought.

The blonde girl was frowning. 'Well, *aren't* you a princess?'

'She must be,' said the other dismissively, as if princesses were two-a-penny. '*All* the bridesmaids are princesses. And she's definitely a bridesmaid or why would she be wearing that dress?'

'Aren't you supposed to be at the rehearsal, or whatever it's called, with all the other bridesmaids?' the blonde girl asked Ava impatiently.

'I . . . I don't know . . .' Ava murmured, flushing. 'I came in here to look for my cat,' she added in a rush. 'You haven't seen her, have you? She's a tabby cat called Cindy.'

'*Cindy?*' The dark-haired girl started to laugh in a mocking sort of way.

'What is it? What's so funny?' Ava asked uncertainly.

'Did you *deliberately* call your cat after our sister?' the girl eventually spluttered. 'You really shouldn't have, you know – our sister is nothing like a cat!'

'No, she's nowhere near as clever,' the

blonde one added spitefully. 'For one thing, she's totally hopeless at catching mice! We used to lock her in the cellar at home and tell her she must catch at least one and wring its neck before we'd let her out again – but she never could!'

'She doesn't like to harm any animal – even a mouse – so we used to make her spend all day in that cellar,' the dark one added. 'Served her right for being such a goody-goody!'

'Such a pity she wasn't shut in the cellar when the prince came by with that silly glass shoe,' the blonde one said crossly.

'I know – and I never did understand why that shoe didn't disappear at midnight along with the rest of that interfering fairy godmother's trickery.'

'Wait a minute . . .' Ava could hardly

believe her ears. 'Is your sister *Cinderella*?'

'Of course,' snorted the blonde one. 'Who else did you think we were talking about?'

'Actually, she's our stepsister,' added the dark one. 'We are not truly related to her, thank goodness. Our dear mother married Cinderella's extremely pathetic father, who soon realized our mother was nowhere near as soppily gentle as his first wife. Soon afterwards he died, and after that it didn't take us long to turn that silly daughter of his into our servant. I am Ermentrude and this is my sister Astrid.'

'The *ugly* sisters!' Ava blurted out excitedly.

As soon as she'd said it she regretted her mistake. Both sisters' eyes flashed menacingly.

'Who do you think you're calling ugly,

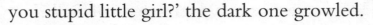

you stupid little girl?' the dark one growled.

The other sister took a few steps closer
and hissed in a threatening voice, 'Perhaps
you'd like to tell us exactly which princess
you are before we throw you into the palace
dungeons?'

Ava felt her mouth go dry. Panicking,
she did the only thing she could think of.
She turned her back on them and stared as
hard as she could into the little mirror in
the music-box lid, wishing desperately to be
transported back to Marietta's shop.

In a matter of seconds the gold dancing
figure began to glow brightly, and soon
Ava's face in the mirror was glowing too. As
the two ugly sisters came further towards her,
Ava closed her eyes – and she didn't open
them again until the bright light had gone.

Ava could feel her heart racing as she

allowed her wobbly legs to lower her trembling body on to the floor, where she sat gradually getting her breath back. She was in Marietta's shop again, in the room at the top of the spiral staircase and she could hardly believe what had just happened to her.

Marietta wasn't crazy after all! The magic was real!

There could be no logical explanation for what had just happened. She didn't even try to think of one. Her mind felt temporarily frozen, as if there was no point in trying to think at all any more. She felt as if all her previous thoughts counted for nothing after what she had just discovered.

As she sat there slowly recovering from the shock, she became aware of Marietta's soft voice in conversation with

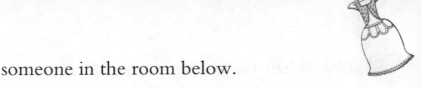

someone in the room below.

'You shouldn't try to stop her, Otto. It's not natural. She has the same gift as you and me and she should be allowed to use it.' Marietta was talking to her dad! He must have discovered she was gone and come looking for her.

Ava heard her father's voice then, low and angry. 'Just because she's *able* to do a thing, doesn't mean she *has* to do it,' he said. 'Now where is she?'

Ava couldn't believe what she was hearing. Her dad clearly knew all about the magic mirrors – and about Ava's ability to use them. And what's more, it sounded as though he might be able to use them himself!

'What makes you think she's still here?' Marietta was asking him.

'She'd better be,' Dad said sharply.

79

'Well, she isn't.' Marietta sounded defiant. 'She's gone travelling!'

'I don't believe she's gone through a mirror already,' Dad snapped. 'She wouldn't be that reckless.'

She could hear her father stomping about angrily downstairs after that, searching for her. Any minute now he would come up the spiral stairs and find her, and then she would be in big trouble for disobeying him. Not only that, but she was sure he would forbid her from using the magic mirrors again – and then how was she ever going to find Cindy.

She looked at the music box, still open on the table.

As she heard her father opening and closing more doors downstairs, Ava knew what she had to do if she wanted to avoid being

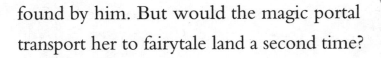

found by him. But would the magic portal
transport her to fairytale land a second time?

As soon as she looked into the mirror, the
light began to glow. Holding her breath, she
closed her eyes, keeping them closed until
the bright light had passed – and when she
looked again she found, to her relief, that
not only was she back in the palace music
room, but that the room was empty.

It wasn't empty for long however. Just as
Ava was starting to look around for Cindy,
an older lady in a plain blue gown came
sweeping in through the door. She was
followed by five pretty girls who all wore
bridesmaids' dresses identical to Ava's. Each
girl had her hair piled up on her head and
wore either a small crown or a tiara and Ava
was certain they must all be princesses.

The ugly sisters were nowhere to be seen, thank goodness.

The older woman (who Ava guessed was some sort of governess) stopped when she saw Ava. 'Our sixth bridesmaid. Excellent!' She walked past Ava to the piano. 'As you can see, girls, here we have some music to practise with.'

'What are we practising?' Ava asked the

 82

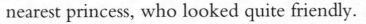

nearest princess, who looked quite friendly.

'Our dance for Cinderella's wedding of course,' the girl replied. 'This is our dress rehearsal.'

'Really?' Ava's head felt spinny with sudden excitement. She could hardly believe that she had arrived in a place where not only was she one of Cinderella's bridesmaids – but she would actually be dancing at her wedding!

The friendly princess giggled as she added, 'You'll never guess who we just met in the corridor. Astrid and Ermentrude! They looked really pale. They said there's a ghost in here – a vanishing ghost who looks like a *bridesmaid*!'

Ava gulped as all the bridesmaids started giggling.

The older woman clapped her hands for

silence. 'I pity *any* ghost who is unfortunate enough to meet those two on its travels,' she said briskly. 'They may be Cinderella's sisters, but they are two of the rudest, most unpleasant, most *hysterical* creatures I have ever met. Now come on, girls . . . Let's move some of this furniture out of the way so that we have room to practise.'

As the princesses started to move chairs and tables to the edge of the room to clear a space to dance, Ava asked them, 'Have any of you seen a little tabby cat with a white patch on her front paw? She's my pet and she's gone missing.'

'A cat as a pet!' one of the princesses exclaimed. 'What a strange thing!' She looked down at the skirt of Ava's dress and added a little snootily, 'Do you know there's a bow missing from your gown?'

'Yes,' Ava replied apologetically. 'I think my cat has it.'

All the princesses started to giggle again then, until the older woman clapped her hands together a second time. Looking sternly at Ava, she said, 'Your Highness, no princess with a less than perfect gown may attend Cinderella's wedding. You must visit the palace seamstress without delay. There is a servant just outside the door and I'm sure he will show you the way.'

Realizing she had been dismissed, Ava headed curiously for the door. She stepped out into a corridor with a plush red carpet and royal portraits hanging on the walls, and immediately saw the servant. He was standing very still, staring straight ahead and wearing smart knee-length breeches, a tight jacket with long tails and a white powdered wig.

'Excuse me,' Ava asked him politely. 'Have you seen a tabby cat anywhere? She might have a gold bow caught in one of her paws.'

The servant looked down at her as if he suspected she was making fun of him. 'There are dozens of cats in the palace grounds, Your Highness, though I have not, as yet, seen one with a bow.' He gave her a cool stare as he added, 'Will that be all?'

'Yes . . . I mean, no . . . Could you please show me the way to the palace seamstress?' she blurted.

'Follow me, Your Highness,' the servant replied in a haughty voice. And he led the way along the corridor, down a flight of spiral stairs, along another corridor, up

two further flights of stairs and along yet
another corridor until he came to a halt
outside a plain wooden door.

'The palace seamstress is within,' he
declared, knocking on the door. Without
waiting for a reply he swung open the door
and stood with his back against it so that Ava
could enter. 'Your name, Your Highness?'
he asked her.

'It's Ava — but you don't have to—' she
began, only to be interrupted by the man's
booming proclamation.

'Her Royal Highness, the Princess Ava!'
he bellowed.

A young servant girl, with big dark eyes
and a single plait that fell halfway down
her back, immediately jumped up from
her stool and curtsied. She looked a few
years older than Ava — twelve or thirteen

maybe. Behind her a small elderly lady, with wrinkled skin and grey hair done in a bun, who was sitting in a chair by the window, put down her needle and thread and struggled to her feet to do the same.

Ava felt embarrassed and very guilty about an old lady curtsying to her like that. 'Please sit down,' she said as the manservant left them.

'*You* must sit first, Your Highness,' the old woman said. 'Here. Take my chair. It is the most comfortable.'

'No, thank you,' Ava insisted. She quickly dropped to the ground, where she sat cross-legged as if she was in her school assembly hall. From there she looked around the

small room, which was filled with clothes in various stages of being made or repaired – all of them much grander than the clothes worn by the seamstress and the girl, who were now exchanging looks as if they thought this was very strange behaviour for a princess.

'I am Dinah, the palace seamstress, and this is Tilly, my apprentice,' the old lady told her, sounding a little guarded. 'Have you a dress or some other garment that needs repairing, Your Highness?'

'Well . . . do you have . . . I mean, do you think you could . . . find another bow for this bridesmaid's dress?' Ava asked, bunching up the material at the front of her skirt to show where the missing bow should be.

Tilly gave a little grin and pulled something out of her sewing box. 'What about this one?' she asked, holding up a gold silk bow identical to the others on Ava's dress.

'That's it! That's the missing bow!' Ava exclaimed. 'Where did you find it?'

'Dinah found it yesterday in the palace kitchens,' Tilly told her. 'She was there speaking to the palace cook, when she noticed one of the kitchen cats had something caught in its claw.'

Ava turned to Dinah excitedly. 'Was it a *tabby* cat?'

The old lady frowned as if she was trying her best to remember. 'I believe it might have been a tabby, Your Highness . . . yes . . .'

'Where is this cat now?' Ava asked, jumping to her feet. 'Is it still in the kitchen?'

'I expect so — Cook likes to keep them there because cats are so good at keeping the mice away.'

'We have to go and look for her!' Ava

exclaimed, taking an impatient step towards the door. 'She's not a kitchen cat, you see. She's my pet cat, Cindy, and I have to find her!'

'A *pet* cat!' Dinah looked surprised. 'Well I never!'

'I can take you to the kitchens if you like,' Tilly offered. She looked at Dinah. 'If you can spare me for a little while.'

Dinah nodded. 'Hurry back though. We've a lot of work to do before the ball tonight.'

'Don't worry. I'll just show Princess Ava the way and I'll come straight back,' Tilly promised.

Ava almost blurted out that she wasn't *really* a princess – because somehow she felt bad about lying to these two servants – but she stopped herself. After all, she was very close to finding Cindy now, and she didn't want to say or do anything that might ruin things.

91

6

Tilly led Ava along the corridor and through
a doorway that led to a narrow flight of
spiral stairs. 'This is the servants' staircase,'
Tilly explained. 'It's the quickest way to the
kitchens. You don't mind, do you, Your
Highness?'

'Of course not,' Ava said.

The staircase went down a long way.
After a while Ava became aware of cooking
smells, and finally they reached the bottom,
where Tilly stopped to push open a heavy
oak door.

Now they were in a vast kitchen full of

 92

servants. It was very like the one Ava had seen when she'd visited a National Trust stately home with her mother. Except that there the servants had been waxwork figures, whereas here they were real. At one end of the room there was a massive stone fireplace with a huge fire that was giving off a terrific amount of heat. An enormous pig

was being roasted over the fire while a maid (who was dripping with sweat) poked at the logs underneath. Elsewhere in the kitchen other maids were standing at big stone work surfaces, chopping up vegetables, rolling out pastry and performing various other tasks with great speed. Two maids stood at a massive cooking range stirring the contents of several huge pans. The noise of all this activity, in addition to the shrill voices of the senior maids shouting orders at the junior ones, was deafening.

Tilly leaned closer to Ava and said, 'I'll ask Cook to come and speak with you.'

Ava watched Tilly dodge across the kitchen, skirting around the hard-working maids in order to approach an older, plumpish woman on the other side of the room, who was overseeing the plucking of

a pair of pheasants. The young maid who
was doing it was obviously too slow for
the cook's liking, because the cook kept
prodding her and shouting that she would
box her ears if she didn't speed up.

Ava thought Tilly was very brave to
interrupt the impatient cook – but clearly
the fact that she had come on an errand for
a princess made all the difference. As soon as
Tilly pointed to Ava, the cook quickly used
her apron to wipe the sweat from her brow
and came to greet Ava with a polite smile on
her face.

She gave a little curtsy before saying,
'Tilly says you're looking for your cat, Your
Highness.'

Ava nodded and the cook shook her head
sadly. 'If only you'd come just a few hours
earlier, Your Highness . . .'

'What do you mean?' Ava asked, starting to feel butterflies in her tummy again.

'Well, only this morning we had a visit from Cinderella's fairy godmother. She was collecting animals, you see. You know how she likes to turn mice into horses and lizards into footman and rats into coach drivers and the like? Well, we gave her all the mice from the mousetrap – she's given us a special one to use that catches them but doesn't actually kill them – and a rabbit that was too skinny to make stew out of, which we kept alive for her too. I mean, after all that, I felt we'd done our bit down here in the kitchens, I really did, but *then* she said she was looking for some cats and dogs as well. I said we couldn't help with the dogs but since we've got quite a few cats here she could have the first one she could catch. Well – that tabby

one went up to her the second she wafted
some fish under its nose.'

'Oh no,' Ava murmured, thinking how
much Cindy loved to eat fish. 'Where did
the fairy godmother take her?'

'I'm afraid I couldn't say, Your Highness,'
replied the cook politely. 'I expect she's
taken her off to wherever it is that she
concocts her spells. Now, if you'll excuse
me, I must be getting back to my work.'

'I *have* to find Cindy before anything
happens to her!' Ava exclaimed to Tilly as
they left the kitchen together. 'You don't
think the fairy godmother would actually
hurt her, do you? After all, she's a *good*
character . . . I mean, *person* . . . isn't she?'
she added quickly.

'She's certainly a character-and-a-half and
no mistake!' Tilly answered, grinning. 'Most

people reckon she *means* well most of the time – but she's very temperamental and she tends to fly off the handle on a regular basis! She's obsessed with inventing new spells and nobody's ever quite sure what she's going to come up with next!'

Ava frowned. Somehow she had expected the characters in fairytale land to be a lot more straightforward – like they were in her fairytale book. 'Do you have any idea where she might be right now?' she asked Tilly anxiously.

'I don't know about right now,' Tilly answered. 'But tonight she'll definitely be at the ball.'

'The ball?' Ava queried.

'The special eve-of-the-wedding ball. Everybody is going to it. And the fairy godmother will definitely be there because

she has to help at the dress competition.'

'The *dress* competition?'

'Surely you've heard about it, Your Highness,' Tilly said. 'When Cinderella and Prince Charming got engaged they announced that there would be a special competition in honour of their marriage – a competition that absolutely anyone in the palace is allowed to enter – even the servants! Cinderella is going to award a prize to whoever makes the most original and beautiful dress – which they may wear tonight to the ball. Cinderella is to choose the winner and the prize will be to have a magic wish granted by the fairy godmother!'

'Wow!' Ava exclaimed. 'That sounds amazing!'

Tilly had a strange look on her face as she

blurted, 'It's a once-in-a-lifetime chance! At least, it *could* have been.'

'What do you mean?' Ava asked, puzzled.

Tilly sniffed and rubbed her nose. 'It's just that I've always wanted to have my own dress shop one day, but – as Dinah says – a poor servant like me could never afford it. So I thought . . . I thought with the help of a magic wish, maybe it *could* happen, so . . .'

'You decided to enter the competition?'

Tilly nodded. 'I've spent all my spare time for the last few months making a dress from the material that was left over after we'd made gowns for the queen and the princesses and the ladies-in-waiting and all the other members of the royal household. Just small scraps that would have been thrown away otherwise – but together they made a beautiful multicoloured dress fit for a princess. I was sure I had a real chance of winning!'

'So what happened?' Ava asked, guessing from Tilly's face that something must have.

'One day last week my dress was stolen from the sewing room. Dinah had gone to lie down because she wasn't feeling well, and I went to measure one of the ugly sisters for a new gown. When I got back the dress was gone.'

'That's terrible!' Ava exclaimed. 'But who could have taken it? And why?'

'I don't know.' There were tears in Tilly's eyes as she continued, 'But now there's no time to make another dress for the competition.'

Ava was looking thoughtful. 'Are the two ugly sisters entering this competition too?' she asked.

Tilly nodded. 'But neither of them can sew very well so I don't think they have much chance of winning!'

'You said you were measuring one of them when your dress went missing?' Ava reminded her.

'That's right – Ermentrude wanted a new gown.'

'Was Astrid there as well?'

'No. She was taking an afternoon nap.'

'Hmm . . .'

Tilly sighed as if she already knew what Ava was thinking. 'You're wondering if Astrid stole the dress while Ermentrude was keeping me distracted with her fitting, aren't you?'

'Well, they *do* seem like the most likely thieves,' Ava agreed.

'That's what *I* thought too. I mean, I know

they can't *wear* my dress, because neither
of them would fit into it. But at least by
taking it they've knocked me out of the
competition, which gives their own dresses
a better chance of winning. But when I
said that to Dinah she said I had to be very
cautious about accusing them, because they're
Cinderella's sisters, which means they're
practically royalty too. She said I'd need to
have proof first – and I haven't got any.'

'I see what she means,' Ava murmured,
thinking about how dangerous it could be
for a servant to get on the wrong side of the
ugly sisters.

'So even if Ermentrude and Astrid did
steal my dress, there's nothing I can do
about it,' Tilly said sadly. 'I guess I've just
got to accept that I'll *never* have my own
dress shop now.'

Ava thought about what *she* did when she wanted something really badly, but couldn't see any way of getting it. 'Have you talked to your mum and dad about it?' she asked.

'My parents died when I was very small,' Tilly told her.

'Oh.' Ava was shocked and didn't know what else to say. 'That's awful,' she finally mumbled.

Tilly nodded. 'But I was lucky because Dinah saw me begging outside the palace that winter and asked if I'd like to learn how to be a seamstress like her. I was very little then and the winter was so cold that year that I'd probably have died myself if it hadn't been for her. Even though I was too young to be much help to her to start with, she still shared her food with me and let me snuggle up in bed while she worked into

the night. She even made me
a doll to play with – a little
ragdoll with buttons for eyes
and soft woollen hair.'

'Dinah must be a very
kind person,' Ava said.

'She is,' Tilly agreed.
'She's taught me everything
she knows, plus she says I have a natural flair
for sewing. Now, because her eyesight isn't
so good and her hands are getting shaky, I'm
better at it than she is – and a lot faster. She
can't even thread a needle very easily any
more so I have to do that for her.'

'It must be an important job being the
palace seamstress,' Ava said.

'Yes it is, but we have to work very hard
and everyone bosses us around all the time,
wanting their clothes to be ready far more

quickly than we can do them. That's why
I'd really love to get away from here one
day . . .' She sighed. 'Never mind. Maybe my
dress wouldn't have won the competition
in any case. But I'd really *love* to be going to
that ball!'

Ava frowned, desperately wanting to help.
'Couldn't you *borrow* a dress to wear?' she
suggested, an idea forming in her head. 'One
that's just as beautiful as the missing dress . . .'

'Where would I possibly find such a
thing?' Tilly asked in a disbelieving voice.

Ava grinned as she replied, 'Leave it to
me – I know of a very good shop near here
where I'm allowed to borrow any dress that
I like!'

After Tilly had sewn the gold bow back on Ava's dress, Ava asked her new friend to show her the way back to the music room.

When they got there, the dancing princesses had left (thankfully) and the music box was still sitting on the table.

'Thanks, Tilly. I'll come and find you later when I've got the dress, and we can go to the ball together,' Ava promised, eager to be alone so that she could make her escape. She hoped her dad hadn't been too worried about her while she was gone. Still, she reassured herself quickly, it wasn't as if he hadn't known where she was – sort of.

Carefully she opened the lid of the music box and stared as hard as she could at her reflection in the little mirror inside. To her huge relief the mirror instantly began to glow. Ava kept looking into it with as much concentration as she could, until the mirror became too bright to look any longer. Then she closed her eyes.

Just as before, the brightness soon passed and after a few seconds Ava nervously opened her eyes again.

'*Yes!*' she exclaimed jubilantly as she looked around and saw that she was surrounded by wedding dresses, safely back in the upstairs room of Marietta's shop.

Incredibly, no time at all seemed to have passed since she'd left – because the first thing she heard was her father's footsteps on

the spiral stairs and his angry voice calling out, 'Ava! Are you up there?'

Desperately Ava looked around for somewhere to hide. It wasn't that she was truly scared of her father — but she couldn't allow him to stop her returning to fairytale land before she had rescued Cindy and helped Tilly.

She ended up crawling under the nearest wedding dress. Its full skirt, which fell to the floor, hid her completely like a tent. She only just got there in time as her dad arrived at the top of the stairs and called her name again. Then she heard him walk slowly around the room.

'Where is she, Marietta?' he asked crossly as Marietta arrived at the top of the stairs too.

'I told you — she's still travelling.'

109 ❀❀❀

'So which mirror did she go through?' Dad demanded.

'I'm not telling you,' Marietta answered firmly. 'You'll only go there and spoil it for her. You'll just have to wait until she gets back – it can't be long now.'

'She's been gone for over two hours!' Dad growled. 'What if something's happened to her?'

Ava listened to this with interest. If two hours had passed since she had last been in Marietta's shop, then time couldn't have stood still after all.

'I expect she's found lots of exciting things to do there,' Marietta said. 'You may as well go home again and I'll ring you when she returns.'

'I've already *been* home,' her dad said angrily. 'And now I'm back and she's *still* not here! It's just not on, Marietta! She has no experience of this sort of thing!'

'And whose fault is that?' Marietta said quietly.

'Don't start that again!' Dad retorted. 'I've done the right thing, keeping her away from all this for as long as I could.'

'Except that you've kept her away from yourself in the process!'

111

'I wanted her to lead a normal life with her mother,' Dad said sharply. 'And she has done – until *now*, that is.'

'She *can't* lead a normal life, Otto,' Marietta said passionately, 'and the sooner you realize that the better. The travelling gift is in her blood! Anyway, I don't see *you* turning your back on it, to pursue a *normal* life, as you call it!'

As the two adults started to walk back downstairs, Ava crawled out from her hiding place. She was intrigued by what she had just heard, and her mind was spinning with questions, but now she had to concentrate on picking out a dress for Tilly to wear for the competition. She also had to choose another dress for herself – a ball gown to wear this evening.

As she got to her feet, all she was thinking

about was how soon her dad was going to leave so that she could ask Marietta to help her.

'AVA!'

She jumped with fright, whirling round to see her father, who had crept back up to the top of the staircase. He must have heard the rustling as she'd come out of hiding.

'Dad,' she said in a shaky voice.

'Ava – where have you been? I've been worried sick!' he exclaimed angrily.

'Sorry,' she mumbled hoarsely. And suddenly his anger on top of everything else was too much – and she burst into tears.

Back downstairs as Marietta gave her a hug and started to say something sympathetic, Dad said crossly, 'You keep out of this, Marietta – you've done enough already!'

He was clearly much more angry with Marietta than he was with Ava, who was still sobbing loudly. He even made an awkward attempt to comfort Ava himself, mumbling, 'There, there – no need for that,' as he pulled out a grubby-looking hanky to mop up her tears.

'Shall I make us all a cup of tea?' Marietta suggested soothingly.

But Dad just glared at her and said that he was taking Ava home immediately.

'But maybe I can help you explain things, Otto,' Marietta said, frowning.

'I am perfectly capable of explaining things myself, thank you, Marietta,' he snapped. 'Come on, Ava. It's time to get changed back into your own clothes.'

Ava had no choice but to do as he said.

Thankfully, by the time she emerged in

her ordinary clothes from Marietta's fairytale changing room, she was feeling a lot more together and a lot more determined. 'Does the time pass just as quickly on the other side of the mirrors as it does here?' she asked Marietta as she pushed back the sparkly curtain to hand her the green and gold bridesmaid's dress, followed by the tiara and the emerald shoes.

As Marietta replied that it did, Dad asked suspiciously, 'Why do you want to know that?'

'Oh, I just wondered,' Ava replied guardedly, but in fact she was trying to calculate how long she had before the ball – and the dress competition – took place that night.

'When we get home I'll explain everything,' her father told her as they left the shop together. 'But I don't want you using the mirrors again. At least not until I think you're ready – do you understand?'

When she didn't answer, he repeated more forcefully, 'Do you understand, Ava?'

'Of course,' she murmured sullenly.

Of course she understood that he didn't *want* her to use them – but that wasn't the same as promising not to, was it?

8

It didn't take them long to get back to the house, and Dad immediately asked Ava to sit down while he made them both a cup of tea.

'I don't like tea,' she snapped, but he ignored her and went into his study, coming back with a small blue tin with a teddy bear on the front.

'This is special tea,' he told her. 'I've had it since I was your age. I'm not sure how it's made exactly, but when I was a boy I thought it was the most delicious drink imaginable. You can taste it for yourself in a minute and see what *you* think.'

'I told you, I don't want any tea,' Ava said impatiently, sure that her dad was just stalling for time. 'I want you to explain everything.'

Dad sighed. 'The fact is — this tea will *help* me explain, because it reminds me of how I felt when I was *your* age.' He spoke very carefully as he continued. 'When *I* was a child I went travelling with my parents from an early age, but it wasn't until my ninth birthday that they let me go on my first trip through a mirror alone.' He smiled as he remembered. 'They arranged for me to go and see Father Christmas. The *real* Father Christmas!'

Ava gaped at him, hardly able to believe he was serious.

'It was the middle of the summer, so he

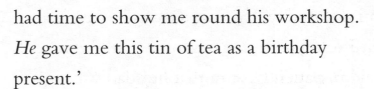

had time to show me round his workshop. *He* gave me this tin of tea as a birthday present.'

Ava just gazed at him incredulously.

'You might think that was a funny sort of birthday present to give a little boy, right?' Dad continued.

Speechless, she nodded, because it was true that she had always imagined Father Christmas's workshop to be full of shiny new train sets and beautiful dolls, rather than tins of tea.

'Well, it isn't just ordinary tea,' her father explained. '*He* called it *fizzy* tea – but in fact it does a lot more than fizz. When you drink

119

it, it can tell what your favourite flavours
are – and it creates them for you!'

'*Magic* tea!' Ava burst out.

'There must certainly be some magic
in the ingredients, yes,' her dad agreed.
'Anyway, I drank most of it as a boy, but I
put the last few spoonfuls away – because I
couldn't bear the thought of it being gone
completely. I've saved what was left for all
these years, waiting for an occasion that was
special enough to bring it out again.'

As he took the tin into the kitchen Ava
followed him, her mind racing. 'But you still
haven't told me about the mirrors, Dad. Are
we a family of witches or something? Is that
how we can travel through them?'

Her dad laughed. 'No, Ava. We aren't
witches. It's just that *we* can use the magic
mirrors whereas most people can't.' He

paused, looking more solemn. 'I know you must be feeling very confused right now, Ava. I guess the first thing you need to know is that you come from a long line of people who have an exceptional gift – the gift of being able to travel through magic portals. It's an ability that seems to be inherited from one generation to the next – a magic gene that gets passed on, if you like. It sounds crazy, I know. Don't worry – I'm going to answer all your questions in a minute. But first I want you to taste this tea.'

Ava watched her father use the end of a teaspoon to prise the lid off the tin. Then he took out a spoonful of tea and showed it to her. It looked exactly like ordinary tea and it didn't smell of anything at all. He placed a spoonful into each mug before filling them with cold water from the tap.

'Shouldn't you use boiling water from the kettle?' Ava asked in surprise.

'Not for this tea. The leaves will heat up the water to just the right temperature for drinking.' He handed her a mug. 'Now watch and wait.'

First Ava heard the liquid fizzing – then she saw it. Inside the mug some sort of special magic reaction seemed to be taking place. As Ava watched, the liquid was changing from clear to brown to green to pink to yellow to blue to red to orange and on and on through every colour Ava could imagine.

'It won't stop changing colour even when you're drinking it,' her dad told her. 'Don't worry – it's perfectly safe.'

Ava took a small, cautious sip. The drink tasted like warm toffee in her mouth.

Her second – longer – sip tasted of lemon bonbons. 'That's amazing!' Ava exclaimed. 'Whenever I'm choosing sweets I can never decide between lemon bonbons or toffee ones. And Mum always gets impatient and moans that they're both equally bad for my teeth!'

Dad's eyes were twinkling – something she didn't often see. 'Take another sip,' he urged her.

She did, and instantly giggled. 'Toothpaste flavour,' she burst out. 'But very *nice* toothpaste!'

'Father Christmas pops in something to help clean your teeth after anything that's very sweet,' Dad said. 'Very conscientious of him, wouldn't you say?'

'Very,' Ava agreed, still giggling. 'Can I drink the whole lot?'

'Of course,' Dad said, taking a gulp of his own drink. 'Liquorice Allsorts!' he exclaimed. 'Delicious!'

Ava smiled, but she still had a lot of questions. 'Why did you never tell me about Marietta and her shop before, Dad?' she asked. 'Marietta wanted you to, didn't she?'

Her father carefully put down his mug. 'Marietta, as you probably already know, can also travel through the

124

mirrors, though her main job is to stay and look after the shop.' He paused. '*She* thinks our ability to travel through the portals is so much a part of us that it's not natural to try and pretend it isn't there. And *she* thinks that children with the gift should grow up knowing about it and using it from the beginning.' He paused again. 'But *I* think differently. *I* think it is too much for a child to understand – especially if one of its parents is a *non*-gifted human, like your mother. I believe it is better to wait until a child has reached adulthood before introducing them to the portals. Then at least they are old enough to assess for themselves all the risks involved.'

'*What* risks?' Ava asked, frowning.

'The gift of travelling is not always an easy gift to have, Ava. It can be exciting, yes, and there are plenty of places I'd love to take you in a few years' time. But the reason I don't want you travelling until you're older is that sometimes things can go wrong on the other side of the mirrors. Not all the places there are good ones, and in some you might experience things that you wish you hadn't.'

'What sorts of things?' she asked curiously.

Her father looked at her steadily, as if he was weighing up whether or not to tell her more. Finally he said slowly, 'Well . . . a few weeks ago, when I visited Victorian Britain, I saw a chimney sweep younger than you die after getting stuck up a chimney.'

'That's terrible!' she gasped.

'It was very frightening – and I wish I hadn't been there. It's one thing reading about that sort of thing in a book – but quite another actually seeing it for yourself.'

He swallowed, and Ava was surprised to see tears in his eyes.

Now she remembered that he was writing a book on Victorian children. 'Is *that* how you do your research for your books?' she asked. 'By using the mirrors and actually *going* back in time?'

He nodded. 'For a long time now I have been using my gift to document what life was like in days gone by. Marietta also has some historical men's outfits in her shop. I use them quite a lot.'

'So when we don't hear from you for ages and Mum says you're travelling with your work – is *that* what you're doing?'

He nodded again. 'Sometimes I live in other time periods for weeks or months on end. It's the only way to get a real feel for that time in history.'

'Does Mum know the truth?' Even as she asked it Ava was sure that her mum didn't.

'No. She isn't a traveller so she'd never understand. That was another reason I didn't want *you* to know yet, Ava – because I didn't like the idea of asking you to keep such a big secret from your mother.'

'Maybe Mum would understand, if *I* explained it to her,' Ava said.

'Or maybe she'd get such a fright that she'd never let me see you again,' Dad replied grimly.

'She wouldn't do that,' Ava said. 'She's always saying that she *wants* me to spend more time with you.'

'You *can't* tell her, Ava,' Dad said firmly. 'Not if you want her to keep letting you come and stay with me. Trust me on this, OK?'

'OK.' Ava listened quietly as Dad went on to talk about how everyone in his family was born with the special gift of being able to travel to other times in history, and even to fantasy worlds that various people had dreamed up at one time or another and which existed in the space between what was real and what was not.

He told how there were many places in *this* world where certain magic energies all clustered together to form magic portals that allowed entry to *other* worlds. And Marietta's shop was one of those places.

'The plot of land where the shop stands has been in our family for generations,' he added, 'though it was an ordinary house rather than a shop when my parents lived there – and my grandparents and great-grandparents before them.'

Ava had never heard her father mention his family before. All she knew was what her mother had told her – that Dad's parents had died a long time ago. Ava had always felt a bit strange asking questions about them, but now seemed like the right moment.

'Dad, how did your parents die?' she asked gently.

He frowned. 'Twelve years ago – not long before I met your mother – my parents went on a trip through one of the portals. They never returned.'

'That's terrible!' Ava exclaimed. 'What happened to them?'

'I don't know. Presumably, they are still living happily ever after.'

Ava was puzzled. 'I don't understand. I thought you said they died?'

'They might as well have done,' her

father said bluntly. 'They left a note saying that they had decided to go and live for good in one particular fantasy land that they'd found. Since such a thing is totally against the laws of our people – and a search party would most certainly have been sent after them to bring them back – they destroyed the portal they had travelled through to make sure no one could follow them. Destroying a portal is very difficult and very dangerous – but it can be done if you know how.'

'It must have been a really wonderful place if they wanted to stay there forever,' Ava said wide-eyed, because however exciting her trip to Cinderella-land had been, she couldn't imagine never wanting to come home again.

'It doesn't matter *how* wonderful it was –

they had no right to do that to me and my sister,' Dad said, scowling.

'*Sister?*' This was news to Ava.

Dad looked at her. 'That's right – a younger sister who was only sixteen when my parents left.'

'A *sister!*' Ava still couldn't believe it.

'We don't always get on very well,' Dad added drily.

'Where does she live? When can I meet her?' Ava asked breathlessly.

Dad was giving her a very sober look now, as if she was being incredibly stupid.

And that's when it dawned on her. 'You don't mean . . . you can't mean . . . ? Dad, is *Marietta* your sister?'

'Marietta and I both grew up in that little corner house,' Dad explained. 'It was Marietta's idea to turn it into a shop after our parents left.'

Ava stared at him in amazement. 'You mean, I had an aunt all this time and I didn't even *know*!' she blurted out.

Her father looked apologetic. 'I didn't want you to find out about the magic portals, and I knew that if I let you meet Marietta she'd see to it that you did. She was meant to be going away for the whole of this summer – the shop was to be closed for a while – but at the last minute she changed her plans. Of course as soon as she heard you were coming she got all excited. I suppose I should have expected that she'd make herself known to you somehow.' He scowled. 'She won't admit it, but I'm sure she deliberately used Cindy to lure you into the shop.'

'What do you mean?' Ava was confused.

'Marietta happened to phone me on the day Cindy went missing so I mentioned to her that we were searching for your cat. She was very interested – asking me exactly what Cindy looked like – and I told her about the white patch on her front paw and that little nick she's got on her right ear. I asked Marietta to keep an eye out for her and to give me a ring if she saw her. Anyway, I think Marietta did more than just keep an eye out. I think she went and hunted high and low for Cindy until she found her. But instead of letting me know, she took her back to the shop and put that notice on the door to tempt *you* inside.'

Ava frowned. 'But how could she guess I'd walk past her shop and actually *see* the notice? I mean, *you* might have walked by and seen it first!'

'Oh, she knows I don't go near her shop when you're staying with me. And she also knows your instincts would soon take you in that direction. The portals are a bit like magnets to people who can travel through them. We sort of get drawn towards them without even being aware of it. You've been sensitive to the magic in the portals ever since you were tiny, Ava – that's why I've always known that the travelling gift has been passed on to you. I don't think you realize the number of times you've started to walk towards Marietta's shop when you've visited me before – and I've always steered you off along another route.'

'Really?' Ava was surprised – and a little bit thrilled at the thought of being drawn towards the magic portals like that. Then she thought about her cat and frowned again. 'But it's not fair of Marietta to use Cindy in that way.'

'I know,' Dad said.

'And *then* she let her disappear through a magic mirror!' Ava exclaimed indignantly.

Her dad nodded grimly. 'That was very irresponsible. I'm sure she didn't mean that to happen.'

Ava sat very still as she let everything sink in.

'Ava, I know you think I haven't been

around for you very much up till now,' her dad said, sounding a little uncomfortable. 'But my priority has always been for you to have what I didn't have – a normal childhood.'

Ava thought about all the times she had worried that it was *her* fault that her dad didn't want to see her more often.

'You could have come to visit me more,' she said in a small voice. 'Or taken me away for a holiday somewhere. Then I wouldn't have had to come anywhere near Marietta's shop.'

'I'm sorry, Ava,' Dad said sombrely. 'I guess I was just afraid that the more time you spent with me the more chance there was that you'd find out my secret. It's very difficult to keep a thing like this from people you're close to.'

'So you thought it was safer if we *weren't* close?' Ava said.

Dad met her gaze as he replied, 'Yes, I suppose I did.'

'So how come you let me stay with you for such a long time *this* summer?' Ava asked quietly.

Dad sighed. 'If I'm honest, I was worried about it at first, but since Marietta was meant to be going away I thought it would be all right, so long as I was careful about what you saw while you were here. I didn't mean to leave those books on magic lying about, for one thing. By the time Marietta told me she had changed her plans, it was too late to stop you coming.'

Ava had a sudden thought. 'Does *Mum* know about Marietta?'

Dad shook his head. 'It was easier not to

introduce them. Marietta thought I was a
fool to marry your mum. She said the two
of us could never be happy because of all the
secret-keeping. The worst thing is that she
was right.'

'But *why* couldn't you tell Mum?' Ava
asked. 'She *might* have understood.'

'Would *you* have understood a thing
like that? Would you have even believed it
was possible before you experienced it for
yourself?'

'I suppose if I actually *saw* a person
disappearing through a mirror in front of
me . . .' Ava murmured.

'You'd assume it was a magician's trick,'
Dad said. 'Think about it, Ava. If a bright
light forced you to close your eyes and then,
when you opened them again, the person
who'd been in front of you was gone, what

would you think had happened? Would you think they had been transported through a magic mirror or would you assume a trick had been played on you?'

Ava was beginning to see his point. 'A trick,' she admitted.

'Exactly – and you wouldn't rest until you found out how it had been done. Only you never *would* find out . . .'

Both Ava and her dad were silent for a few moments, thinking about Ava's mother. Then Ava said, 'But now that *I*'ve found out, Dad – and now that I've travelled through a portal myself – I *have* to go back to Cinderella-land.'

'That's where you were?'

'Yes. And I *have* to go back there to find Cindy.'

Her dad looked solemn. 'I don't think

that's a good idea. Fairytale land isn't as
safe as you think, Ava. There are plenty of
baddies in fairytales – and
they are usually very bad
indeed. Think of the
wicked witch in the
story of Hansel and
Gretel – or the evil
queen who poisoned
Snow White!'

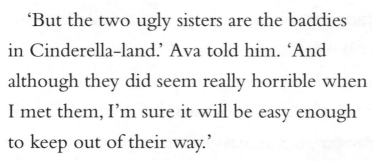

'But the two ugly sisters are the baddies
in Cinderella-land.' Ava told him. 'And
although they did seem really horrible when
I met them, I'm sure it will be easy enough
to keep out of their way.'

Her father looked at her sharply. 'You've
met the ugly sisters already?'

Ava nodded. 'I think they must be staying
in the palace for Cinderella's wedding.'

She frowned because there was something that was puzzling her about Astrid and Ermentrude. 'Dad, why does everyone call them the *ugly* sisters? I mean, they're not all *that* ugly.'

'The description isn't to do with their appearance,' her father explained. 'They are called that because they have very little beauty or goodness *inside* them. And they are *extremely* ugly on the inside, believe me, judging by some of their past actions.'

'Like when they shut Cinderella in the cellar, you mean?' Ava said.

'That . . . and . . . well . . . it's never been proven, but apparently many people in fairytale land don't believe that the death of Cinderella's father was an accident.'

'What? You mean they think the ugly sisters *killed* him?' Ava asked, wide-eyed. In her fairytale book there had been no details given of exactly *how* Cinderella's father had died, she remembered.

'So I'm told. I haven't been to fairytale land myself for a long time, but Marietta heard that he fell down the cellar steps and broke his neck one day while the ugly sisters just happened to be alone in the house with him. They claimed to have nothing to do with it of course, and Cinderella believed them because Cinderella *always* believes the best about people.' He shook his head a little impatiently. 'I know she can't help the nature she's been given, but sometimes I think Cinderella has too *much* goodness inside her. I mean, why on earth would she invite her stepsisters to the wedding?'

'I guess she must be *very* forgiving,' Ava said.

143

'*Too* forgiving, if you ask me,' her dad grunted. 'Like I said before, none of the rumours have ever been proven – but if *anyone* should go back to fairytale land to fetch Cindy, it should be Marietta or myself, not you.'

'No, Dad. *I* have to be the one to go,' Ava insisted. 'It's not just to fetch Cindy. There's a girl there whom I promised to help too! Don't worry – I'll be really careful to stay away from the ugly sisters. *They're* scared of *me* now, in any case, because they think I'm a ghost!'

'A ghost?' Ava's dad was clearly about to ask more, when the phone started ringing.

He quickly went to answer it. 'Hello, Marietta . . . Yes, I've told her . . .' There was a long pause while he listened. '*What?* . . . Are you sure? . . . OK, OK, just

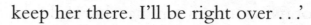

keep her there. I'll be right over . . .'

'What's wrong?' Ava asked when he came off the phone.

'Marietta has a visitor in her shop,' he said, frowning.

'What visitor?' Ava asked curiously.

'A nanny whom I met on my last visit to Victorian London. She's a travelling person like us and she must have been watching the last time I came back through the portal because she followed me through it. And now that she's discovered it, the daft woman seems to think she can come and go as she pleases.'

'But why shouldn't she – if *she* has the gift too?' Ava asked, puzzled.

'Because for *her*, this is the future. And it is forbidden for any of us to visit the future.'

'Really? Why?'

'It's complicated. All you have to know for now is that it's against our laws, Ava. Even when we travel *back* in time, we have to be careful not to give too much away about where we come from. If this nanny gets discovered here, Marietta's shop might be closed down.'

'That sounds serious.'

'It is – which is why I have to go there at once.'

'Can I come too?' Ava asked, excited at the prospect of getting to meet a real nanny from Victorian times.

But her father shook his head. 'The less contact the nanny has with people here, the better.'

'You can't just leave me in the house on my own,' Ava pointed out, a little sulkily.

'Fine. You can come with me to the

shop, but you'll have to wait for me in the front room while Marietta and I sort this out.'

Marietta gave Ava an excited hug when she greeted her at the door, clearly delighted that she could now be open about the fact that Ava was her niece. Ava found it difficult to suddenly think of Marietta as her aunt – but she guessed maybe that would come in time. After all, *she* had only just learned about Marietta, whereas Marietta had known about *her* ever since she'd been born.

'Wait here, Ava,' Dad said, pointing to a small, uncomfortable-looking chair in the dreary front section of the shop. 'Hopefully this won't take *too* long.' He turned to Marietta and asked, 'Where is she?'

'Follow me.'

After they had both disappeared through
the beaded curtain, Ava got up and went
to peer through it herself. They weren't in
the fairytale room on the other side, so Ava
could only assume Marietta had taken Dad
to a room even further back inside the shop.

Ava quickly pushed through the curtain
and went to look for a dress for Tilly.
It would have been better if she could
have asked Marietta's permission before
borrowing another dress, but she couldn't
do that without alerting Dad. Besides, she
had a feeling Marietta would approve of
what she was doing in any case.

After several minutes of trying to make
up her mind, Ava pulled out the four dresses
that looked like they would fit Tilly the
best. One was yellow with cream bows, one
was pale blue with a lacy bodice, one was

pink and quite
frilly, and the
fourth was
cream with
silk violets
embroidered
on to the
skirt and a
simple bodice
that laced up
at the back
with violet
ribbon.

This is the
prettiest,
Ava
thought, slipping the cream and violet one
from its hanger.

She then had to choose a dress for herself,

149 ❀❀❀

and her eye caught a child's ball gown that was remarkably like one that she had for her Princess Barbie doll at home. It had a long red skirt with a stiff red petticoat underneath, which made the skirt stick out without having to wear any hoops. The simple red bodice had a pretty heart-shaped neckline and was attractively decorated with shimmering gold beads.

Excited, Ava quickly found a pair of shoes to match each dress, before disappearing into the changing cubicle. Hopefully the Victorian nanny would keep Marietta and her dad occupied long enough for her to change without being discovered. She felt slightly guilty about disobeying Dad like this – but only slightly. He didn't always know what was best for her, she decided. It was *her* job to rescue Cindy and help Tilly – and besides

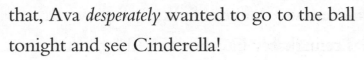

that, Ava *desperately* wanted to go to the ball tonight and see Cinderella!

Once she was ready – and she was delighted with how glamorous she looked in her new dress – she hurried up the spiral staircase and found to her relief that the music box was exactly where she had left it. Holding on tightly to Tilly's shoes, and with the cream and violet dress draped carefully over her arm, Ava opened the lid of the box.

Would the ball gown she was now wearing transport her through the mirror in the music box, just as the bridesmaid's dress had done? It came from Marietta's fairytale collection too, so surely it should. But would it matter that she was carrying with her an extra fairytale dress? Unfortunately Ava just didn't yet know all the rules when it came to travelling through the portals – and there was nobody she could ask.

Feeling nervous, she looked into the mirror, holding her breath as she waited for the magic reaction to start up. There was nothing left to do now but take a chance . . . and keep her fingers crossed that nothing would go wrong.

As soon as Ava arrived back in the palace music room she heaved a huge sigh of relief. Her new red ball gown had made the magic happen just as well as the bridesmaid's dress had done – and Tilly's dress and shoes had also passed through the portal unharmed. But she decided that it was best to play it safe from now on, by keeping the music box in her possession. That way she knew she could return home through the portal at any time she chose.

The clock on the wall told her that it was nearly half past six already, which meant that if she was to get Tilly's outfit to her in time for the competition she would have to hurry.

'Look who it is!' a snide voice exclaimed as she stepped out of the music room into the corridor.

Ava froze as she found herself face to face with Astrid and Ermentrude.

Unfortunately they no longer looked frightened of her.

'She doesn't look much like a ghost now, does she, Ermentude?' the blonde-haired sister sneered.

'No,' the dark one snapped. 'It was obviously some sort of trick.' She glared menacingly at Ava. 'And now we're going to make you tell us how you did it!'

Astrid suddenly spotted the music box, half concealed by Tilly's dress. 'What's that?' she snarled, reaching out and grabbing the box before Ava could stop her. 'Look, Ermentrude! She's clearly a thief!'

'I was only borrowing it!' Ava protested. 'Please give it back!'

Ermentrude laughed nastily. 'Let *me* see the box, Astrid. Is it valuable?'

'I don't know, but *I'm* keeping it! It will look perfect on my dressing table!' Astrid grinned slyly at Ava. 'If anyone notices it's missing we'll tell them *you* stole it! After all, *you'll* be too scared to tell them anything by the time *we've* finished with you!'

Ava started to feel frightened, but fortunately at that moment Ermentrude made a grab for the box herself, snarling, '*You're* not keeping it, Astrid. I'm the older

sister so *I* should have it!'

Ava seized her chance to escape while they were still bickering. She lifted up the long skirt of her gown and rushed as fast as she could away from them.

'After her!' Astrid yelled at once – but the ugly sisters weren't very quick on their feet and Ava soon managed to outrun them.

She headed for the sewing room, trying not to let the feelings of panic overwhelm her. The ugly sisters had the music box! And for as long as they had it she wouldn't be able to return home again! She *had* to think of a way of getting it back from them – but what if she couldn't? Did that mean she would be stuck in fairytale land forever?

'Princess Ava!' Tilly exclaimed in surprise, starting to curtsy as she opened the sewing-room door to Ava. 'Are you all right? You look as though you've just had an awful shock.'

Ava's stomach was churning as she thought about the music box, but she couldn't explain that to Tilly. 'I'm fine,' she said, doing her best to sound normal. 'I found you another dress to wear. Look.'

Tilly looked uncertain as Ava held up the cream and violet ball gown to show her. 'It's lovely, Your Highness, but I don't know. I've been thinking about it. Wouldn't it be cheating to enter a dress into the competition that isn't my own creation?'

Ava supposed that it probably *was* cheating. But after her most recent encounter with the ugly sisters – who were almost certainly the ones who had stolen Tilly's original dress – she felt determined

that they shouldn't get to ruin *everything*.

'Oh, but it's only fair that you get to go to the ball after all your hard work,' she insisted.

Tilly was slowly inspecting the gown. 'I *would* really love to go to the ball,' she said. 'And I suppose it can't do any harm to wear this dress tonight if it fits me, since I'm sure it won't actually win.' She flushed as she added quickly, 'It's really pretty – but I'm sure the winning dress has got to be a bit *different* from normal dresses – more *original*, if you see what I mean. Don't you think so, Dinah?'

The elderly seamstress nodded, looking thoughtful as she said, 'Yes, Tilly, I do. That dress is very pretty – but I've seen many others just like it.'

Tilly agreed to try on the dress, and while

157

Dinah was helping her to change, Ava suddenly remembered something important. 'Tilly, do you think Astrid and Ermentrude will *definitely* be at the ball tonight?' she asked.

'Oh yes. Like I said before, they are both entering the dress competition.'

'Good,' Ava murmured under her breath. For Ava had remembered what her dad had said about people with the travelling gift being *drawn* towards the magic portals. If that was true, then all she had to do was follow her *instinct* and she would be *taken* to wherever the ugly sisters had hidden the music box. And as long as they remained out of the way at the ball, Ava would have the chance she needed to escape home with Cindy – presuming she had found her by that time of course.

She would just have to make sure the ugly

sisters didn't actually see her tonight, that was all.

'You look lovely!' Ava exclaimed when Tilly was ready.

'It's certainly an excellent fit,' Dinah said.

Making a big effort to smile bravely, Tilly said, 'Thank you so much, Princess Ava. At least now I can go to the ball.'

'That's all right.' Ava replied, smiling back. 'But it must be due to start very soon, isn't it? Hadn't we better get going?'

'The ball starts at seven o'clock, but the competition isn't until eight,' Tilly said. 'I'll come along then because I need to help Dinah finish off some needlework first.'

'OK, but I think I'd better go now if I'm to find the fairy godmother.'

'Just be aware of the fact that she might

have used your cat in a spell already,' Dinah said warningly.

'Dinah!' Tilly exclaimed.

'I just want Princess Ava to be prepared, that's all,' Dinah said defensively. 'It's better to be prepared than to get a nasty shock. I've had a good few nasty shocks in my life, so I know what I'm talking about.'

'It's OK, Dinah. I *am* prepared,' Ava reassured her.

But as she headed on her own to the palace ballroom, taking care to follow Tilly's directions precisely so as not to get lost, she started to feel as if she wasn't prepared in the slightest. After all, it wasn't every day you had to rescue your cat from Cinderella's fairy godmother, was it? I mean, how could anyone be truly prepared for *that*?

The ball had already begun by the time
Ava got there. Lively music could be
heard coming from the ballroom, where
an important-looking manservant in a
white curly wig and gold-coloured jacket
and breeches was standing at the door
announcing all the guests. Nervously Ava
joined the small queue waiting to enter the
room, and she was pleased to see the friendly
young princess she had spoken to earlier,
who waved to her.

All the young princesses except Ava
seemed to be accompanied by their parents,

and Ava was given a strange look by
the manservant as she stood alone in the
doorway.

'Your name, Your Highness?' he enquired.

'P-P-Princess Ava,' Ava stammered,
cringing and going bright red as she said it.

But the manservant didn't bat an eyelid
as he effortlessly announced at the top of his
voice, 'HER ROYAL HIGHNESS THE
PRINCESS AVA!'

A few guests turned to look at her,
but most were too busy with their own
conversations to wonder why a child
princess had come to the ball alone.

Doing her best to rein in her nerves, Ava
walked into the ballroom holding her chin
up high as if she was balancing books on top
of her head – which was something she had
once heard all princesses were taught to do.

The ballroom, the walls of which were
made up entirely of mirrors, was beautifully
decorated, with glitter balls hanging from
the ceiling in between massive crystal
chandeliers. Free-standing candleholders
stood around the periphery bearing
enormous shimmering candles. The music
Ava had heard was coming from a string
quartet at one end of the room, and a few

❁❀❁

guests were already dancing, the richly dressed women creating a colourful display in their beautiful gowns and sparkling jewellery as they waltzed with their handsome partners.

Around the edges of the dance floor, other guests were seated on ornate chairs, sipping glasses of champagne or fruit punch, while neatly dressed servants served delicious-looking finger food from silver trays. At the end furthest from the musicians four throne-like chairs had been placed, and Ava guessed that was where the King and Queen, and Cinderella and Prince Charming would sit when they arrived.

She started to scan the room for the fairy godmother, but since she didn't know what she looked like, it wasn't easy. How old was she, for one thing? And would she have visible wings like a regular fairy, or would they be hidden under her clothes? Might she be flying about the room waving her wand, or would she be trying to blend in with the other guests?

Ava decided to go and ask the princess she had spotted earlier for help.

The young princess was sitting on a seat beside her mother, looking at the diamond watch on her wrist and frowning.

'Hello.' Ava greeted her shyly. 'Isn't it a wonderful ball?'

The young princess looked up and gave her a friendly smile before saying in a hushed voice, 'It's quite pretty, I agree – though as it's my tenth ball this summer I must say I'm getting a little tired of them.' She sighed. 'Mama says it's something all princesses have to endure – the endless parties and balls. I expect *you* feel a bit fed up with the whole thing too, don't you? What kingdom do you come from, by the way?'

Ava thought very fast. Avoiding the last part of the question, she gushed, 'Well, the thing is, I'm especially excited about *this* ball because I really want to meet Cinderella's fairy godmother. I'm not sure where she is though. Do *you* know?'

'Oh, I believe she's helping out with the dress competition. Cinderella was worried some of the entrants might cheat by wearing dresses they'd actually got someone *else* to make for them – so each entry is to be checked over by the fairy godmother first. Apparently she's got a magic spell which can tell her whether or not each dress was truly made by the person wearing it.'

'Oh no!' Ava blurted.

'What's wrong?' the princess asked in surprise.

'Nothing!' Ava replied quickly. 'I just really want to speak to her, that's all, and . . . and it sounds like she might be too busy.'

'Oh, look – there she is!' the princess exclaimed suddenly, pointing across the room at a plump, middle-aged lady who was holding a lace hanky over her nose as she ordered a maid to remove a large vase of pink flowers from a nearby table – complaining that the ghastly things were making her sneeze. She had curly white-blonde hair with

glittery bits in it and she was wearing a
large purple and red ball gown with a huge
skirt. As she turned slightly, Ava saw that
her shimmering gold-coloured wrap was
covering something bulky attached to her
back, which Ava guessed must be her wings.

Ava thanked the princess and slowly
approached the fairy godmother, desperately
trying to think of a tactful way to ask her
about Cindy.

'Excuse me, Fairy Godmother,' she said
timidly.

Immediately the fairy godmother whirled
round and peered at her suspiciously
through her round gold-rimmed spectacles.
'Don't tell me you're *another* of my
godchildren?' she exclaimed. 'They seem to
be cropping up everywhere I go these days!
Just because I helped Cinderella to marry a

prince, doesn't mean I intend to do the same for the rest of you, you know! Now, which one are you and what do *you* want?'

'I'm Ava,' Ava told her nervously. 'And I'm actually *not* one of your godchildren.'

'You're *not*? Then why did you just call me godmother?'

Ava flushed. 'Because . . . because that's what Cinderella calls you and I don't know your real name.'

The fairy godmother looked slightly friendlier as she said, 'So you're a friend of Cinderella's, are you? Good. At least you're on *her* side and not the prince's.'

'Her side?'

'For the ceremony of course. His family is far larger than hers and he has many more guests at the wedding than she does. I'm afraid it's going to look very uneven inside

169

the church. That's the only reason I didn't try and stop her inviting those dreadful stepsisters of hers — because at least they will boost the numbers on our side.'

'Well, I'm *supposed* to be a bridesmaid,' Ava began, 'so I'm not sure if that means—'

But she was interrupted by the fairy godmother letting out an annoyed grunt as she exclaimed, 'Just look at that!'

Ava followed her gaze and saw that Cinderella's stepsisters were standing in the doorway, being announced by the important-looking manservant. Ermentrude was in a very bright, very tight dress that she seemed to be having a lot of trouble walking in and Astrid was in an orange and lime-green ball gown that looked extremely lopsided.

As they watched, a maid directed the

sisters to a table on the other side of the room. The table had a gold banner attached to one end which read: 'COMPETITION ENTRANTS, PLEASE GATHER HERE!'

'They must have decided to enter the dress competition,' the fairy godmother said. 'Well, there's no way either of them will win in those monstrosities, even if they did make the dresses themselves, which I very much doubt! Still – I suppose I shall have to go and test them just the same.'

'Please can I ask you a question first?' Ava said quickly.

'I'm *not* granting any more magic wishes, if that's what you're after,' the godmother said impatiently. 'Honestly! Some people seem to think they can treat me like a genie in a lamp!'

'It's not that,' Ava said at once. 'The

question I've got is about my cat.'

'Your cat?' The fairy godmother looked surprised.

'Yes – she accidentally got into the kitchens the other day and the cook said she gave her to you to practise your spells on. Her name is Cindy and the thing is, I really want her back.'

'Oh, you do, do you?' The fairy godmother paused for a moment. 'I presume you are talking about that very hot-headed female tabby. She's an excellent mouser, so she says.'

'She *is* – unfortunately,' Ava agreed. 'Wait a minute – she actually *told* you that?'

'Oh yes. She also mentioned that at home she is called Cindy – though among other cats she goes by the name of Lucinda Wet-Whiskers the Third.'

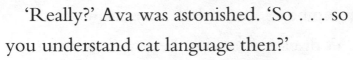

'Really?' Ava was astonished. 'So . . . so you understand cat language then?'

'Goodness, no! She told me all this over a nice cup of tea – after I'd changed her into human form.'

Ava gulped.

'Well, perhaps she drank more milk than tea,' the fairy godmother continued, 'but in any case it was all very civilized. Until she smelt my mice, that is, and then she seemed to forget that I had turned her into a human. Clearly my spell needs some refining. Anyway, you can certainly take her away with you if you want. But you'll have to wait until the ball finishes at midnight.'

'Why? Where is she now?' Ava asked.

'The King and Queen were a bit short of staff tonight so I turned your cat into a maid and a couple of the kitchen mice into

serving boys. They're all here somewhere.
I told the head maid to keep a close eye on
them.'

As she talked, she had been walking
towards the table where Cinderella's
stepsisters were sitting, and Ava had been
obliged to walk with her. The ugly sisters
were now close enough to recognize Ava,
but luckily before they could, the fairy
godmother produced a wand from a pocket
in her dress and waved it at them.

Ava quickly dodged out of sight as
Cinderella's stepsisters screamed, causing all
the other guests to turn and stare at them.

Ava couldn't tell at first why they were
screaming — until she suddenly realized that
the fairy godmother's magic had caused
their dresses to vanish. The ugly sisters were
standing there, looking totally mortified,

wearing nothing but their tight corsets and frilly underclothes.

'Stop that awful noise and tell me who made those dresses,' the fairy godmother commanded, prodding both girls in the ribs with the end of her wand. 'It certainly wasn't you! I know that much or they wouldn't have disappeared!'

Bright red, and staring fearfully at the wand (which was still giving off some dangerous-looking sparks), the sisters answered, 'Our m-m-mother . . . But she's not very good at sewing . . .'

'I can see that!' The fairy godmother

175 ✿❀✿

looked like she was enjoying herself now. 'Well . . . perhaps your punishment should be that you remain at the ball tonight – without any dresses on at all!'

The ugly sisters squealed even louder, and as some of the other guests who had overheard started to laugh and clap at that suggestion, they let out loud sobs and rushed out of the ballroom.

Ava was just wondering whether she ought to follow them and see if they would lead her to wherever they had hidden the music box – after all it might be better not to depend *totally* on her instincts – when she noticed one of the senior maids scolding one of the serving boys. It looked as if he had been caught eating whatever it was he was meant to be serving to the guests from his large silver platter.

'That boy is one of my mice,' the fairy godmother whispered to Ava. 'I hope they haven't given him the cheese straws to hand round. I *told* them what would happen if they did. Oh no! Just look at Cindy over there with the smoked-salmon canapés!'

Ava looked across the room and saw a maid with very strange hair (that could best be described as tabby-coloured) balancing a silver plate of mini pancakes that had smoked salmon on top. Only instead of offering them to the guests, the maid was biting the fish off the top of each one before allowing any of the guests to touch them. Ava watched as she licked her lips, then lifted her fishy fingers to her mouth to lick them clean too.

'Is that girl . . . is that really *Cindy*?' Ava exclaimed, and for a moment she was so fascinated that all she could do was stand and stare.

'Why don't *you* go and speak to her?' the fairy godmother suggested. 'Try and distract her from eating any more of the guests' food. Oh dear,' she murmured, as Cindy put down her tray and started to follow the serving boy who had been eating the cheese straws. 'It was probably unwise to use a mouse and a cat in the same experiment.'

Judging by the way Cindy was now sniffing at the serving boy from behind, Ava assumed the fairy godmother's spell hadn't entirely removed the *smell* of mouse from her subject.

'She looks like she's about to tuck into him too,' the fairy godmother said nervously. 'You've got to stop her, Ava. Otherwise there will be a terrible scene and Cinderella's party will be ruined.'

'*Me* stop her?' Ava exclaimed. 'Can't *you* do something?'

But the fairy godmother was already sitting down at the table, where more contestants were arriving to have their dresses tested for authenticity.

That's when Ava knew that it was up to *her* to stop Cindy pouncing on the manservant – or mouse-servant as she reckoned he ought to be called. But how was she going to do it? And besides that, she urgently needed to stop Tilly from coming to the ball and making a complete fool of herself in her borrowed dress. And she *still* had to think of a way of getting the music box back from the ugly sisters . . .

'Cindy, it's me – Ava,' she whispered, gently tapping Cindy-the-maid on the shoulder as she approached her from behind.

The maid whirled round and let out a strange noise that sounded a bit like a purr. 'Ava!' Her voice was like that of a human female, but very throaty. 'What are you doing here?'

'I came to find you and take you home,' Ava said, hardly able to believe she was having an actual conversation with her cat.

'I don't want to come home,' Cindy said in rather a snarly voice, keeping one eye firmly on the serving boy. 'I'm having too much fun.' The boy was now scuttling towards another servant who was holding a tray of cheese vol-au-vents.

'Cindy, I know you won't change back into a cat until midnight, but I really think we should leave the ball *now*. Before you attack that boy and get us both into terrible trouble.'

Cindy-the-maid gave her the same sort of look that Cindy-the-cat gave her when she yelled at her to stop scratching the stair carpet.

'Don't be ridiculous, Ava. I have no intention of attacking anyone. But we have some delicious herring pâté on crackers coming out of the kitchen at any moment. And then I believe we have some prawns. I certainly intend to sink my teeth into some of those!' Cindy started to dribble a little at the thought of yet more fish.

Ava had to think fast. What did Cindy like to eat even more than herring and prawns?

'OK, but first there are some *tuna* sandwiches that need collecting from the kitchen,' she lied.

Cindy's nose started to twitch. Tuna was her favourite fish of all. 'What are we waiting for?' she purred.

Cindy looked so pleased that Ava started to feel guilty at tricking her like this. But as soon as she got Cindy home again she would make up for it by giving her the biggest bowl of tuna she'd ever had.

They were almost at the door when Cindy picked up the scent of the mouse-turned-manservant again – and this time everything happened so fast that there was no time for Ava to stop it.

Cindy's nose twitched again and she let out a strange half-cry, half-growl. Then,

shoving two princesses and a duchess out of
the way, Cindy hurled herself tiger-like at
the other servant. The skinny young man
fell to the floor, where he squeaked in fear as
Cindy – who had thrown herself down on
the ground with him – sank her teeth into
his collar and started to drag him towards
the door. Despite being the same size as her
victim, Cindy seemed to have ten times the
strength.

As the surrounding guests screamed, the
fairy godmother came rushing over. 'No
need to be alarmed, everyone! It's just a little
party trick – a little charade we've put on to
entertain you!' she trilled.

'Can't you *do* something?' Ava whispered
to her as Cindy started to play with her
terrified prey, letting him go for a few
seconds, then pouncing on him again.

'I'm afraid I can't change either of them back to normal before midnight,' the godmother replied. 'We'll just have to wait until the spell wears off.' She bent down closer to the cat-turned-maid, shouting, 'Do you hear that, Cindy? Let go now and you can eat then if you want.'

As the manservant squeaked even louder, Ava decided that enough was enough. 'Let *go*, Cindy!' she yelled, in much the same stern voice she used whenever Cindy caught a mouse at home.

But Cindy completely ignored her, just as she always did at home, and continued to swat the boy around the head while growling excitedly.

'Get her some more salmon or something!' Ava shouted, but everyone else was backing further away, including the fairy godmother.

'Perhaps I should call the palace doctor —
or the vet,' the godmother was mumbling.
'Oh dear — I don't know which would be
most appropriate . . .'

Desperately Ava grabbed Cindy by the
hair and tugged as hard as she could, and for
a second Cindy loosened her grip on the
manservant for long enough to spit and hiss
at Ava instead. Ava jumped back in fright as
she saw that the maid's fingernails were as
sharp as a cat's claws.

'Get her some FISH somebody!' Ava
yelled again, now on the verge of tears.

Suddenly she heard a familiar voice
calling her name and she looked up to
see a handsome man dressed in a very
princely purple and gold outfit and wearing
a powdered white wig pushing his way
towards her through the crowd of guests.

185

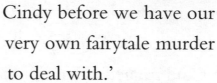

'DAD!' she exclaimed in amazement.

'Here,' he said, as he reached into his jacket pocket. 'You'd better give this to

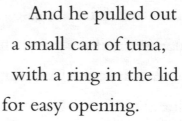

Cindy before we have our very own fairytale murder to deal with.'

And he pulled out a small can of tuna, with a ring in the lid for easy opening.

11

Ava watched her dad – with his back to
the rest of the guests – tear off the lid using
the ring pull, then take out a large silk
handkerchief. Carefully shielding the can
from view, he tipped its contents into the
hanky, which he placed on the floor close to
Cindy.

'Cans of tuna don't exist in fairytale land
so we mustn't let anyone see this one,' he
whispered to Ava, slipping the empty tin
back into his pocket.

Thankfully, as soon as Cindy smelt the
tuna she let go of the manservant and

pounced on the fish-filled hanky instead.

'Dad – what are you *doing* here?' Ava asked, as the terrified manservant scrambled to his feet and bolted for the door.

'Rescuing *you*,' her father replied sternly. 'I *told* you things could get dangerous in fairytale land, didn't I?'

'Cindy would never hurt *me*,' Ava said defensively. 'I wanted her to stop attacking that poor little mouse-servant, that's all.'

As she spoke Ava glanced across the room to where there was now a long line of girls in beautiful dresses waiting for the fairy godmother to check them before letting them enter the competition. Ava was relieved to see that Tilly wasn't there yet, but she knew she had to find her immediately to warn her to stay away.

'We can't take Cindy home through

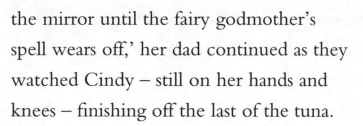

the mirror until the fairy godmother's spell wears off,' her dad continued as they watched Cindy – still on her hands and knees – finishing off the last of the tuna.

'We have to find the music box first!' Ava said anxiously. She started to tell him about the ugly sisters taking the music box for themselves, but he interrupted her.

'I realized something like that must have happened when I arrived through the mirror and found I was inside the wardrobe in their bedroom. Luckily for me they weren't in the room themselves, or I'd have had a lot of explaining to do.'

'Of course!' Ava heaved a sigh of relief as she realized that her father would have to have travelled here the same way she had. Which meant he would have arrived wherever in the palace the music box happened to be. 'Where's the music box now, Dad? You did bring it with you, didn't you?'

He nodded. 'I hid it out in the corridor before I came into the ballroom. We'd better go and fetch it. Then I want you to use it to go straight home, Ava.'

'*No*, Dad!' Ava protested. 'I'm not ready to go back yet. I still have to find Tilly and warn her not to come to the ball. If she does and the fairy godmother totally humiliates her in front of everyone, it will be all my fault!'

'What are you talking about?'

She quickly explained to him what had happened with the competition dresses.

After he had listened to the whole story, her dad sighed. 'Ava, we have to be very careful how we help the people we meet on the other side of the portals. Helping someone by bringing them something from *our* world often *causes* more problems than it solves.'

'I'm sorry, Dad,' Ava said, frowning. 'But *that's* why I need you to take me with you when you go through the portals – so you can teach me what's allowed and what isn't.'

Dad sighed again. 'I think I'm beginning to see that, Ava.'

Ava's heart skipped a beat. 'You *are*?'

'Yes. Now that you know about your gift – however much I wish you didn't – I think I owe it to you to teach you how to use it responsibly. As Marietta says, you're a sensible girl – *most* of the time. Perhaps I just have to trust you more. In any case I intend to explain to you in much more detail how the magic-portal system works – and answer *all* your questions about it.'

Ava tried not to look too excited. After all, she didn't want Dad to think she *wasn't* sensible. But in fact she was so thrilled right at that moment that she felt like dancing about in a way that was totally and utterly crazy!

'So you'll let me stay here long enough to help Tilly?' she asked.

He nodded. 'So long as we keep together.'

Cindy was back on her feet, looking a lot calmer now that she had a full stomach.

'That includes you too, Cindy,' Dad said. 'You need to stay close to us from now on. Come on – I think it's time we left this ball.'

'I'm thirsty,' Cindy complained, eyeing a tray of drinks being carried by a nearby waitress.

'It's all that salty tuna, I expect,' Ava said quickly. 'Come with us, Cindy, and we'll soon find you a nice cool drink of water.'

So Cindy accompanied them out of the ballroom into the corridor, where Dad immediately went to retrieve the music box, which he had hidden behind a suit of armour that was on display in a nearby alcove.

'Not the best hiding place, but I was in a bit of a hurry,' he murmured as they set off towards the sewing room – with Ava leading the way and Cindy following in a maid-like fashion a short distance behind them.

Ava decided now would be a good time to ask a question she had been meaning to ask Marietta. 'Dad . . . I've been thinking . . . this isn't the *only* fairytale land we can visit, is it? I mean, there are a lot more fairytales apart from *Cinderella*, aren't there?'

Her father nodded. 'You're beginning to understand how complicated all this is, Ava. Cinderella-land is not the *only* fairytale land in existence, but it's the only one we can visit from Marietta's shop. There are many more shops like Marietta's however – and a lot more magic portals in other places as well.'

'Do you know where all of them are?' Ava asked curiously.

'I know where a lot of them are, yes. For instance, there's a little shop not too far away from where you and your mother live where I go when I want to be transported back to Tudor times. And I've heard they *also* have a portal that takes you to Snow White's cottage.'

'Wow!' Ava exclaimed excitedly. 'Can we go there after this?'

Her father laughed. 'All in good time, Ava.'

'Have you been through *all* the portals in Marietta's shop yet?' Ava wanted to know.

'At one time or another – yes.'

'So when did you last come to Cinderella-land?'

'Oh, it must have been about fifteen years ago or so. I found myself in the middle of a ball the King was throwing for the Queen's birthday. Prince Charming was only a little boy back then, and Cinderella was a very small child living happily in a nearby village with her mother and father.'

Ava was puzzled. 'You mean not everybody comes to Cinderella-land at the time that Cinderella is getting married?'

'Oh, no. It's a bit of a mystery how the fairytale lands work, but they extend a long way, time-wise, on either side of the actual

stories we read about in fairytale books.
You've been exceptionally lucky, Ava,
to arrive here at the most exciting part of
Cinderella's story.'

'I'm *so* glad I did!' Ava gasped. For even
though she wouldn't have minded meeting
Cinderella as a child – or even as an old
woman – the Cinderella she most longed to
meet was the fairytale princess she knew and
loved from her storybook.

Dinah was alone in the sewing room
when they got there, and she immediately
started to struggle to her feet upon seeing
Ava and her father.

'Dinah . . . please . . . you don't have to
curtsy to me,' Ava told the old lady quickly.
'This is my dad, but he's not royalty or
anything, so you don't have to curtsy to him
either.'

'Oh?' Dinah sounded confused – perhaps wondering how Ava could be a princess if her father wasn't a king or a prince. 'I'm very pleased to make your acquaintance, sir,' she murmured, giving him a sort of half-curtsy anyway.

'And I yours, Dinah,' Ava's father replied, bowing his head politely. 'And thank you for helping my daughter.'

'Oh – it was a pleasure, sir.' Dinah looked curiously at Cindy as she lowered herself back on to her chair. 'And I presume this is . . . ?' She trailed off politely as Cindy gave the back of her hand a careful lick to remove a remaining flake of tuna.

'This is Cindy, my cat,' Ava told her. 'The fairy godmother changed her into a maid for the ball. She's not due to change back again until midnight. Do you mind if she stays here until then? Oh, and do you have a drink of water we could give her, please?'

Dinah pointed to a stone jug with two cups sitting on the table. 'There's some water. Does she know how to use a cup?'

'Of course I do, old woman,' Cindy interjected indignantly. 'At the fairy godmother's house I drank milk from a china teacup!'

'Cindy, don't be so rude!' Ava exclaimed, embarrassed.

'It's all right,' Dinah said, trying not to smile. 'Cats aren't the most humble of creatures after all.'

As Dad poured out some water for Cindy, Dinah added in a warning sort of voice to Ava, 'You do realize Cindy might not be quite the same when she changes back again?'

'How do you mean?' Ava asked in surprise.

'Well, the fairy godmother isn't as good at spells as she makes out, you know. This whole glass slipper thing with Cinderella was a mistake, for one thing. I have it on good authority that Cinderella's whole outfit was meant to change back to rags at midnight. Instead, one of her shoes — the one that fell off — stayed as a glass slipper. Of course it all worked out very well for Cinderella in the end, with the prince taking the slipper round to all the houses in the neighbourhood, promising to marry the first girl it fitted! But it wasn't *meant* to happen.' She paused to take a breath. 'So I'm just warning you that when Cindy changes back into a cat, there's a chance that she might not change back *entirely*.'

As Cindy looked alarmed, and Ava looked upset, Ava's dad said quickly, 'Isn't that being rather pessimistic, Dinah? Let's worry about that if it happens, shall we?'

Dinah sniffed. 'Personally I like to be prepared for bad things happening. As I'm always saying to Tilly, at least if you *expect* bad things to happen then you don't get too many nasty shocks.'

'Where *is* Tilly?' Ava asked now.

But Dinah was looking suspiciously at Cindy, who had picked up a freshly mended velvet cape and was rubbing her cheek against it. 'Perhaps it's not such a good idea to keep Cindy in here with all these expensive fabrics,' she told Ava nervously.

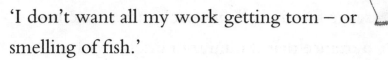

'I don't want all my work getting torn – or smelling of fish.'

Ava had to admit she had a point. To make matters worse Cindy was now looking with interest at a small hole in the floor that looked like it could be a mouse hole.

'Is there somewhere else we can take Cindy while we wait for the spell to wear off?' Ava's dad asked Dinah.

Dinah looked puzzled. 'Can't you take her to your guest room, sir?'

Quick as a flash Ava's father replied, 'Of course, but for now I should like her to remain here in the servants' part of the palace. She is a maid, after all.'

'Well . . . you are welcome to take her up to my room, if you want somewhere quiet,' Dinah offered. 'I can show you where it is. I've just been up there helping Tilly get ready for the ball. When I left her she was putting the finishing touches to her hair. Ever so pretty she looked! She should be on her way to the ballroom by now.'

'Oh no!' Ava exclaimed. 'Dad, we have to stop her!'

'Why?' Dinah asked, frowning.

'The fairy godmother is using a special spell to check if the girls entering the competition have made their own dresses or not,' Ava explained to Dinah.

Dinah looked horrified.

'Don't worry. I'll go straight back to the ballroom and fetch her right now,' Ava added, stepping towards the door.

But as she did so, Cindy let out a loud, very *un*maid-like growl of protest.

'Don't worry, Cindy,' Ava said. 'Dad will look after you while I'm gone.'

'Oh no – I'm coming with *you*!' Cindy spat out. 'I don't trust humans who don't like cats.'

Ava stopped in surprise. 'But Dad *does* like cats. Don't you, Dad?'

'Well . . .' Ava's father replied, looking awkward. 'It's not that I *dis*like them, but I suppose, if I'm honest, I *have* always been more of a dog person . . .'

'See what I mean!' Cindy looked disgusted. 'A *dog* person!'

'I tell you what, Ava,' Dad suggested hurriedly as Ava gave him an exasperated look. 'Let's do this the other way round. You and Cindy can stay in Dinah's room, where you'll both be safe – and *I'll* go and fetch Tilly.'

'You can't,' Ava said dismissively. 'You don't even know what she looks like!'

'I'll come with you, sir, after we've taken

Princess Ava and Cindy up to my room,'
Dinah offered at once. 'They won't let me
inside the ballroom, but I can stand in the
doorway and point Tilly out to you.'

'Thank you, Dinah.' Dad was looking at
her gratefully. 'Ava, trust me – it's better
if you stay out of the way of the fairy
godmother. If she finds out that *you* gave
Tilly that dress, who knows what she might
do to you.'

'*I'm* not scared of the fairy godmother,'
Ava said stubbornly.

'Well, you should be,' Dad replied firmly.
'Look what she did to Cindy!'

'Your father is right,' Dinah said. 'It is
safer to stay well away from that woman.
Oh, she *means* well enough most of the
time, but her spells have a habit of going
wrong – sometimes dangerously wrong!

And if she loses her temper there's no telling what she'll do with that wand of hers. She always calms down again afterwards, but by then it's usually too late!'

As Cindy went to lie down for a catnap on one of the narrow beds in Dinah's room, Ava started to look around for a place to temporarily hide the music box. Her dad had slipped it to her when Dinah wasn't looking, and whispered that she should put it somewhere out of sight until he returned. But where?

The room was very small, containing only the two beds, a chest of drawers and two wooden trunks – one at the bottom of each bed. Ava quickly moved the things off the top of the trunk nearest her and opened the lid. The trunk was almost completely full with blankets and various items of clothing that, judging by their size, belonged to Dinah rather than Tilly.

Ava lifted out some folded clothes in order to make some space for the music box. That's when her eye was caught by a brightly coloured piece of fabric sticking out from the folds of one of the blankets at the bottom of the chest. Curiously Ava opened up the blanket and found, hidden inside it, a neatly folded girl's dress. As Ava held up the dress and shook it out, she saw that it was no ordinary item of clothing. It was the most unusual, most perfectly made gown she had ever seen – and it seemed to contain all the colours of the rainbow.

'*This* must be the dress Tilly made for the competition!' Ava exclaimed in amazement. 'But what's it doing *here*?'

12

Ava carefully hid the music box inside the chest and closed the lid, wondering what to do next. She knew that she had to get the dress to Tilly as soon as possible. But how?

The safest option seemed to be to wait here until her dad got back — hopefully with Tilly. After all, if she went off to look for Tilly herself, she might very well miss her and Tilly might arrive back in the servants' quarters while she, Ava, was looking for her at the ball. No, the most sensible thing was definitely to wait.

Ava only hoped there would be enough

time for Tilly to wear her dress to the competition. The dress was so beautiful and so different from all the other dresses Ava had seen in fairytale land that Ava could see now why Tilly thought it had a really good chance of winning. But for that to happen, Tilly had to get here soon.

At last the door opened and Tilly appeared, still wearing the violet and cream dress from Marietta's shop.

'Thank goodness!' Ava said, standing up and sighing with relief.

'Your father came and found me in the queue before I got too near the front,' Tilly said. 'He and Dinah explained about the fairy godmother's spell.'

'That's great, but look!' Ava turned to point at the rainbow-coloured dress, which she had draped over the only chair in the room.

'*My dress*!' Tilly exclaimed, rushing over and lifting it up. 'You *found* it! I can't believe it! Where was it?'

'That's the strange thing. It was . . .' Ava paused, suddenly unsure how to explain *why* she had been looking inside Dinah's wooden trunk. 'I'll tell you later, but shouldn't you hurry up and change, if you're going to wear it to the ball?'

Tilly was beaming with excitement as Ava started to help her out of Marietta's dress. 'I can't believe it!' she kept saying over and over. 'You've got to tell me where it was!'

'I will tell you,' Ava promised. 'But let's wait until Dad and Dinah get here. Where *are* they anyway?'

'Your father is escorting Dinah back to the sewing room. He's a very kind and well-mannered gentleman, isn't he?'

Ava flushed a little as she answered, 'Yes, I suppose he is.' Dad seemed very different here from how he was at home, she thought. In the real world he never seemed to mix much with other people or be very interested in making friends. Here he seemed a lot more *involved* with those around him. In fact, it was almost as if *this* was where he felt most comfortable.

'What do you think?' Tilly asked, after she had carefully pulled on her dress and smoothed down the creases with her hands.

The rainbow-coloured dress appeared to be made of several overlapping layers of fine material. It had a simple, perfectly fitting bodice, long elegant sleeves and a stunning multicoloured sash tied at the waist, beneath which the long flowing skirt billowed out in a mass of rippling colour.

'I've never seen anything like it before!' Ava gasped. For the dress seemed to come alive in an almost magical way as Tilly twirled round, the colours merging with each other like those of a real rainbow.

'Good,' Tilly said grinning. 'Come on. Let's go down to the sewing room and show Dinah.'

Briefly Ava worried about leaving Cindy – who was still asleep on the bed. But she couldn't bear to wake her up and have her cause lots of trouble again. Besides, she reassured herself, in her cat-form Cindy could sleep for hours at a time if she was left undisturbed.

The two girls hurried along the corridor and down the servants' staircase to the sewing room, where Tilly burst into the room excitedly. Ava's father was there with Dinah and when he saw Ava he frowned.

'What are you doing here?' he demanded sternly. 'I told you to wait with Cindy.'

'Cindy's fast asleep, and I'm sure she won't wake up again for ages,' Ava said. 'Dad, I just found Tilly's dress. The one she really *did* make herself! Doesn't she look beautiful in it?'

They were interrupted by an exclamation of concern from Tilly. 'Dinah, what's the matter?'

Both Ava and her father turned to look,

and saw that Dinah had gone very pale. Judging by her face, anyone would think she had just seen a ghost – a *real* ghost – thought Ava.

'Your dress . . .' Dinah murmured, staring at Tilly. 'I'm so sorry . . .'

'It's all right – there's still time to wear it to the ball,' Tilly said, cheerfully. She turned back to Ava and asked breathlessly, 'Where did you find it, Princess Ava? Did the ugly sisters have it?'

Ava slowly shook her head. 'I found it . . . I found it . . .' she began, but something about the look on Dinah's face made her stop.

'It's all right, my dear. Let me tell her,' Dinah said shakily. Slowly she turned to Tilly and continued, 'Princess Ava found your dress in *our* room, Tilly – hidden inside my trunk. The truth is, *I'm* the one who took it.'

'*You?*' Tilly looked disbelieving.

'I was worried about what would happen if you won the competition,' said Dinah. 'To have a wish granted by the fairy godmother seems like such a *risky* prize. You know how unpredictable her spells can be. But it wasn't just that. It was the thought of you going away and leaving me that really made me do it.' Dinah started to cry.

'I don't understand. Why would you think I would leave you?' Tilly asked, still looking incredulous.

'If the fairy godmother grants your wish to have your own dress shop, then of course you'll go,' Dinah replied.

'Don't be silly!' Tilly protested. 'If that happened you could come and work in my dress shop *with* me. I'm not old enough to

❀❀❀ 214

run a dress shop all by myself in any case.'

Dinah shook her head sadly. 'You'll soon be old enough, Tilly, and by then I probably won't even be able to sew properly any more. I already need your help to thread my needles. The fact is, I'll be worse than useless as a seamstress soon.'

'But, Dinah, I'd want you to come and live with me even if you *couldn't* sew any more!' Tilly exclaimed. 'You're my family, and I would never just go away and leave you! Why would you even *think* that?'

Dinah sniffed. 'Because . . . because . . .' She trailed off, seeming unable to answer.

In the painful silence that followed, Ava's dad said softly, 'Is it because you always expect the worst thing to happen, Dinah?'

Before Dinah could reply, Tilly exclaimed, 'But how could you expect the worst of *me* like that? I'd never just abandon you, after everything you've done for me. I don't know how you could possibly think I would!' She sounded angrier as she added, 'And I don't know how you could be so mean as to steal my dress!'

Dinah hung her head. 'I'm sorry, Tilly,' she said. 'It *was* mean – and I feel terrible about it.'

'No you don't! You wouldn't have said anything if Ava hadn't found the dress. I'll never forgive you for this, Dinah. Never!' And with tears streaming down her face Tilly burst out of the room.

Ava would have gone after her if her dad hadn't put his hand on her shoulder to stop her. 'Leave her for a few minutes, Ava. She needs time to calm down. And I think Dinah has more to tell us.'

He looked questioningly at Dinah who was still looking very pale and teary-eyed.

'What else is there to tell?' Dinah said hoarsely. 'I was afraid, that's all. I've *always* been afraid of losing the people I care about . . . ever since . . . ever since . . .' She broke off.

'Ever since *what*?' Ava asked anxiously.

Dinah sniffed, looking at Ava with a faraway expression in her eyes. 'When I was a small child my parents were so poor they hardly had enough food to feed themselves, let alone me,' she began slowly. 'Nevertheless I loved them and trusted them – just like most children do their parents. One morning they left me on my own to sit and beg by the side of the road. My mother was very tearful that morning but she wouldn't say why. They said if I

217

waited there, they'd come back for me later that day. I started to cry and my father promised that if I was very good they would bring me back a fresh loaf of bread to eat. So I did as they said and I waited. But darkness came and they still hadn't returned. I waited all night for them but they still didn't come. Eventually I realized that they'd abandoned me.' She sniffed again. 'I became a beggar-girl after that and somehow I survived to grow up – but . . . well . . . I suppose I've always been on my guard for bad things happening ever since.'

Ava stared at Dinah speechlessly, hardly able to imagine such a terrible thing happening to a small child. 'Is that why you took Tilly in?' she eventually whispered. 'Because she was left on her own just like you were?'

'Yes, and because I was lonely and I wanted someone to keep me company. Now of course I love her like I would my own daughter. So when she started telling me about her dream to go off and run her own dress shop, I suppose I just panicked.' Dinah's voice was very choked as she added, 'The thing is, Tilly's had just as difficult a start in life as I did. Her parents loved her very much and she missed them terribly after they died. I don't expect her to feel sorry for me — or to forgive me.'

There was a long silence in the room, broken only by the sound of Dinah's weeping.

Ava's dad was looking thoughtful. 'It sounds to me that at least Tilly has always felt *loved* — first by her parents and then by you, Dinah. Perhaps that might help her to forgive you.'

As Dinah looked across at him, still crying but with something like a flicker of hope in her eyes, Ava found herself wondering again why she had never seen this side of her dad before.

'Come on, Ava,' Dad added, putting one hand on her arm. 'We have to go and check on Cindy. We'll come back and say goodbye to Dinah before we leave.'

After they had left the room Ava said in a small voice, 'I don't understand, Dad. This is fairytale land, isn't it? I thought that only good things would happen here.'

'Fairytales always end happily for the main characters, like Cinderella and the Prince,' her dad said. 'But some of the other characters don't get quite such a good deal, I'm afraid.'

As he spoke, Tilly stepped out into the corridor from one of the rooms behind them. Her face was still smudged with tears, although she was obviously trying hard to put on a brave face. 'Princess Ava – wait! I want to come to the ball with you!'

Ava and her father both turned, but before Ava could reply her dad said, 'Ava isn't going to the ball, Tilly. But you mustn't let that stop *you*.'

As Tilly's face immediately fell, Ava begged, '*Can't* I go with her, Dad? Please?'

'We can't leave Cindy on her own for any longer,' Dad said firmly. 'And don't ask if I'll stay with Cindy while *you* go to the ball without me, because the answer is no.'

'*I'll* go and sit with Cindy, if it would help, sir,' said a nervous voice – and they looked round to see Dinah standing in the doorway of the sewing room. She still looked pale but she had stopped crying.

'That way you can escort both the girls to the ball. And –' she turned to look timidly at Tilly – 'and afterwards I'd like to try and explain things a bit better to you, Tilly – if you'll hear me out. I know I don't deserve it but . . .' She swallowed.

Tilly frowned uncertainly as she met Dinah's gaze, but after a few moments she slowly nodded.

Ava turned eagerly to her father, who looked like he was weighing up his options.

Eventually he asked Dinah, 'Do you think you can handle Cindy if she turns back into a cat before we return?'

'Oh, I'm sure she'll be *easier* to manage as a cat than as a maid,' Dinah replied. 'Don't worry, sir. I'm perfectly capable of handling her either way.'

Dad turned back to Ava, who was giving

him her most pleading look. 'I suppose there isn't any real danger in letting you go to the ball, so long as I'm with you,' he admitted slowly. 'Since Tilly is no longer wearing the dress you lent her, she shouldn't get into any trouble with the fairy godmother.'

'No – and if she wins the competition, then I *really* want to be there to see it!' Ava said, beaming.

'What time do they announce the winner?' Dad asked Tilly.

'At midnight,' Tilly said. 'Cinderella is to select the winner herself.'

'*Cinderella?!*' Ava gasped. After everything that had happened she had totally forgotten that Cinderella would be at the ball too. And she started to feel light-headed with excitement as she realized that at long last she was going to meet her favourite fairytale princess!

13

The ballroom was packed when they got there. The footman who had been announcing all the guests was still at the door, stifling a yawn and looking grumpy and exhausted. He recognized Tilly and waved her inside impatiently without bothering to announce her, but he clearly expected to formally introduce Ava and her father.

Ava's dad grinned – looking unusually playful all of a sudden as he murmured something to the footman.

'His Royal Highness the Crown Prince

Otto and his daughter, Princess Ava!' the servant boomed out as they entered the ballroom.

Ava gaped in disbelief at her father.

'That's what I called myself when I came here fifteen years ago, so I decided I'd better stick with it,' he told her. Once they were inside the room he seemed to know exactly how to deal with all the other guests, she noticed, as she watched him bow his head politely to an elderly duke and kiss the outstretched hand of his rather haughty-looking, much bejewelled wife.

The ball was now in full swing even though the royal family had yet to arrive. The musicians were playing a fast waltz very energetically, and the couples on the dance floor were whirling round the room – a mass of shimmering colours.

Tilly had already gone over to the table where the fairy godmother was sitting. There was only one other young girl left in the queue, waiting to have her dress tested.

Ava waved to her friend, mouthing, 'Good luck!' and Tilly gave her a nervous smile of thanks back.

Ava looked across to where the other contestants were all gathered together waiting for the competition to begin. 'I don't think any of the other dresses are as beautiful as Tilly's, do you?' she said to her father.

'Maybe not, but don't get your hopes up too much, Ava,' he replied warningly. 'We don't know for sure that she'll win.'

'Now you sound exactly like Dinah,' Ava complained, pulling a face.

Dad laughed. 'Oh dear.'

Over at the table, the fairy godmother was already pointing her wand at Tilly and for a few seconds Ava held her breath – but there was no need to worry. Tilly's dress passed the test and she was soon being waved across to stand with the other contestants.

The fairy godmother then raised her hand to signal to the musicians. The music stopped at once and all the guests who had been dancing were asked to leave the floor.

The fairy godmother waited for the dance floor to empty completely before going to stand in the middle of it. 'If I could have your attention, please, lords and ladies, dukes and duchesses, princes and princesses, counts and countesses, earls and . . . hmmm . . . yes . . . well . . . For the next dance I would like *only* the girls in our dress competition to take to the floor. I need to see their dresses more closely before I can decide which six are good enough to make it through to the final – which Cinderella is to judge herself.'

'Where *is* Cinderella?' one of the male guests called out.

'She and the royal family will be here in their own good time, Duke Drink-a-lot,' the fairy godmother replied sharply.

'Yes, well, it's taking them a very *long* time, if you ask me,' muttered the duke grumpily, as he tipped his champagne glass up and downed it in one, before snapping his fingers for a servant to bring him some more.

'He's got a very silly name, hasn't he?' Ava whispered.

Her dad grinned and pointed to a fat man in a gold-trimmed blue velvet suit, who was eating his way through a whole tray full of pork pies. 'That's his friend Earl Eat-a-lot over there. They both looked a lot younger – and a lot slimmer – fifteen years ago.'

Ava giggled as the earl let out a loud burp.

The head footman suddenly stepped into the middle of the floor beside the fairy godmother and cleared his throat loudly. He was holding a scroll of paper in one hand. 'The King has asked me to make some announcements before the royal family make their entrance.' He cleared his throat again before unrolling the paper. 'By royal decree, there is to be no

229

burping or wind-breaking of any description in the presence of the royal family,' he declared, looking pointedly at Earl Eat-a-lot.

This brought an amused titter from the audience and an indignant 'Well, really!' from the earl.

'By royal decree, no one must tread on the toes of any member of the royal household while dancing,' the footman continued.

'I say, do we get thrown into the dungeons if we do?' exclaimed Duke Drink-a-lot jokily – but nobody else laughed.

'By royal decree, no one with bad breath is permitted to dance with their royal highnesses,' the footman added, fixing his gaze firmly on the duke so that nobody could be in any doubt as to who *that* announcement referred to.

The footman went on making announcements, which Ava barely took in because she was so excited. 'I can't *wait* to meet Cinderella,' she whispered to her dad, who was looking at his watch. 'Do you think I'll be allowed to actually *speak* to her?'

But before her dad could reply there was a loud crash as a tray of champagne glasses clattered to the floor just behind them.

'*Mouse!*' a terrified princess shrieked, stamping her feet up and down to try and crush the creature that had disappeared under the long skirt of her gown.

'I say – that servant over there just vanished!' called out another guest in a high-pitched voice. 'Look – those are his clothes!' He was pointing to a pile of servant's clothes on the floor, close to where the tray had fallen.

Other guests started screaming too as panic quickly spread about the room.

'Dad – *look*!' Ava said, pointing to the servant who Cindy had attacked earlier. She had just noticed him standing very still amid all the activity and his appearance was changing as they watched. Grey hair was growing on his face, and long white whiskers were growing out from either side of his mouth. Two pointy grey ears were sprouting from the top of his head, his nose was turning black and wet, and his eyes seemed to be shrinking. And poking out from underneath his jacket was a very fast-growing tail.

A few seconds later the servant

was gone and in his place was a second heap of clothes and another small squeaky mouse.

'Catch him!' yelled the fairy godmother.

The dress competition was totally forgotten as chaos descended on the ballroom, with the fairy godmother tearing round the room in a frenzy, lifting up the skirts of all the ladies to see if there was a mouse hiding underneath any of them. As all the lady guests shrieked with indignation, their husbands and fathers shouted angrily for the fairy godmother to stop.

In all the commotion, nobody noticed that the footman at the door was trying to make an important announcement. 'Pray be upstanding for His Majesty —' he began, but nobody heard him. 'His Majesty the —' he tried a second time — but still no one was listening.

'*WHAT* is going on here?' a loud voice

suddenly bellowed above the din.

Immediately the whole room froze, for it was the King himself who had spoken.

'For *His Majesty the King!*' the footman finally burst out.

Ava found herself staring in awe at the large man in the glittering crown standing in the doorway as the hushed words, 'Your Majesty,' echoed round the room.

The King nodded regally at his guests as they curtsied and bowed to him, before turning to glower at the fairy godmother, whose face was flushed as she got up from looking under a nearby princess's skirt. 'Well, madam?' he demanded impatiently. 'What is the meaning of this?'

'Your Majesty, there's been a small problem with the servants I brought to help out at the ball,' the fairy godmother replied breathlessly. 'I'm afraid my spell has worn off too soon and they've already turned back into . . . well –' she coughed politely – 'their original forms. It's really most inconvenient and I have to find them straight away.'

'I do believe she's talking about those *mice*,' said an anxious-sounding princess.

'If you ask me, the only good place for mice is cooked inside a pie!' declared Earl Eat-a-lot heartily.

'Hear! Hear!' agreed Duke Drink-a-lot. 'Though a mouse-shake is even better in my opinion!'

'If there are *mice* at this ball, I think I'd rather go home,' exclaimed the nervous duchess standing next to him.

As several of the more panicky guests started to agree with her, the King spoke again.

'There will be no more talk of mice, Fairy Godmother!' he ordered. 'I will not have my guests upset like this! You will forget about your spell and get on with judging the dress competition. The Queen will be here shortly with Prince Charming – and of course Cinderella.'

As he went to sit on the largest of the throne-like chairs, Ava whispered urgently to her father, 'Dad, what about Cindy? If the *mice* have changed back already . . .'

'I was just thinking the same thing,' her dad replied. 'Dinah's with her of course, but I still don't think we should stay here much longer. I'm starting to get rather a bad feeling about this ball.'

'What do you mean?'

But before he could answer, the fairy godmother appeared as if from nowhere at

Ava's side. 'Princess Ava – *what* have you done with my maid?' she demanded angrily.

'Cindy's not your maid! She's *my* cat!' Ava protested.

'Maid or cat – I want her back!' the godmother snapped. 'I *must* find out if she has changed back too soon like those wretched mice!'

'We can certainly find that out for you,' Ava's father said quickly, 'if that's all you need to know.'

'Of course it's not *all* I need to know,' the godmother replied, sounding irritated. 'I shall have to conduct further experiments on Cindy to help me perfect my spell. Princess Ava may have her back when – and *only* when – I am finished with her!'

'*If* she's still alive by that time of course – which I seriously doubt!' came a snooty voice from behind them.

Ava turned and gasped in shock as she saw the two ugly sisters standing there. They weren't so much glaring at *her*, Ava realized, as at the fairy godmother.

'What are *you* doing here?' the godmother snapped at them. 'I thought I banished you from the ball!'

They were wearing different ball gowns now, and Astrid was sneering boldly at the fairy godmother as she replied, 'We've spoken to Cinderella about how you humiliated us in front of everybody, and she felt *so* sorry for us that she's given us permission to come tonight after all.'

'Yes – and when she hears about the chaos *you've* just caused, I expect *you'll* be the one banned from the ball – not us!' Ermentrude put in.

Astrid laughed as she continued cattily, 'Even Cinderella is getting tired of the mess you always make with your ridiculous spells! And as for the Queen and Prince Charming – well, they've quite lost patience with you! In fact, they seemed quite interested when we suggested that you be sent away to one of those boarding schools where clumsy fairies are taught to do magic *properly*. The Queen thought you were too old to get a place in such a school, but *we* told her that we know of one that will make an exception for particularly *stupid* fairies!'

Astrid and Ermentrude both burst out laughing, watching gleefully as the fairy godmother's face turned bright red with rage.

'You . . . you . . . wicked girls!' the godmother exclaimed angrily. '*I'll* show you how good my spells are! I shall banish *you* to a boarding school right now – a school on the other side of the kingdom where they specialize in teaching nasty, rude girls better manners!' And before anyone could stop her she was waving her wand high above her head as she shouted out a stream of unintelligible words that seemed to be causing the air around the ugly sisters to sizzle with orange sparks. At the end of her spell she spat dramatically on the end of her wand, at which point there was a loud bang as a cloud of orange smoke totally engulfed the screaming Astrid and Ermentrude.

'Look! They've vanished!' several of the stunned guests exclaimed as the smoke cloud started to clear.

For several seconds nobody spoke. The whole room was staring in amaze-ment at the fairy godmother – who was

still shaking with rage.

Then the silence was broken by a loud, slow clapping. The King had risen to his feet and was actually applauding the fairy godmother. 'Good riddance!' he announced. 'Well done, Fairy Godmother!'

And little by little the whole room started to clap along with the King.

Ava was hugely relieved that the ugly sisters were gone, but suddenly she found herself feeling even more afraid for her cat. 'Dad, we *can't* let her have Cindy back to experiment on her!' she hissed fiercely to her father – but unfortunately the fairy godmother overheard her.

Quick as a flash she turned and pointed her wand at Ava. '*You'll* do as you're told, young lady – unless you want to join Cinderella's sisters.'

'Now, now . . . there's no need for that,'
Ava's father intervened hurriedly. 'You can
have Cindy back if you want her that badly,
Fairy Godmother – of course you can.'
He ignored Ava's protests as he continued,
'But don't you have to judge this dress
competition first? Look – it's already begun.'

The King had just signalled for the music
to start and all the girls whose dresses were
to be judged had started to dance.

The godmother frowned. 'Wait here,' she
ordered them before sweeping across the
room to take her place as competition judge.

'The fairy godmother isn't a totally *good*
character like she is in my fairytale book, is
she, Dad?' Ava said shakily as they watched
her go.

'She's certainly someone you don't want
to get on the wrong side of,' her dad agreed.

'Come on, Ava. We'd better leave now, while she's distracted.'

But Ava had also become distracted by what was happening on the dance floor. In particular she was distracted by Tilly, who was twirling round very fast. Some multicoloured sequins on her dress, which had been barely noticeable before, were now catching the light, and she reminded Ava of a beautiful rainbow sparkling in the sun.

'Can't we just stay long enough to see if the fairy godmother picks Tilly?' Ava begged.

'Ava, there isn't time,' her dad replied firmly. 'If we're still here when the fairy godmother has finished the judging, she'll make us give up Cindy.'

'No, she *won't*,' Ava said defiantly. 'She

can threaten me all she likes, but I still won't tell her where Cindy is!'

'That's very brave, Ava, but the next time she threatens you with her wand, then *I* shall be telling her straight away,' Ava's dad said, taking hold of her hand before she could protest any more. 'Now come with me, please.'

As the fairy godmother requested a temporary halt to the music so that she could shout instructions to the contestants, Ava and her dad began to edge cautiously around the room towards the door. At the open doorway they saw the footman, who seemed to have fallen asleep on his feet. His eyes were shut and he was swaying alarmingly.

As Ava and her dad attempted to slip past him unnoticed, he woke up with a start, took one look at them, and in his half-awake state mistook their exit for an entrance. Even half asleep he clearly had an excellent memory for names because he immediately boomed out at the top of his voice, 'His Royal Highness the Crown Prince Otto and his daughter, Princess Ava!'

Ava and her father froze as everyone in the ballroom turned to look in their direction.

They stayed like that for only a few seconds. As the furious fairy godmother raised her wand to point it at them, Ava's dad clutched her hand more tightly and shouted, 'RUN!'

14

'Stop!' shouted the fairy godmother, who was very close behind them. 'Stop or I'll turn you both into mice!'

'Keep running,' Ava's dad gasped.

'I'm going to put a spell on your legs to *make* you stop!' the angry godmother yelled, raising her wand just as Ava and her dad came to a place where two of the main palace corridors crossed each other.

Coming down the other corridor towards them, behind an escort of two slow-stepping footmen, was a well-groomed older lady with a crown on her head, dressed in a

glittering purple gown. Behind her came a
handsomely dressed smiling young man, also
wearing a crown, and, on his arm, a beautiful
young girl wearing a stunning blue ball gown.

It was the Queen, Prince Charming and
Cinderella herself!

'Dad, look! It's Cinderella!' Ava burst

out, momentarily
forgetting
everything else as
she strained to get
a proper look at
her heroine.

'Keep
going!' Ava's
dad barked,
tightening
his hold
on

her wrist as he pulled her across the other corridor directly in front of the royal party.

'Arrest them!' yelled the fairy godmother, waving her wand in a furious manner.

But the footmen had come between the fairy godmother and her targets just as she was pointing her wand. Seconds later the two footmen's legs were completely frozen and they stood rooted to the spot, their arms waving frantically in the air.

The Queen started to scream as Prince Charming shouted angrily at the flustered fairy godmother. Only Cinderella herself remained calm, doing her best to soothe everyone in a soft, sweet voice.

Ava would have loved to stay and meet Cinderella, but of course she couldn't. This might be their only chance to escape – and her dad suddenly seemed to have a good

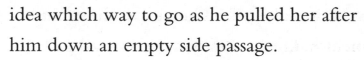

idea which way to go as he pulled her after
him down an empty side passage.

Thankfully they managed to find their
way to the servants' quarters – after
stopping briefly to ask a surprised maid for
directions – and once they got there, Ava
quickly found the right door.

Inside the little room, Dinah was sitting
on her bed with Cindy on her lap.

'Thank goodness!' Ava gasped, running
over to pick up her beloved cat, who purred
loudly as she started to stroke her. 'Is she
all right? There aren't any bits of her that
haven't changed back, are there?'

'None that I can see,' said Dinah. 'I got
a bit of a shock when it happened, though.
I thought she wasn't going to change back
until midnight!'

'Something went wrong with the fairy

godmother's spell,' Ava said, tickling Cindy under her chin. 'Oh, Cindy, I'm so glad you're a cat again!'

'She's certainly much *nicer* as a cat,' Dinah agreed. 'So . . .' She looked a little anxious now. 'How is Tilly? How is she doing in the competition?'

'We're not sure. The competition hasn't really got started properly,' Ava told her.

'The fairy godmother has been chasing after *us*, instead of getting on with the judging,' Dad explained. 'She's trying to force us to give her Cindy so that she can discover what went wrong with the timing of her spell.'

'I *told* you her spells hardly ever go according to plan,' Dinah grunted. 'I always make sure I steer well clear of her whenever she waves that wand of hers – and I wish Tilly would too!'

'She just did a very *successful* spell on the two ugly sisters,' Ava pointed out, but before she could explain further her father cut in.

'*We* need to steer well clear of her from now on too, Dinah – which means we have to leave immediately!'

Dinah looked him straight in the eyes. 'I expect you'll be needing your music box then.'

Ava gasped out loud, while her dad was momentarily speechless.

'I couldn't understand what made you open up my wooden chest, Ava,' Dinah continued. 'So I had a look inside myself, and I found that you'd been in there for a reason that had nothing to do with Tilly's dress.'

Ava flushed as her dad said quickly, 'It's not how it looks, Dinah. Ava wasn't trying to *steal* the music box. It's just that—'

But Dinah swiftly raised a hand to silence

him. 'Don't worry. You don't have to explain.' She paused. 'You see, a long time ago – twelve years or so, I'd say – there was another girl who came here pretending to be a princess. *She* needed the music box to get home too.'

'*What* other girl?' Ava blurted, glancing sideways at her dad, who had suddenly become very still.

'She called herself a *travelling* girl,' Dinah continued. 'She was quite a bit older than you – sixteen or thereabouts. Very pretty, she was, with long reddish hair. She was rather an angry, mixed-up sort of girl, but I understood why. You see, just like me, she had been abandoned by her parents.'

Ava's mouth fell open and she looked questioningly at her dad. Could it be . . . ?

'She wouldn't tell me where she came

from or anything about the magic she used to get from place to place,' Dinah went on. 'But she did say that she was running away from home – from an older brother she didn't get on with. He was very bossy and overprotective, she said – always fussing about where she was and what she was doing. But he was her only family since their parents had left them – and I told her she was lucky to have him. I was alone in the world at the time, you see, so I knew what it was like to be completely without family. It was before I adopted Tilly.'

There was a short silence. Ava glanced at her dad and was taken aback to see tears in his eyes.

Without looking at Ava, her father murmured quietly, 'I'm very grateful to you for helping her, Dinah.'

'I thought you might be related to her

when I found the music box,' Dinah said.
'You're her brother, aren't you?'

Silently he nodded.

Dinah smiled in a knowing sort of way.
'I've heard a lot about you over the years.'

'You have?'

'Oh yes. Marietta has become quite a
frequent visitor. After all, we have a lot
in common, both being dressmakers. I'm
surprised that she hasn't mentioned me
before now . . .'

'Yes, well . . .' Ava's dad grunted. 'Marietta
makes it a rule to tell me very little about
her travels. She says she's afraid I'll *interfere* if
I know too much. Where she gets *that* idea
from, I don't know . . .'

Dinah was trying not to smile. 'She did
mention something about you disapproving
of some of her friends in the past – and that

she'd felt rather embarrassed when you made it your business to tell them so! Anyway,' she added hastily, 'it will be absolutely *lovely* to see her tomorrow at Cinderella's wedding!'

'*Marietta's* coming to the wedding?' Ava exclaimed in surprise.

'Oh yes. She's made herself a very beautiful new dress to wear, I believe.'

Ava immediately remembered the raspberry-coloured gown she had seen hanging up in Marietta's shop, but before she could tell Dinah about it her dad was continuing in an urgent voice, 'Dinah, about this music box . . .'

'Oh, don't worry about that. *I'll* take it back to the music room after you've gone,' Dinah offered at once. 'I've done that many a time for your sister.'

'Are you sure? I don't want to get you into any trouble.'

'Oh, I won't get into trouble. If anyone sees me with it, I'll just say that some guests borrowed it and asked me to return it for them,' Dinah said.

'But, Dad, we *are* coming back here tomorrow for Cinderella's wedding, aren't we?' Ava asked anxiously, watching her father open Dinah's wooden chest and take out the music box. 'I still have to meet Cinderella properly! And I'm to be a *bridesmaid* at her wedding, remember!'

'Ava, we can't risk another encounter with the fairy godmother,' he said. 'I'm sorry. Marietta can do what she likes of course, but it's not safe for *you* to go to Cinderella's wedding now.'

'But, Dad, that's not fair!'

'It's the way it has to be, I'm afraid, Ava,' her father said firmly.

'But I don't want to go home yet!' Ava's lower lip trembled and tears pricked her eyes.

'Ava, it won't take long for the fairy godmother to find that maid who gave us directions. Then she'll know we were heading for the servants' quarters. And if she catches us here, not only will she take Cindy and do goodness knows what to her, but Dinah will be in big trouble for helping us. That's not what you want, is it?'

Ava sniffed. 'Of course not, but—'

'Good – now listen carefully.' He opened the music box. 'You go first, with Cindy. I'd take her myself but I think she'll be calmer with you. And I'll be following right behind you so don't worry.'

'Don't forget these, Ava,' Dinah suddenly said, holding out the dress and shoes Ava had lent Tilly from Marietta's shop. Dinah had a thoughtful look on her face as she handed over the dress – stroking the silk violets on the skirt as if they had given her an idea – but whatever she was thinking, she didn't say anything.

As Ava took her position in front of the music box with Cindy she was struggling not to cry. 'Will you say goodbye to Tilly for me, Dinah?' she said miserably. 'Tell her I hope she wins the competition!'

Dinah gave her a hug. 'I'll tell her – and don't be too disappointed about having to go home, my dear. After all – you never know when something good may be just around the corner.'

This was so unlike Dinah that for a moment Ava stared at her in surprise, wondering if the fairy godmother had cast some sort of spell on *her* – one that had

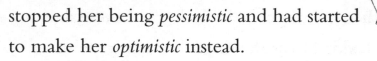

stopped her being *pessimistic* and had started
to make her *optimistic* instead.

Then Ava's dad was ordering her to look
in the mirror and concentrate . . .

Feeling as if she hadn't fully returned yet
to the real world, Ava sat quietly on the
floor in the upstairs room of Marietta's
shop – with Cindy curled up in her lap –
waiting for her father to arrive through the
mirror. When he didn't appear after another
few minutes, Ava started to worry, and
decided to go and find Marietta.

'You're back!' Marietta exclaimed in
delight when she saw Ava. 'And Cindy too!
Wonderful!'

As Marietta spoke, Cindy jumped out
of Ava's arms on to the settee, where she
settled herself against a cushion, lazily licking

her paws as if she was cleaning them after an everyday trip out into the back garden.

'*She* doesn't seem any the worse for her travels, in any case,' Marietta said, smiling as she turned to Ava. 'So what about you? Did you have a good time?'

'Yes,' Ava replied, 'but I'm worried about Dad. He was supposed to be following me back through the mirror straight away.'

'Oh, I shouldn't worry about *him*,' Marietta said reassuringly. 'Otto can usually take care of himself – *and* everybody else! He's rescued me out of a few scrapes in my time, I can tell you. Now, tell me about your visit. Did you meet Cinderella?'

'Not properly – but we met Dinah and Tilly,' Ava said.

'Really?' Marietta looked momentarily taken aback. 'Your father met Dinah too?'

Ava nodded. 'She told us that you're
going to Cinderella's wedding tomorrow.'

'That's right. Isn't it exciting? I've been
waiting years for it to happen — and now
you and I can go together!'

Ava shook her head sadly. 'Dad won't let
me.'

'Why ever not?'

Ava was about to explain when they
heard footsteps above them, and seconds
later Dad appeared on the spiral staircase.

'Dad, I'm so glad you're back!' Ava cried
out, rushing to give him a hug.

'Ava was getting worried about you,'
Marietta told him lightly when he looked
surprised.

'Really?' Ava's dad stroked her hair a
little awkwardly as he explained, 'I'm sorry,
Ava. I stayed behind for a bit longer because

261

Dinah wanted to discuss an idea she thought might interest us.'

'What idea?' Ava asked curiously.

But before he could answer Marietta said in a rush, 'So, Otto . . . you've met Dinah?'

'Yes, Marietta, we have,' he replied crisply. 'And I gather she's known *you* since you were a teenager.' He was giving his younger sister rather a stern look, considering she hadn't actually *been* a teenager for quite some time, Ava thought.

Marietta laughed, a little self-consciously. 'She told you about when we first met?'

'She certainly did.'

'Ah, well . . .' Marietta sighed. 'It was a very long time ago, Otto. I was young and headstrong and I didn't like being bossed about by my ultra-sensible older brother!'

'I did *not* boss you about,' Ava's dad said, sounding irritated.

'You wouldn't let me leave school and go off travelling like I wanted to,' Marietta pointed out.

'You were too young to drop out of school! Anyway, *someone* had to give you some guidance – and it wasn't as if our parents were there to do it!'

'I know that, Otto,' Marietta said. 'And I'm very grateful to you for trying so hard to take their place – really I am.' She spoke sincerely, though she also had a twinkle in her eye. Turning to Ava, she added, 'I was a bit of a wild child when I was younger, Ava. Your dad was always looking out for me and stopping me getting into *too* much trouble.'

As Ava looked at them both she suddenly felt that there was much more she wanted to ask them about their lives when they were young – and about her missing grandparents.

But right now the thing she was most interested in was what Dinah had just said to Dad that sounded like it involved *her*. 'So what *was* Dinah's idea, Dad?' she prompted him.

Her father turned to look at her. 'Dinah's idea? Ah, yes . . . well . . . Dinah knows how much you were looking forward to being one of Cinderella's bridesmaids, but she agrees with me that it's too dangerous as things are at the moment. The ugly sisters may be out of the way but there's still the fairy godmother to consider. However, she has another idea. Apparently the fairy godmother has one weakness – flowers!'

'Flowers?' Ava was puzzled.

'Yes. According to Dinah, not only do flowers make the fairy godmother sneeze,

but she is quite unable to perform any magic
on a person who is carrying more than a
hundred of them.'

'A *hundred*!'

'Yes – it's all to do with some flower
spell she once did that went badly wrong.
Anyway, what Dinah suggested is that rather
than going to Cinderella's wedding as her
bridesmaid, you should go as her flower girl
instead. What do you think?'

'Great! But how will I hold that many
flowers?'

'Oh, you don't have to *hold* all of them,'
Dad replied, smiling. 'Does she, Marietta?'

'Of course not,' Marietta said, smiling
too. 'All we need to do is find the right
flower-girl dress for you to wear, Ava – and
I believe I have just the one! Come on! Let's
go upstairs and you can try it on right now!'

15

'So what do you think?' Ava asked her dad the next morning as she pushed back the sparkly curtain of the changing cubicle and gave a little twirl.

'You look beautiful,' he declared, smiling proudly.

Ava's flower-girl dress was made of very swishy cream silk, on to which dozens of pretty silk flowers of all different colours were sewn. On her feet she wore sandals that were also totally covered with silk flowers, and on her head was an elegant headband that had beautiful silk daisies sewn on to it.

'I can hardly believe they're going to turn into real flowers when I go through the portal!' Ava exclaimed. 'Marietta says she used a very special type of magic thread to sew them on. Look – you can actually see it sparkling.'

Dad glanced at the thread she was pointing to and nodded matter-of-factly. 'Has Marietta checked that you have *enough* flowers?' he wanted to know.

'She says when I get my flower basket I'll have well over a hundred, so I'll be quite safe,' Ava reassured him. She frowned slightly because there was something she wanted to ask and she wasn't sure how Dad would react. 'Dad, I've brought my camera with me . . . and . . . well . . . do you think you could take a photograph of me in this dress so I can show Mum? It's just that I really wish she could be here to see it too.'

'Of course we can take a picture,' Dad said at once. 'As long as—'

'As long as I don't tell her where I got the dress,' Ava finished for him. 'Don't worry. I know I mustn't say anything about Marietta's shop.'

As she spoke, Marietta came down the spiral staircase to join them. She was wearing the raspberry-coloured fairytale gown that she had modelled on the music-box princess's. It had a snug-fitting bodice and a massive skirt, which swayed regally when she walked. She had a sparkling tiara in her hair and a matching necklace around her neck. On her feet she wore shoes made of raspberry-coloured glass, each of which had a glass rosebud on the front that matched the silk rosebuds decorating her dress.

'I believe glass slippers are the "in" thing now in fairytale land,' she told them, smiling. 'I must say they are not the most comfortable of shoes, so goodness knows how I shall dance in them – but they do look stunning!'

'*You* look stunning,' Ava's father said warmly. 'Now promise me, both of you, that you'll be careful while you're away. I'd come with you, except that I don't think the fairy godmother would be very pleased to see me. Besides –

269 ✿❀❋

weddings aren't really my thing!'

'We promise,' Ava said, smiling.

'So long as *you* promise to be polite to my customers, if there are any while I'm gone, Otto,' Marietta added as she pulled on a pair of cream silk gloves.

Dad laughed. 'I'll do my best. And I'll *also* do my best not to lose Cindy again while you're away. Now, if you fetch your camera, Ava, I'll take that photo you wanted. Then I think you two princesses had better get a move on, if you don't want to be late for the big event!'

Ava arrived on the other side of the mirror to find herself not in the palace music room, as she'd expected, but outside in the royal gardens. Marietta, who had travelled through the magic portal first, was standing

on the grass waiting for her, her red hair glinting in the sunshine.

'Look at my dress!' Ava exclaimed. The silk flowers that had decorated it before had magically blossomed into beautiful, sweet-smelling real ones.

Before Marietta could reply, a familiar voice behind Ava called out, 'Wow! You look really . . . *flowery!*'

Ava turned to see Tilly in her rainbow-coloured dress, beaming at her. The palace music box was sitting on the grass at her feet, glowing slightly.

'Tilly!' she exclaimed, delighted to see her friend.

'I won the competition!' Tilly told her breathlessly. 'And it's all thanks to you, Ava, for finding my dress!'

As the two girls hugged, Tilly added, 'And

271

guess what? Since the fairy godmother's spells have been going a bit wrong lately, Cinderella suggested I choose a different prize. Dinah told me about the music box and why it was so special, so I asked Cinderella if I could have that and she said yes! We're going to keep it in the sewing room, so you and Marietta can come and visit us whenever you like without worrying about running into the fairy godmother. *Or* the ugly sisters – if they ever come back here, that is!'

'That's great, Tilly – but what about your dress shop?' Ava asked in surprise.

'Well, Cinderella likes the dress I made so much that she's asked me to be her personal dressmaker after she marries the prince. Then, when I'm older, she's going to help me get set up in my own shop, with a little flat above it for me and Dinah to live in.'

'So you and Dinah are friends again?'

Tilly nodded. 'I know Dinah's really sorry for taking my dress, and it's difficult to stay angry with her after everything she's done for me.'

'Girls, I know you have a lot to catch up on, but we mustn't forget we have a wedding to go to,' Marietta interrupted them now. 'I've waited all this time for Cinderella to get married – and I don't want to miss it!'

'Don't worry. It's not due to start for another half an hour, over there in the big walled garden,' Tilly said, pointing to the far side of the lawn, where they could see a high brick wall with a door set into it. The door had been propped open and servants were hurrying in and out, carrying cushions and extra chairs.

'I thought the fairy godmother said the

273

wedding was to be in a church,' Ava said.

'It was, but at the last minute Cinderella and Prince Charming decided it should be outside in the open air instead. Come on. I'll show you,' Tilly said.

Marietta and Ava followed Tilly towards the walled garden. As they got closer they could hear the sound of lots of people chattering.

'Wow!' Ava gasped as they reached the door and looked in.

The walled garden had been turned into a very beautiful open-air room. The guests were seated in rows on either side of a red carpet that had been placed down the centre to create an aisle. Where the carpet ended there was an archway with beautiful flowers laced through it – under which the young couple would take their marriage vows. The four walls of the garden were covered in rambling pastel-coloured roses, which gave off a very sweet scent.

'The fairy godmother was very cross about all the flowers – but Cinderella insisted,' Tilly said, grinning.

Along the tops of the walls, small animals

had started to gather. Ava saw red squirrels, grey rabbits, white doves, three baby owls with their mother, a robin (even though it was summertime) and some lively fox cubs who were being miaowed at to sit still by a cross mother cat who was there with her four kittens.

'Cinderella has befriended a lot of the animals who live in the palace grounds,' Tilly explained. 'And they all want to see her get married. She's even having a choir of bluebirds perform – they're just tuning up down in the vegetable garden.'

'Hadn't you better go and join the bridal party now, Ava?' Marietta said.

'I'll take you,' Tilly offered at once. 'Dinah is with them and she'll give you your flower basket.'

'Tell Dinah that I'm looking forward to

catching up with her after the wedding,'
Marietta said.

'I'll tell her,' Tilly replied. 'Come on,
Ava. But watch out for the fairy godmother!
She's in the garden somewhere too,
practising her confetti spell. She wants to
make confetti fall out of the sky immediately
after the wedding ceremony – but every
time she tries it, she makes it pour with rain
or start snowing instead!'

Ava followed her friend across the grass to
the palace – thankfully *without* encountering
the fairy godmother – and into a huge light
room which had glass doors along one side
that opened out on to the palace gardens.

Inside, Dinah was ordering the excited
bridesmaids to stand still as she gave their
dresses a final inspection. 'Oh, there you are,
Tilly! And Princess Ava is with you! How

lovely!' She came over to Ava and gave her a kiss on the cheek. 'You look beautiful, my dear . . .' she said, adding in a low voice, 'Now, there's nothing to worry about. I've already told Cinderella that you're going to be her flower girl, and your flower basket should be arriving at any minute.'

'Where *is* Cinderella?' Ava asked eagerly, looking around the bustling room and seeing no sign of the bride.

'She said she needed to get some fresh air,' Dinah told her.

'I bet I know where she is,' Tilly said. 'Come on, Ava.'

Tilly led Ava through the glass doors out into the garden. 'There's a spot on the other side of that bush where Cinderella often goes when she wants to be on her own,' Tilly told her, pointing at an extremely large bush with big orange flowers growing all over it. 'Why don't you see if she's there now?'

So Ava left Tilly and headed across the grass, her heart pounding.

'Oh!' she gasped excitedly, because standing on the other side of the bush, gazing dreamily into the distance, was Cinderella herself, looking just like she had stepped out of a fairytale book.

The full skirt of her wedding dress was made from several layers of crushed

white silk draped over a hooped underskirt. The bodice was also white silk, with dainty little flowers embroidered on to it. On her feet Cinderella wore what looked like her original glass slippers. Her golden hair was piled up high on her head and decorated at the back with tiny white jasmine flowers.

'Excuse me,' Ava began in a shy whisper, 'but . . . but . . .' She found herself unable to speak because her throat had gone so dry.

Cinderella saw how nervous she was and gave her an encouraging smile. 'You must be Ava, my flower girl,' she said sweetly. 'Your dress is so . . . so . . .'

'Flowery?' Ava finished for her.

Cinderella laughed. 'Yes. But very pretty too.'

Then Ava found herself gushing, 'Cinderella, I've been wanting to meet you for ages! You're my favourite of all the fairytale princesses! And you must be *so* excited about marrying Prince Charming! He's *very* handsome, isn't he?'

'You are very kind,' Cinderella replied graciously. 'And yes, I am looking forward to marrying Prince Charming very much. He is the sweetest person I have ever met – even if he does get a little flustered by the antics of my godmother!' She frowned slightly. 'But I must confess, Ava, that I am rather anxious about the wedding itself. I only hope I don't let everybody down. There will be so many people there looking at me. What if I get so nervous that I can't speak? Or what if I trip up on my way down the aisle – or do something else silly that will make everyone laugh at me?'

'Cinderella!' Dinah's voice called out

urgently, making them both jump. 'It's nearly time to go!'

'You mustn't worry,' Ava reassured her heroine earnestly. '*You* could never do *anything* that would make people laugh at you. You're *Cinderella*!'

Cinderella sighed. 'The thing is, Ava, I'm just an ordinary girl really, underneath all these fancy clothes.'

'Cinderella, you will *never* be ordinary!' Ava told her firmly.

And neither will I, Ava thought to herself as she accompanied Cinderella back across the garden to the palace. For now that she had discovered Marietta's shop, and with it the amazing truth about her dad – and about herself – Ava knew that her life was going to be anything *but* ordinary from now on!